HIDDEN WITHIN THE SECRET HEART

DESPERATE DISGUISE BOOK 4

TESSA COLE

Gryphon's Gate Publishing

Hidden Within the Secret Heart

Gryphon's Gate Publishing
550 King St. N.
PO Box 42088 Conestoga
Waterloo, ON
N2L 6K5

Print ISBN: 978-1-990587-67-2

A Quick Recap

When I took my brother Sawyer's place as a sacrifice to the Black Guard, I knew my life would never be the same again.

What I didn't expect was to find myself trapped between two worlds.

In the Gray, I was Sawyer — a nobleman hated by the other guardsmen. They saw me as entitled and weak, and every day was a battle to survive their "lessons" and hide my secret.

In the Garden, every time I fell asleep, my spirit manifested as a fae woman.

And that fae woman was kidnapped and almost forced into unwanted mating bonds by a bunch of fae men led by Wells and Crane.

My Fantasy Man, Rider, Talon, and Quill saved me, and I killed Wells in the struggle, but Crane and three others escaped. On top of that, I was trapped in the Garden by a magical bracelet Wells had put on me, and the power in my mating marks grew out of control, overwhelming me with desire.

But my Fantasy Man, Ash, helped me, caring for me and protecting me like he'd always done despite me learning that he was another Captain of the Black Tower, and despite the fact that he thought I'd reject him for the horrible scars marring his face and body.

But I could never reject him. I believed he wouldn't abandon me like Talon and Quill had when Rider had commanded I run on the running trail until I threw up. I'd already seen Ash's soul and knew it was beautiful. It didn't matter what he looked like.

Rider and the others brought a fae knight to hear my testimony and a healer to help me, who thankfully put my blazing mating marks to sleep. Sure, my sleeping marks might never wake up, but I didn't care. I wasn't fae. I wasn't supposed to be searching for my mates to begin with.

The only downside: because of what had happened to my marks, the overwhelming desire I'd experienced before they were put to sleep could still flare up, making me desperate for sexual relief.

With that settled — and absolutely nothing else, like the bracelet still trapping me in the Garden — the High Priestess summoned me to her throne room.

Standing before her, surrounded by courtiers who stared at me like I was prey, I realized the ruler of the Garden was even more dangerous than the men who'd attacked me. She was a powerful ruler who liked to play games with people's lives.

She assigned a massive knight named Sir West as my protector, spirit-linked him to me against my will so he'd know whenever I entered the Garden and exactly where I was, and bound me to a spirit anchor so I always manifested beside him.

At least she gave me a nice dungeon cell— I mean guest suite.

At dawn, when I was getting nervous about someone walking into my room in the Black Tower and discovering my spiritless body, a magister finally arrived and removed the bracelet.

I woke exhausted and sore from having run for hours on the running trail. Kit, Payne, Lewin, and Grefin were banging on my door, wanting to check on me before they retired to their rooms from their night shift.

They discovered I didn't feel safe bathing with all the other men in the bathhouse in the basement of the Black Tower and invited me to use the private bathing room in their elite team suite while they were on patrol that night. They didn't know the real reason I avoided the bathhouse, and I wasn't going to tell them, but I still accepted their offer with gratitude.

Except while I soaked my sore muscles in their tub, a horrific vision of the team being attacked by shadow bears crashed through me.

Kit and Lewin were bleeding out on the tables in the Tower's infirmary, and Payne was going to die from a shadow poison infection that only *I* now knew about...

CHAPTER 1

Sage

I SCRAMBLED out of the tub, sending water sloshing over the side. I had to hurry. Kit and his team were in the infirmary of the Black Tower right now.

Payne was dying. Right now.

And no one knew.

I threw on my shirt, not bothering to dry myself off or bind my breasts, added my jerkin, and half hopped, half staggered into my pants before running out the door. My jerkin was just going to have to be thick enough to cover the soft swell of my chest because my soul screamed that every second counted.

I bolted through the maze of halls back to the stairwell near the great hall. There were probably stairs closer to the infirmary, but I didn't know anything about this wing of the Black Tower and couldn't afford to get lost.

Hurry. Hurry.

I had to save him.

With his healing magic, Flint could save Kit and Lewin. He had to. But no one knew Payne was poisoned.

I reached the main floor and raced down the wide hall, away from the great hall, past the quartermaster's rooms, and crashed through the infirmary doors into a nightmare.

The metallic, sour, rancid reek of blood, sweat, and I don't know what else filled the room, making me gag. The guys were covered in gore and mud, and blood was splattered everywhere. So much blood.

My gaze landed on a trail leading from the door that opened out to the bailey to the tables and all the bloody footprints stark against the pale stone floor.

Kit's torn jerkin and shirt lay in a bloody heap on the tiles a few feet from the table where he lay, his ruined body pumping blood everywhere. Lewin lay on the table beside him. More blood. I jerked my attention to Grefin and Payne and the blood streaks on the wall near them and on the floor.

Flint barked orders at the two other guardsmen, who rushed to obey, while Kit screamed in pain, Lewin moaned, Grefin rambled about the bears, and Payne hissed, "Save him," over and over again.

Father, I'd never seen anything like it, and my stomach roiled at the true horror of being a guardsman.

This was what I was training to do, to fight monsters so powerful they left elite swordsmen like Kit and Lewin in bleeding agony.

Bile burned the back of my throat and a chill swept over my still-damp skin. I never wanted to face even a glimpse of what I'd seen in my vision, that flash of those shadow bears attacking Kit, Payne, and the others.

But if I and the men of the Black Tower didn't face those horrors then it would be people like Sawyer and the cook at Herstind Castle, and her son Dodd who did. They wouldn't stand a chance. They'd be slaughtered without any hope of survival, and the only way to prevent that was for someone to stand up and fight.

"I need two drams of wistellel," Flint barked, jerking me out of my stunned shock.

Shit. What was I doing? I couldn't just stand there like an idiot.

I opened my mouth but had no idea what to say. It would take too long to explain... if anyone would even listen to me. I was a nothing nobody sacrifice who was more trouble than he was worth. As far as anyone knew, I was useless, particularly in this situation.

I glanced at Payne. His complexion was gray, but that could be attributed to shock. His mate was dying, and I had no idea if fae men who took mating vows had a similar magical link like the men who were mated to a fae woman. Even if anyone was paying attention there were no clues that Payne had been poisoned.

"Save him," he prayed. "You have to save him."

"He's losing too much blood." Flint grabbed Kit's severed hand from Payne but didn't pause to look at the man before using his magic to reattach the limb.

Lewin screamed, his breaths turning into short, sharp gasps.

I was running out of time.

"Damn it." Flint jerked away from Kit and placed his hands on Lewin.

I rushed into the room, heading for the cabinet filled with jugs of medicine. I had to get Payne the antidote before Kit knocked over the rolling table.

My bare foot hit a blood pool, slipping out from under me, and I windmilled my arms, fighting to keep my balance, as I careened toward the large, wooden cabinet.

"—splint that hand."

I toppled over, cracking my elbow on the stone floor and sending pain jolting through my body. My knees slammed into the bottom of the cabinet, shocking more pain through my aching muscles. Inside, the glass contents rattled, sending my heart into my throat, but somehow nothing fell over or broke.

"How the fuck were there five of them?" Grefin moaned.

I scrambled to my feet.

Kit was going to scream any minute now and knock over the table.

The cabinet had two large doors, and I threw both of them open and stared at all the neat rows of jugs and jars and glasses. There were easily over a hundred containers, each neatly labeled in small but clean writing, and half a dozen different sized glasses, some with etched lines on the side indicating different amounts.

Shit.

Which one was the antidote? How much did I give him?

"Please," Payne said. "Save him."

I closed my eyes. I didn't have time to read every label. I *saw* the guardsman pull out a jug and start to pour it into a glass. I knew which one I had to take. I just needed to remember.

It was...

Which one was it, damn it? I didn't have time to figure this out.

On instinct, I blindly reached out and grabbed a jug and glass. The label listed the jug as an antivenom.

Please let it be the right stuff.

I started to pour but realized I never *saw* the amount, and the glass I'd taken from the cabinet had three lines etched into the side.

I didn't know if the antivenom was dangerous. Too much of some medicines were also deadly.

Shit shit shit.

I couldn't just pour and pray. I needed someone to tell me how much.

"He needs to drink," one of the guardsmen said.

My pulse lurched. That came just before Kit's scream.

With jug and glass, I scrambled back across the room to Payne's side, barely missing the blood pool I'd slipped in before.

"You're poisoned," I told him as I held up the jug and glass. "How much?"

"Save him," he moaned, his gaze locked on Kit as if he hadn't heard me.

"Payne," I snapped.

His attention swung to me, slowly, too damned slowly, and his eyes were unfocused. "Sawyer?"

"You're poisoned." Please, listen to me. "I don't know how much to give you. I—"

Kit screamed, wrenching Payne's attention back to his mate. The rolling table crashed to the floor, sending medical supplies flying, and the guardsman trying to give him the medicine grunted and stumbled back.

Now.

I had to save Payne now.

If I was going to change the future, I had to do it now.

I filled the glass to the top with the antivenom and shoved it against Payne's lips. "Drink."

"What the fuck are you doing, runt?" Grefin dropped the towel he'd been holding against the side of his head, grabbed my jerkin, and tugged, making me stumble back.

The antivenom sloshed over my hand, and I wrenched back to Payne and shoved the glass to his lips.

"Please. Drink," I begged. "You've been poisoned."

"We fought bears, not serpents," Grefin snapped.

Payne groaned and his dazed gaze dropped to meet mine.

"Please," I insisted, trying to will him to understand that I'd explain everything once he drank. He had to drink. "He needs you."

"Shit," Payne gasped, and he grabbed the glass and downed the medicine even as his legs gave out and he collapsed to the floor.

He dropped the glass and clutched his chest, his eyes wide, his breathing suddenly sharp and shallow, and my pulse lurched.

Was I too late?

CHAPTER 2
Sage

"FUCKING HELL." Flint shoved me aside, knocking me onto my butt, and grabbed Payne's hand. He closed his eyes, his expression hard. "Shadow venom? I thought you said you fought bears."

Grefin stared at me, his eyes wide. "We did. Just bears."

"Then how?" Flint grabbed the jug of antivenom from my hand. "It's over here," he called out to the guardsman who'd run to the cabinet for the medicine the moment he'd heard the words "shadow venom."

The healer looked from the jug to me and frowned then grabbed Payne's hand again and closed his eyes. A flicker of light, barely bright enough for me to see, danced over Flint's fingers for a quick moment before he released Payne.

"You got it to him just in time," Flint said as he stood and rushed back to Kit. "Another heartbeat and it would have been too late."

Oh, thank the Father.

I sagged back, my body throbbing in pain from the sudden overexertion, and a strange giddiness bubbled in my chest.

I did it.

I'd changed the future.

Which meant I had proof that if I kept my secret long enough, Sawyer would be safe...

Except I hadn't seen Sawyer safe. I'd only seen that I'd taken his place and was murdered in the Gray instead.

But I had to cling to the hope that it was possible. I could change my fate. I could survive the attack that was coming and Sawyer would be safe.

Please, Father.

Grefin grabbed my wrist, yanking me closer. "How did you know?" he demanded as he glared at me. "How did you know Payne was poisoned?"

"I—" I glanced at Payne, who stared at me, his color already improving as the antivenom aided by Flint's magic coursed through him. His eyes were wide with a different kind of shock from before.

This shock was disbelief, and I couldn't blame him. I had no way of knowing he'd been poisoned, and I didn't know how to explain it.

Sure, there were fae-touched humans — those who possessed a magical ability and not the men who were attracted to other men. But the gift was so rare, and I had no doubt being able to see the future was even more unlikely.

"There weren't any serpents," Grefin pressed. "There's no way you could have known."

His gaze dropped to my bare feet then jumped to my waist where I hadn't secured my sword.

I wrenched free of Grefin's grasp and crossed my arms, praying he wouldn't notice my chest. Despite wearing a shirt and my jerkin, I now felt naked, like they'd discover the truth at any moment.

"Where are your boots?" He pressed his free hand against the side of his head and groaned.

"I was—" I bit the inside of my cheek.

I had to tell the truth. Once the chaos in the infirmary had calmed down, Flint and the other guardsmen would ask questions, and there wasn't anything I could say other than the truth... and there was a chance they wouldn't believe the truth either.

My stomach tightened and my mouth went dry.

There was also a chance they *would* believe me and want to use me, and I wouldn't be able to help them because I couldn't control my magic.

And what was done was done. I couldn't take it back and I wouldn't. Payne was alive, and I would deal with whatever came next.

"I'm fae-touched."

Grefin rolled his eyes. "That doesn't explain why you're here or how you knew."

Payne tipped his head back against the wall and closed his eyes. "It does if by fae-touched you mean you've been blessed with magic."

Grefin's head snapped toward Payne, his eyes wide.

"You have the sight. It's the only way you could have known we were here and that I was poisoned," he huffed a bitter laugh. "I didn't even know I was poisoned until it was almost too late. I thought—" He pressed a hand over his heart and looked at Kit on the table. "I thought our bond..."

Flint held Kit's hand, his eyes closed in concentration, while one of the guardsmen stitched and bandaged his numerous injuries, and the other worked on Lewin.

"So you just knew?" Grefin asked.

"I was soaking in the tub and saw you collapse," I told Payne.

"You could have prevented all of this," Grefin said, his voice gruff as he jerked his chin toward Kit and Lewin, the men working to save them, and all that blood and pain.

I wished with everything I had that I could have stopped it, but my visions didn't work that way. Hell, before a few days ago, I hadn't even had visions. All I had was a sense that something bad was going to happen.

"Why didn't you stop this?" Grefin demanded as he lunged at me, his expression wild.

I jerked back but wasn't fast enough. Grefin landed on me, his weight pinning me to the floor, and he grabbed the front of my jerkin, yanking me up and making my muscles scream in protest at the sudden movement.

"Why didn't you stop this?" He wrenched his arm back, his hand clenched in a fist.

I flinched and brought my hands up to protect my

face, but Payne grabbed Grefin's arm and yanked him off me.

"It doesn't work that way," Payne said, shoving Grefin away from me. "It's a miracle he managed to save me in the first place."

"I can't control what I see," I said, my voice shaking as I scrambled back to put more distance between me and Grefin. "And I can't control when I see it. Tonight was the first time I've ever been able to change something."

Flint looked up from where he was working on Kit, his expression grim. "And we're grateful for that. Thank you."

Grefin's shoulders slumped, and he pressed the towel back against his head wound. The fight seemed to drain out of him as quickly as it had flared up.

"You need to tell Rider, though," Flint added, his expression clear: if I didn't tell Lord Rider, he would. "Two of the three fae ever recorded to have the sight went mad, unable to tell reality from vision."

A chill swept through me. "And the third?"

"Was a woman, and her bonded mates kept her sane," Payne said.

So if I didn't want to lose my mind, I needed to reawaken the mating marks that weren't guaranteed to ever reawaken and that I wasn't supposed to have in the first place.

CHAPTER 3

Rider

MY WOLF SNARLED as I raced through the Black Tower's left wing toward the infirmary. There were too many hunting teams down already, and now Kit's...

The gate guard had caught me just before I'd headed up to my suite to send my spirit to the Garden, but his words had sent me running in the opposite direction. "Serious injuries" translated to "might not survive" in guard-speak, and I needed to assess the damage no matter how much my wolf heaved inside me, desperate to get to the Garden.

Protect, he snarled within me. *Now now now.*

He didn't care about the Gray or even that Kit was my cousin. In his mind Kit would either live or die, there was nothing he could do about it now, but he sure as hell could protect Sage if he got to West in time.

But I couldn't shirk my duties as the Lord Commander of the Black Guard just because my wolf was fascinated with a woman.

She wasn't my mate, damn it. And she never would be.

I clenched my jaw and swallowed back my wolf's growl of frustration as I reached the infirmary. The copper stench of blood and the sour reek of healing herbs hit me before I'd even shoved the door open.

Inside was controlled chaos. Blood streaked across the pale stone floor from the bailey entrance to the center of the room and had splattered on the floor beneath the tables where Kit and Lewin lay. Kit was unconscious with Owun, one of the two guardsmen assisting Flint this evening, securing a splint that immobilized Kit's wrist, while Lewin moaned and gasped as Evrat, the other guardsman assigned to the infirmary, stitched a gash on his arm — another, larger injury on his thigh already bound in white linen.

Near the door, both Grefin and Payne sat on the floor, Grefin holding a bloody towel to his head while his calf oozed blood, and Payne leaning against the wall, his complexion too pale — although given the state of his mate, I wasn't surprised to see the man in shock.

Then there was Sawyer, slumped on the floor staring at Flint with a stunned expression. The boy's feet were bare, he didn't have his sword, his hair was damp, and there was no logical reason for why he was in the infirmary.

Sure, he liked Kit, Payne, and Lewin, but I doubted anyone in the guard would have told him in the middle of the night that the team had been injured. Hell, given how much the guardsmen seemed to hate him, I doubt anyone would have told him in the middle of the day, either.

The boy was a problem for later.

"Report," I ordered, crossing to where Flint worked on Kit.

"Everyone will live," Flint said without looking up from stitching a gash in Kit's chest. "But Kit and Lewin are down for at least four rotations. Maybe more. And Payne doesn't leave tonight. He had a close call."

Flint stopped working and looked at Sawyer. The boy went still. They stared at each other in some kind of silent conversation and Flint raised an eyebrow.

Sawyer opened his mouth, closed it, and looked at the floor. Flint's jaw tightened. He wanted the boy to do or say something. That much was obvious. But Sawyer was probably still terrified of me after I'd made him run on the trail until he puked.

I bit back a sigh. Whatever he wanted the boy to say, it could wait. I didn't have time for whatever was going on, and I could deal with it in the morning. I had to get to the Garden before Sage did.

But Flint huffed and gave Sawyer a pointed look. "Sawyer has the sight. Payne was poisoned with shadow venom and Sawyer foresaw that he'd die."

"Because we fought bears," Payne said. "I still don't know how I got poisoned."

The boy had the sight?

I went cold and had to fight to keep my breathing even.

I knew Sawyer was fae-touched because Talon had

said so when his shadow had attacked him by the running trail a few days ago, but this— This was the worst possible gift. The sight meant madness, visions bleeding into reality until he wouldn't be able to tell which was which.

I hadn't witnessed it firsthand, but all the stories talked about seers who couldn't stop screaming about disasters that they couldn't change and others who stood frozen in place, trapped in their visions. And those had been fae.

The only one to survive the gift without going crazy had been a woman and only because of her bonded mates.

Sawyer was human. And a man. The Goddess wouldn't give him any bonded mates, and his mind was more fragile than a fae's since humans weren't supposed to have magic.

Fuck.

But that wasn't my biggest problem. While Sawyer had potential, he was just a single guardsman.

No, Payne said they were attacked by bears, except Payne had been poisoned. "And no one saw a serpent?"

Shadow monster activity had increased, but we were fucked if they were also undergoing a transformation of some kind.

"I didn't see a serpent. Kit or Lewin might have." Payne's gaze slid from me to his mate lying on the table, his expression tight with worry.

"I didn't see one either," Grefin groaned. "But everything happened so fast. Those bears came out of the trees like an ambush."

Shit. This wasn't good. The fact that an experienced guardsman like Grefin felt like the shadow bears' behavior had changed was beyond concerning.

Ambush. The word stuck in my mind. Shadow monsters didn't coordinate. They hunted, they attacked, they fed—but they didn't *plan*.

Except first there'd been the increasing numbers, then the daytime attacks that never used to happen. And now five bears attacking an experienced team like they'd known exactly how to strike.

Something was changing in the Gray. Something was making them bolder. Smarter.

And we had no idea what.

My wolf heaved under my skin, jerking me a step toward the door and reminding me that I didn't have time to deal with any of this right now.

Goddess be damned!

At least Kit and his team would live. That was something. Except now I was down another hunting team, which meant cutting lieu time for the rest of my men. Again. They were already stretched thin, and morale was shit even before this latest disaster.

My wolf clawed inside my chest. *Garden. Now.*

Fuck. I needed to get to Sage before—

No. I needed to deal with Sawyer first. The boy had the sight and didn't trust me. Not that I blamed him.

Even if he did open up, I was the worst possible

person to help him. I didn't have the patience or the skills to help him manage his gift or stay sane.

No. Quill would have to deal with the boy. He had a better temperament for it, and Sawyer was more likely to trust him than me or Talon.

We needed to know exactly what Sawyer had seen in his vision: how he'd known Payne was poisoned, if he'd seen anything about those bears that explained their behavior, and any other detail that might explain what happened.

And more importantly, Quill needed to teach him fae meditation techniques, so maybe, just maybe, we could keep his mind from shattering.

I clenched my jaw against a growl, my wolf now pissed that the boy was not only endangered by the Gray and the other guardsmen, but by his own magic.

Sawyer shifted, his posture tense, his arms crossed over his chest, and his mouth pinched tight like he was bracing for whatever came next.

"You're dismissed." I jerked my chin toward the door, indicating he should go. "Meet Captain Quill here tomorrow after the fifth bell to discuss your... gift."

He flinched at the word gift and stood. "I can't control it, Lord Commander."

"You might never," I told him.

His shoulders inched down, some of the tension in his posture relaxing, and I realized he'd been afraid that I'd demand he use his abilities to protect the guard, something I'm sure the humans would have jumped at.

And knowing the humans, they wouldn't have

understood his ability and would have punished him for not being able to do what they wanted. No wonder he was so reluctant to say anything.

"Here. Tomorrow."

I hated that I was assigning him something to do on his second lieu day, but he was still being punished for threatening to murder his fellow guardsmen even if they had deserved it. A conversation with Quill while confined to the Black Tower would probably do him good since he might not get much conversation out of Kit, Payne, and Lewin, given the circumstances.

"Yes, Lord Commander." He hurried out of the infirmary, and I turned my attention to the others in the room.

"Nothing said here leaves this room," I said, making sure to catch the eyes of both of the human guardsmen assisting Flint. They didn't know Sawyer like Kit's team did or even Grefin, and the last thing the boy needed was his gift becoming fodder for barracks gossip, especially given how we were still dealing with the fact that he'd come through the ring after dark and pissed off everyone in the guard.

Owun and Evrat exchanged glances, but I couldn't tell what it meant. It would be a Goddess-given miracle if it meant they were starting to accept the boy. He had, after all, saved a fellow guardsman's life.

"Sawyer's fae-touched abilities are not up for discussion. Foresight isn't something that can be controlled or commanded," I continued, keeping my voice hard enough that they'd remember this. "It's not a gift. It's a curse. The visions come when they come, show what they show. The fact that Sawyer managed to change what he saw and save Payne's life is nothing short of a miracle. Don't expect it to happen again."

The guardsmen nodded their understanding, and Owun opened his mouth like he wanted to ask something, then shut it, clearly thinking better of it.

"I'm just glad he saw something," Payne said, his expression tight with exhaustion. "I don't even know where I was bit."

"No shit," Grefin said. "Never thought I'd be grateful for the runt." He winced as he adjusted the towel on his head, blood seeping through the fabric.

"Once I'm done here, you'll need to strip," Flint said. "If we can find the bite, maybe we can figure out how big that serpent was."

"It had to have been small," Payne replied. "That's the only way I could have missed it."

Grefin huffed. "With the way things went down, I would have missed anything smaller than a hound."

Which was saying something, since Grefin was an experienced guardsman and usually kept his head in battle.

My wolf heaved inside me, reminding me that I'd stood there for too long. Fine. Everyone would live and everything else could wait.

I stormed out of the infirmary, back into the silent halls. At this hour, anyone who wasn't on the wall, out in the Gray, or in the infirmary was asleep, something I should be doing. But first, I needed to make sure a stunned, stunning redhead was protected.

I hurried up the stairs, taking them two at a time, to the top of the Black Tower. A hint of light, only really visible because of my wolf-enhanced eyesight, shone through the skylight above, illuminating the floor's unusual design. The hole in the center guarded by a railing offered light to the library below, a small-scale reproduction of some of the towers in the White Tower in the fae realm.

I shoved open my suite door and marched through the sparse sitting room to my equally sparse bedroom. With a growl, I dropped onto my bed, and sent my spirit to the Garden, praying I hadn't wasted too much time and there was a chance we could convince West not to say anything to the High Priestess about Sage's marks.

CHAPTER 4

Rider

I MANIFESTED in a partially hidden alcove near a side door to the Divine Residence, the closest I could get to being inside since it was forbidden to manifest inside without special permission from Her Brilliance, the High Priestess.

Vines with the Garden's softly glowing pink and white flowers curled along the half-stone half-wooden archway at the front of the alcove, but few were inside, filling the space with shadows.

Movement by the back wall caught my attention as Quill stepped forward from where he'd been waiting. He wore a two-toned gold jerkin instead of his usual green and gold, probably chosen to remind West that he was the High Priestess's son and hoping that West wouldn't remember that Her Brilliance had essentially disowned her son when she learned he didn't have any magic.

I peered deeper into the alcove's shadows then glanced through the arch toward the path. No Talon.

Where the heck was he? We didn't have time to wait around. We were all supposed to meet in the alcove and face West together.

"Where's Talon?" I asked.

"He went ahead. Said you were taking too long."

My wolf heaved inside me, pissed that Talon hadn't waited, but it made sense. I'd been delayed, and since we didn't know when Sage would manifest, every second counted. If we could figure out West's motivations before she arrived, we'd be better able to figure out if we just needed to convince West to keep his mouth shut or if we needed to permanently silence the knight.

That, and Talon was the most charming of us. With his shadow's allure, he could probably seduce West, where I'd be more likely to rip the man's throat out... which wasn't great if we wanted to try negotiations first.

Hell, even Quill would be a better choice than me.

Why was I here again? Given how my wolf heaved inside me, I should stay the hell away until things with West were sorted.

But my wolf didn't give a fuck about that. He needed to ensure Sage was safe, and if that meant tearing West's throat out, he would gladly do it.

I strode through the arch toward the side door, unable to hold my wolf back as well as my own desire to get to Sage.

"So?" Quill asked as he followed me.

I shoved through the side door into the Divine Residence's magical opulent architecture with stone that blended with wood, polished floors that gleamed, and sparkling chandeliers radiating steady light. And this was a little-used side hall. The main halls in the Residence were even more impressive.

And while most fae were used to it, I knew Sage wasn't, not just because she was new to the Garden but because I'd overheard something I shouldn't have, that she'd been raised in the human realm.

"Rider?" Quill asked, his tone sharp, and I jerked my attention to him, realizing that I was growling.

Swell.

"If we're going to convince West to listen to us, you need to stop growling."

Right. I raked my hands through my hair, pulling apart my topknot because it felt good easing the pressure at my temples, and because I could reform the knot with just a thought.

Quill grabbed my arm, stopping me before we started climbing the stairs up to Sage's suite. "Is this something to do with what kept you? Is Sawyer all right?"

Of course he'd think it had something to do with the boy. He didn't know how Sage affected me, how much my stupid wolf thought she was ours... which. She. Wasn't. Damn it.

And it would be best to keep Quill and everyone else thinking that.

"Yeah. Kit's team was attacked." I tugged out of Quill's grip and took the stairs two at a time, forcing him to hurry after me. "A pack of bears. Somehow Payne was poisoned and the boy foresaw it."

"He *foresaw* it?" Quill missed a step and grabbed the

railing to keep from falling. "His fae-touched ability is the sight?"

Horror flashed through his expression, his reaction similar to mine when I'd first learned the truth.

"I need you to handle him," I said. "He needs to learn meditation. The sooner the better."

"Do we even know if meditation will help?"

"Do we have any other option?" There wasn't a fae alive who could remove someone's gift, not even Her Brilliance. Our only hope of saving Sawyer's sanity was to pray he could handle fae meditation techniques and that his magic wasn't strong or still growing.

We reached Sage's suite to find West leaning out the door, using it like a shield along with his large body to block the view inside. His expression remained grim and unreadable while one hand gripped the side of the door and the other rested on the hilt of the sword at his hip.

Talon stood in the hallway, his jaw tight and shoulders squared. Clearly, he'd been at this for a while and wasn't getting anywhere.

Fuck.

"I'm just asking if she's manifested yet?" Talon huffed, any hint of pleasantries absent in his tone.

West raised a single eyebrow as if to say, "are you an idiot? The answer hasn't changed since last you asked." His gaze shifted to me and Quill, and the muscles in his jaw flexed.

We weren't going to get anything out of him. Everything I'd heard about West said he took his duty seriously. Too seriously. He followed every command exactly, even if the situation demanded flexibility.

On top of that, it didn't seem like Talon's allure had influenced the knight at all. And I had no doubt Talon had tried to use it first before resorting to whatever was happening now.

Most fae men were as equally attracted to males as they were females since only a quarter of the fae population was female and we didn't have much option if we wanted a sexual partner. Of course, there were exceptions to the rule. Sexuality was a spectrum after all.

Unfortunately for us, it looked like West was one of the exceptions.

Damn it. How long had Talon been standing here? How long before Sage manifested and this whole thing went to shit?

Goddess, I could picture it clearly: that red gauzy thing that clung to every curve and left nothing to the imagination.

Quill had told me Sage hadn't been able to change her spirit clothes, and I doubted she'd manifest in anything other than her usual dress.

The moment she appeared it would be obvious to West that her marks were asleep and we couldn't afford for him to tell the High Priestess.

And while I didn't know what game the High Priestess was playing with Sage and West, I knew it wouldn't be good. And there was no way I, or my wolf, would let Sage face Her Brilliance's ire.

On top of that, Crane, and three of the men who'd tried to force a mating bond on her, were still out there.

Sure, the Order of the Sacred Grove had started an investigation, led by Ash's pompous, arrogant cousin, Yarrow, but that didn't guarantee Sage would get justice, not if it defied a direct order from the High Priestess.

Ash had a few men watching him as best as they could, but so far it didn't look as if Yarrow had found anything.

My wolf snarled at the thought. Crane and the others were out there, hiding and waiting. No doubt planning. Maybe they still wanted to force the bond. Or maybe they wanted revenge for Sage killing Wells. Until they were dealt with, Sage wasn't safe in the Garden, not even in the Divine Residence with West at her side.

Quill stepped closer to West, his posture straightening into the authority he didn't really have anymore and never liked to use in the first place.

"We've already proven that we aren't a threat to Sage," he said.

West's sapphire gaze slid to him, but his expression stayed grim, his mouth in a tight line.

He wasn't going to budge. We weren't going to get in.

Except we had to. We *had* to protect Sage.

The need to ensure her safety clawed at my insides, and my wolf snarled and thrashed at West's refusal to let us in.

Mine. Protect.

"Sir West," Quill's voice took on the formal tone he

used when pulling rank. "As my mother's son, I command you to let us through."

For a moment, something flickered across West's face. But it was too quick to read just like with all of West's emotions, before his expression returned to hard, grim, and unreadable.

"Lady Sage hasn't given her permission, Your Highness."

Except by the time Sage gave her permission it would be too late.

"What if you just stepped into the hall?" Talon suggested.

The strategy to get West out of the suite, if only long enough to convince him to not report Sage's condition to the High Priestess was a good one. If we were in the hall with the door closed, we'd at least be able to stall him from seeing her when she manifested since with the spirit link he'd know the moment she appeared in the Garden... assuming, of course, that the spirit anchor didn't make her manifest right beside West.

"We could talk without—"

"No," West said, cutting Talon off, that one word making my wolf snarl.

No?

We were running out of time and this stubborn bastard wasn't moving.

My breath turned short and sharp and every muscle in my body coiled tight.

Enough talk. Make him submit.

Except we couldn't afford to make a scene. The High

Priestess was already too interested in Sage. Fighting West in the hall would make her ask more questions and we were trying to avoid that.

No. My wolf wrenched inside me and seized control, shoving my consciousness aside. It needed to protect Sage, and West was standing in its way.

I lunged at West, slamming into him and driving him into the suite.

West staggered back but recovered fast, faster than I liked, and his fist slammed into my jaw. Pain exploded through my skull and my teeth rattled.

Mine. Mine. I had to make him submit and protect my mate... who Goddess be damned was *not* my mate.

I drove my fist into his ribs, the impact jarring up my arm and doing little to move the massive knight. All I got was a grunt before the man reached for my throat.

I ducked, both my wolf and I knowing if he got his hand around my neck, I was done for. I rammed my shoulder into his gut. The breath whooshed out of him and he stumbled back a step.

My wolf huffed in satisfaction and dodged out of the way of West's knee.

Were West's strikes getting faster?

They seemed to be getting faster, which meant up until now he hadn't been using his physical enhancement magic to fight me.

Shit.

West's fist flew toward my face, and I barely jerked out of the way in time, his knuckles skimming my ear.

Mine. My wolf snarled, not giving a shit that West

had just become more dangerous. The knight wasn't the only one who could increase their strength.

Fur raced over the back of my hands and up my forearms, and my claws extended from my fingers. My wolf threw me forward, growling and swiping our claws.

West dodged my first strike, but my second caught in his armpit, slipping into the joint where his armor didn't protect him and tearing fabric and flesh.

With a grunt, and no other reaction, not even a flinch in his stony glare, West turned, whipping his foot out in a kick so fast I could barely see his movements.

I wrenched down. West's leg skimmed the top of my head, and I lunged forward. I had to get him contained, had to make him submit before it was too late.

My body slammed into West's, and we crashed through the low table in the seating area with a thunderous crack, sending wood flying in all directions.

West's elbow caught me in the ribs, knocking the air from my lungs. He rolled, trying to get on top of me, but I twisted, getting behind him and wrapping my arm across his neck.

He heaved and jerked, trying to break free, but I held on tight. No way in hell was I letting go.

CHAPTER 5
Sage

THE SHARP CRACK of wood breaking jerked me awake. What the—?

Something thudded, someone grunted, and I blinked hard, trying to focus through the disorientation of manifesting.

Pieces of— Was that a table?

Whatever it was, the pieces lay scattered across the floor, one of the legs digging uncomfortably into my side, and Lord Rider and Sir West grappled on the floor.

Rider had West in a chokehold from behind, his forearm covered in thick fur and his fingers ending in sharp claws as if he were starting to turn into a wolf.

My pulse pounded and my thoughts whirled. None of this made sense. Why were Rider and West fighting?

West rammed his elbow back into Rider's ribs. Hard. The impact made a dull thud, and Rider release a sharp grunt, his grip loosening, letting the massive knight break free and roll off him… right toward me.

Crap.

I scrambled back, hands and feet flailing, desperate to not get crushed.

The movement caught West's attention, and his sapphire eyes locked with mine. His gaze raked down my neck to my cleavage and his eyes widened.

It was barely a fraction of an emotion, a flicker of something that wasn't just grim resignation, but from what I'd seen from West so far, it was practically a full emotional declaration.

"Your marks," he said, his voice deep and harsh.

My marks?

Oh shit, my marks!

Everything froze. I froze. West froze. Rider froze half-raised from where he'd been grappling with West.

Even the air seemed to still and drop in temperature.

In that brief moment between where I was Sawyer, now terrified that I was going to lose my mind because of a magic I didn't want and couldn't control, and waking in the Garden as Sage into the middle of a fight, I'd forgotten Zinnia had put my marks to sleep and I didn't want anyone to know about it.

It was bad enough Quill had learned the truth, but now Sir West and Lord Rider?

And with my revealing lacy dress, the one I couldn't change no matter how much I wanted to, West could see all my plain, lifeless spots where there should be light and power and the promise of a potential mate.

Worse, some of them were green, possibly indicating that my soul had already picked its first mate, which it hadn't because I wasn't fae and I couldn't bond mates… and if I thought that enough times, maybe I'd eventually believe it.

Father, how was it possible for things to keep getting worse? At some point, I had to reach rock bottom, but I really didn't want to see what that looked like. Things were bad enough as it was.

And now everyone knew I wasn't just a novelty by being a new arrival. I was one because my mating marks had been put to sleep. They'd ask questions I couldn't and didn't want to answer and talk about me when all I wanted was to be invisible and bide my time in the Garden and the Gray until Sawyer was safe.

West stared at me, his expression unreadable. What was he thinking? What would he do? The frozen moment stretched longer and longer.

Then Rider snarled and tackled West, pinning the knight to the floor with his claws digging into the man's throat.

"Don't look at her," he growled, but West's gaze remained locked on me. "I said don't look."

Rider jerked West up by the neck of his armor and slammed him back down on the floor, drawing an "umph" from the large knight and making him blink.

The sudden lack of eye contact shattered whatever had frozen the moment between us and I scrambled farther away from the fight until I bumped into something and a soft blanket fell over my shoulders.

"Here," Lord Quill said, wrapping the blanket and his arms around me.

"Thank you." I clutched the blanket at my neck, hiding my marks even though everyone had already seen them.

And that everyone also included Talon, who stood by the door as if to block it. Swell.

Of course, I'd known I wouldn't have been able to keep it a secret forever, at least not from West since I couldn't control the clothing I manifested in, I'd just hoped...

I wasn't sure what I'd hoped for.

A small part of me was furious that Lord Rider, Talon, and Lord Quill were even in the suite, and yet a much larger part was grateful that I wasn't alone with West.

I still wasn't sure I trusted the leaders of the Black Guard, but I trusted them more than the grim knight who'd been spirit linked to me that I knew nothing about.

"Listen," Talon said as he strode across the sitting room with breathtaking grace and knelt beside Rider and West.

As usual, his long white hair was pulled back at his temples with half a dozen braids on each side, accentuating his sculpted facial features and his delicately pointed ears, and my core throbbed with the remembered heat and yearning of his allure while my chest ached at his beauty.

But his beauty, like a lot of beauty I'd discovered in the fae realm, was a lie. It didn't mean he was kind or generous or caring. It just meant he was pretty,

I fought to ignore the sensations, determined to not be attracted to him.

"We just want to have a conversation," he said.

West's sapphire gaze shifted to Talon, and his eyes narrowed.

"We've already demonstrated we care about Lady Sage's safety," Talon continued. "We want to help you with your duty."

"You have your own duties," West replied, his voice a low, dangerous rumble.

Talon frowned and his expression turned calculating for a moment before it smoothed back to calm and concerned. "We do, but you're still going to have to allow men access to the lady so they can court her."

"Barging into her room and assaulting her guard isn't courting behavior," West replied.

"Are you sure?" Talon glanced at Rider.

The knight huffed. "I stand corrected."

"I'm not—" Rider growled, but Talon shot him a hard look, and the Lord Commander of the Black Guard snapped his mouth shut.

"We're all interested in courting Lady Sage. We all intend to spend time here with her." The mesmerizing swirl of pink, blue, and purple in Talon's eyes captured me, and my unwanted desire warmed again. "If the lady will allow it."

I knew for a fact neither Talon nor Rider were interested in courting me.

Except if they were here to protect me from Sir West and the other fae, then they'd need an excuse to be near me, and courting me was one everyone would accept.

"You can meet her in the court gardens and sitting rooms like everyone else," Sir West said.

Rider snarled and jerked his face closer to West's, his canines sharp and wolf-like. "That isn't safe."

"I can protect her," West rumbled back.

"Not if everyone knows about her marks," Quill said, and Sir West's attention jumped back to him and essentially back to me.

I fought the urge to shrink in on myself under the knight's cold glare. Zinnia had assured me I could be as strong and as forthright as I wanted and I wouldn't be punished. But a part of me still struggled to believe that.

Especially since she'd only mentioned it yesterday and the behavior from Wells, Crane, and those other men belied that information.

"So you'd keep her to yourself? You can't even court her," West said to Lord Quill.

Quill stiffened at the reminder that because he didn't have any magic the Goddess wouldn't bond him to a woman.

"Not the point," Talon said, his tone suddenly harsh. "Sage's marks were affected by whatever Wells and Crane did and sharing that information with anyone, even Her Brilliance, will only shame her."

"The power will return when the Goddess wills it," Quill added. "It's just a matter of time. You wouldn't want to shame someone who's already been traumatized?"

West's eyes narrowed and with his set grim expression I couldn't tell if Lord Quill and Talon's argument was working.

"Please," I said. "Magister Zinnia said it's only temporary."

Or at least Zinnia had *hoped* it was temporary.

I hoped it was permanent because I couldn't afford the complication of having a fae mate, not when I was human and didn't belong to the fae realm. It was bad enough some of my marks had already turned from my hair color to my eye color indicating that I'd already bonded a mate.

Regardless, what I really needed to stop attracting any more attention was to keep the state of my mating marks a secret. I didn't want to think about what the High Priestess would do if she found out, but I knew without a doubt it wouldn't be good.

CHAPTER 6
Sage

"I WON'T LIE to Her Brilliance," Sir West said, and my heart sank.

He was going to tell the High Priestess everything and soon the most powerful woman— hell, the most powerful person in the entire fae realm would know there was something wrong with me. That would cascade into her investigating me and learning the truth: that I was a human and didn't belong in the fae realm.

West's sapphire gaze locked with mine, his expression still unreadable. "But I won't answer questions that haven't been asked."

"Your word," Lord Rider growled.

"On my oath," West replied.

With a huff, Rider jerked away from Sir West and strode to the door leading to the hall. He raked his hands through his hair, tugging apart his topknot and making his black shoulder-length locks fall around his ruggedly handsome face. The fur on his hands and forearms receded back under his skin and his claws sank back into his fingernails.

I didn't understand why Sir West would help me, but I was grateful I wouldn't have to deal with questions about my magicless mating marks.

"Her Brilliance will still expect you to make public appearances," Quill said to me as if he could read my mind and knew I planned to spend all of my time in the Garden hiding in my suite.

Of course she would. Nothing in the last few days had been easy, and it was foolish to think something simple was finally coming my way.

It had been clear when the High Priestess had talked down to me, literally from her raised throne and figuratively with her condescension, that I was a toy, a plaything to amuse her. A part of me was hoping she'd forget about me, but I knew that hope wasn't realistic, not unless something more entertaining happened.

"It won't be right away," Rider said. "But you should be prepared to leave this suite at some point, and you'll want to change your spirit clothes when you do."

I tightened my grip on the blanket around my shoulders.

"One of us will always be with you," Quill said, his arms still around me, holding me close.

West rubbed his throat and stood, his presence a reminder that he would be with me as well whether I wanted and trusted him or not.

"I don't know if I can change my spirit clothes," I

said, fighting the urge to look at my feet and make myself smaller like I'd been taught in the human realm.

Father, I was so tired of feeling weak. But if the day before yesterday and last night had proven anything, it was that I *was* weak.

I'd tried last night and failed to change my spirit clothes, and I wasn't sure if Zinnia's theory that the magic that was affecting me from Wells's spell or the artifact that had trapped my soul in the Garden had actually prevented me from changing my clothes or not. Or if I couldn't change my clothes because I was really a human and didn't have the same abilities as a fae.

"Try changing them now?" Rider suggested.

Lord Quill released me and took a step back, giving me space, and I closed my eyes. What should I change my lacey, gauzy dress into? Just like before, I immediately thought of the dresses I was used to in the human realm with high necklines, long sleeves, and floor-length hems.

No. If I was fae, I wouldn't know what human women wore. I couldn't change my dress to one like that.

I tried to remember what Zinnia's robe had looked like. The fabric had been thick and the collar so high it had brushed her jaw.

I imagined myself wearing Zinnia's robe.

It didn't feel like anything happened.

I peeled the blanket away from my chest just enough to confirm I still wore the same red dress.

All right. I sucked in a sharp breath and closed my eyes again.

This time I imagined my dress transforming into the

robe, the gauzy fabric thickening and spreading up my neck and down my arms.

Nothing.

I imagined my dress melting away and a new robe wrapping around me.

Still nothing.

I clenched my jaw, my eyes squeezing tighter with frustration. I had to figure out how to change my clothes or everyone would know my marks had been put to sleep. I had to stop drawing attention to myself.

"Hey," Quill murmured as his hand brushed my shoulder, making my eyes fly open.

Rider huffed, but I couldn't tell why. Probably because I still hadn't changed my clothes and it was supposed to be easy.

"The magic affecting her last night could still be affecting her," Talon said, his gaze intense as if he were looking at something inside me.

Lord Rider took a step closer, his attention also locked on me. "Not everyone can control their spirit form right away."

Even Sir West was staring at me.

I shifted back, bumping into Lord Quill. I didn't like the way everyone was looking at me. They were going to figure out I was human and then they were going to put all the pieces together and figure out I was pretending to be Sawyer.

It would all come crashing down and—

No.

Zinnia had said that as a fae woman I could stand my

ground, that what had happened with Wells and Crane wasn't typical behavior. I needed to stop acting like a scared human. The more I acted like one, the faster they'd learn the truth, and I needed to hold out as long as possible to ensure Sawyer's safety.

I squared my shoulders, prayed this would work, and thought about glaring at them but couldn't make myself do it.

"Please stop staring," I asked, proud I'd managed to keep my voice even and clear.

Rider's eyes widened, and a hint of color stained his cheeks before he looked away and cleared his throat, while Talon gave a slight bow of his head in apology.

West continued to stare.

"All right," Quill said, his voice gentle. "Why don't we practice without the audience?"

He grabbed my shoulders and nudged me toward the fancy bedroom with the enormous bed. We crossed the threshold into the room, and Sir West took a step forward as if he were going to follow, but Quill shot him a hard look. The enormous knight grunted, grabbed the door handle, and shut the door instead, leaving me alone with Lord Quill.

The memory of what Quill and I had done last night flooded me and heat bled across my cheeks. I'd taken my pleasure from him without any regard for his, and then I'd cried in his arms.

I jerked my attention away from the bed, my gaze darting over the room at the opulent furnishings, uncertain where to look. The desire from my marks wasn't spiking, not even being so close to Talon, so I wasn't desperate, but I also couldn't deny how handsome Quill was and how much the kindness in his gaze made me want to believe he actually cared.

Which I suppose wasn't fair. For all I knew he did care... as much as one stranger could care about another.

I just knew that if Lord Rider gave him an order, he'd follow it, regardless of how it hurt me.

My chest tightened. I wished Ash were with me instead. I felt safe with him. Desired. Comforted.

But the High Priestess had banned Ash from the Divine Residence because of his scars.

The thought made me furious. I didn't know how Ash had been burned, but given how kind and caring he'd been toward me, I doubted it had been because he deserved it. He'd said he wasn't a very good man, but I couldn't make myself believe that. And while yes, Ash was also one of Lord Rider's captains in the Black Guard, my soul assured me I could trust him, that he'd pick me over Rider.

Perhaps that was foolish.

I didn't really know these men, and they certainly didn't know me. If they did, I'd doubted they'd be trying to protect me.

What I really needed to learn was how to control when I manifested in the Garden. If I could keep my spirit in my body when I went to sleep, I wouldn't have to worry about the added complications of pretending to be a fae woman.

"Let's sit." Lord Quill's gaze dipped to the bed, and a

hint of color stained his cheeks and the tips of his delicately pointed ears.

His blush made my face heat more, knowing that he was thinking the same thing I was, and the yearning that seeing the bed had inspired within me, burned a little hotter.

It wasn't the crazy, demanding desire I'd experienced last night. It was more natural than that. Quill was so handsome and kind, and the blush brought out more of his boyish charm.

His gaze rose to meet mine and for a breathless moment I was trapped in his emerald orbs, surrounded by his desire, yearning, and resignation.

Ash, when I'd only known him as my Fantasy Man, had told me the fae's goddess would never bind Quill to a woman because he didn't have any magic, and for a moment, I could feel Quill's heartache. I was the thing he yearned for that he could never have. So close and yet forever out of reach.

I closed my eyes, severing the connection between us.

It wasn't *me* he wanted. It was a fae woman, and I just so happened to be the only one in the room. He didn't know me. Only my brother, Sawyer, had ever known me and, if the Great Father was kind and ensured his safety, I'd never see him again.

CHAPTER 7

Sage

I TURNED toward the small seating area by the windows where Zinnia and I had talked last night. If we didn't leave the room, the bed would always be an enormous presence reminding us of what we'd done, but we didn't have to sit on it.

"How about here," I suggested as I settled on the window seat.

Thankfully, the chair Zinnia had pulled up was still there even though the bed had been made, indicating that someone had entered the room and tidied up while I'd been awake in the Gray.

"Right." Quill cleared his throat and sat in the chair. "Why don't we start with something smaller than trying to change your whole dress? Let's try adding sleeves."

"Sleeves," I murmured, closing my eyes. "Just simple sleeves."

I pictured my red lacey dress with long, elegant sleeves that would cover my arms. I tried to imagine the weight of the fabric, how it would feel against my skin, the way the lace would extend down to my wrists in delicate patterns.

Nothing.

All right. Maybe if I started even smaller. I imagined half a sleeve, just enough to reach my elbows. I thought about using a simple material, not a delicate lace. Maybe lace was too complicated for me.

But I still couldn't feel fabric on my shoulders or around my biceps.

I cracked open one eye and glanced at my still bare arms.

No. Damn it.

I could do this. I *had* to do this.

I squeezed my eyes tight again and concentrated. The lacey fabric straps on my shoulders *would* turn into sleeves. I imagined the fabric growing — nothing — then suddenly appearing — nothing — then rising up through my skin — nothing — then draping over me — still nothing.

I imagined the fabric glowing with power, whisp thin then thickening. I imagined it any way, every way. Still no god-damned thing.

"All right." Quill leaned forward. "What about jewelry? A ring or a necklace. Something you're adding, not changing. That might be easier."

"Sure," I said, my hesitation clear in my tone.

I wasn't sure if adding something would be easier, but I was willing to try.

"It can be anything you can wear or hold." He held

out his hand, and a delicate white ceramic cup appeared in his palm. It looked real, like everything else in the Garden.

"It's empty," I said. "Could you put water in it?"

"Only if it's water from the Garden." He turned the cup over. "You can manifest any object you can wear or realistically hold, but not food or water. You can't manifest anything living, like a horse."

I raised my eyebrows at that, making him chuckle.

"Not that you'd be able to hold a horse, but you wouldn't be able to manifest... say... a bird or a mouse, either. And—" He set the cup on the window seat beside me and it disappeared. "If you let go of it or it stops touching you, if disappears."

"But I should be able to manifest a ring?" I dropped my gaze to my bare fingers.

I could imagine a simple gold ring. I knew what that looked like. It wasn't overly complicated.

I closed my eyes and pictured a simple gold band around my index finger.

Nothing.

I clenched my jaw in concentration. A ring. Simple. Gold. Smooth. It encircled my finger.

Still nothing. I imagined it's weight, it pressing against my skin, it wrapping around my finger, it appearing out of nowhere, just showing up on my hand like Quill's cup had shown up in his.

Nothing nothing nothing.

My eyes burned with frustrated tears that I didn't want Lord Quill to see.

He'd already seen enough of my tears, and this was such a silly thing to cry over. For all I knew the magic that Zinnia had said was affecting me still influenced me. She and Magister Aster had said the magic was fading but hadn't said how fast.

Maybe tomorrow I'd be able to do it... if, of course, the magic was the reason I couldn't change my spirit clothes.

"Hey, it's all right," Quill said, his tone overly kind. "You'll get it soon enough. And in the meantime, I'll arrange to have clothes ready for tomorrow night or the night after."

"Right." I turned my attention out the window to look at the lights and softly glowing flowers in the impossible tree-castle that made up the Divine Residence and the garden below.

My insides twisted. Everything could come crashing down at any moment.

"Maybe that strange magic is... you know." I shrugged then brushed my fingertips over my sleeping mating marks. "Or what Zinnia did to put them to sleep..."

The worry in Lord Quill's gaze deepened into concern, and I prayed that what I'd said had been enough to make him reject any thoughts about me being unusual or suspicious.

"For now..." Quill stood and strode to the wardrobe on the other side of the large bedroom. He opened one of the intricately carved wooden doors and pulled out the silk robe I'd worn last night.

I stood and he returned to slide the sensual material over my shoulders, that snap of lightning that always zinged through me when we touched sending a shiver of desire racing down my spine.

The memory of his gentle hands washing my heated skin rushed through me, and a soft gasp slipped from my lips. I ducked my head in what I already knew was a futile attempt to hide my blush, but I just couldn't help myself.

Meeting Lord Quill's gaze was too embarrassing right now, especially since Zinnia had told me a fae woman wouldn't be embarrassed about her sexual activity, and doubly not embarrassed because my mating marks had compelled me. It was the nature of being a fae woman, and there wasn't any shame in it.

"You're presentable," Lord Quill said. "Would you like to return to the sitting room?"

I glanced at the closed bedroom door. I hadn't heard anyone leave, but that didn't mean Lords Rider and Talon hadn't left.

Regardless, West was still out there, and he'd either witness my awkward conversation with Quill or my awkward conversation with Quill, Rider, and Talon when all I really wanted to do was hide... or better yet, go to sleep and return to my body.

What were the chances West would leave me alone in the bedroom with the door closed?

Maybe leaving the door open just wide enough so West could see inside but not wide enough that I would feel exposed would be enough so I could fall back asleep.

"I think I'd like to rest."

Quill's expression softened and he glanced at the bedroom door.

"If we leave it open a bit, hopefully that will be enough for Sir West," I said, knowing what his look at the door meant.

"As you wish." Lord Quill stood and left, leaving the door open by a hand's width.

A shadow stepped in front of the opening, and a masculine voice, too quiet for me to make out the words, said something. The shadow moved away. Sir West didn't come barging in and the door remained ajar. Thank you, Lord Quill.

I turned my attention to the bed. It could be seen from the doorway and the thought of lying there, with Sir West staring at me even if I couldn't see him, made my insides squirm. It felt too exposed, too vulnerable, even if all I really wanted was to lie down, close my eyes, and go to sleep.

Except I had a feeling if I didn't move into sight soon, West would come in, and I really didn't want that.

Keeping the robe wrapped tight around me, I got up from the window seat and moved to the bed. I pushed back the top sheet, crawled underneath, and lay down.

I could feel his gaze on me.

I rolled over and squeezed my eyes shut.

I was tired, my body still ached from all the physical activity I'd done in the past few days and the injuries I'd sustained from being attacked by Wells and Crane even in my spirit form.

Father, I didn't want to think about how much I'd

hurt when I woke up in my room in the Black Tower. I was sore before I'd gone to sleep, and I knew I was going to be sore for days. But at least I wasn't constantly being watched.

And, from the silence beyond the bedroom door, I couldn't tell if West was the only one left in the sitting room.

I didn't want to be alone with him. Of course, I wasn't sure I wanted to be alone with Lords Quill, Rider, or Talon but for completely different reasons.

With a huff, I rolled to my other side.

My mating marks weren't compelling me to have sex anymore, but I still couldn't deny my attraction to them. And Father help me if I had another desire spike...

A chill swept through me. What if I had a spike and only Sir West was around? Would I throw myself at him? Would he want me to?

Was that the High Priestess's plan all along?

No. It couldn't be. She didn't know about my mating marks, which meant she didn't know I could have sudden, overwhelming spikes of desire while the magic in my marks was shut down.

And shadows, that desire—

The memory of how I'd ached to be touched and kissed and filled bled through my worry.

Lord Quill had slid his hands up my thighs, parting me before pressing his lips to my core in this very bed, and I'd been helpless to deny him. It hadn't mattered what my mind had wanted, my body had craved him, needed him, desperately.

Heat bled across my cheeks and low in my gut, and my hand slipped between my thighs inside my robe and cupped my sex over my dress. Even with my body sore and aching from physical exertion, the memory of his touch and the kindness and desire in his gaze burned within me.

My fingers pressed against my sensitive nub like how his tongue had pressed and flicked, driving me crazy.

Except it hadn't been enough.

No, I'd needed him inside me, needed to feel his hard length stretching and filling me.

The heat inside me fluttered stronger, and I sucked in a sharp breath and jerked my hand away.

I had to stop thinking about how it felt to have him inside me, how it had been as amazing as when I'd had sex with Ash and yet different at the same time.

My heart twisted. Shadows, I missed Ash. I ached for him even more than I did for Lord Quill. Yes, I yearned for the comfort and concern that Quill had given me, but I needed the surety and safety I got from Ash more.

I rolled over again and squeezed my pillow. I had to stop thinking about having sex with Lord Quill, with Ash, with anyone. I had to fall asleep and return to my body.

Jeez, why couldn't I get comfortable? Why couldn't I—?

A bell tolled, a loud, deep resonant bong.

I jerked up, my body screaming in pain at the sudden movement. The agony devoured the heat of my desire, pushing it thankfully back to just a memory. The plush mattress beneath me had hardened, and the soft, smooth sheet had become coarse.

Footsteps pounded outside my door, and I blinked a bleary gaze around my small room in the Black Tower. A hint of light bled from between the crack of the closed shutter as well as from the fae crystal in the wall. The towel I kept in my room to clean up was still crumpled on top of the chest at the foot of my narrow bed where Lewin had dropped it, and I wore my Black Guard uniform, not a lacey red dress and a silky robe.

I was back. It was morning. And I didn't feel rested at all.

I flopped back onto the bed, sending another shock of pain racing through me. It was my second lieu day. I didn't need to get up or do any—

Actually, I had to meet Lord Quill in the infirmary at the fifth bell because now everyone — since I was sure no one in the Black Tower could keep a secret despite Lord Rider's orders — knew I could see the future.

Maybe staying in my room until I had to meet with Lord Quill was the best plan.

I closed my eyes, but the fear that I'd fall back asleep and return to the Garden made them fly open again. Lords Rider, Quill, and Talon would be awake right now being the Lord Commander and Captains of the Black Guard, which meant if I fell asleep now and went to the Garden it would be just me and Sir West.

Yeah, not a great idea.

With my aching muscles throbbing in pain, I got up. I shrugged out of my heavy jerkin and shirt and retied the strips of fabric from my ruined dress to flatten my chest. I'd been too afraid someone would walk in on me when I'd returned to Kit, Payne, and Lewin's suite to grab my boots and sword that I'd done a rush job wrapping the strips. I wouldn't have wrapped the strips at all, but I hadn't wanted to walk from one wing of the Black Tower to the other carrying them, not when I should have been in bed.

Of course, no one had walked in on me, since Kit's whole team was still in the infirmary, but I couldn't convince myself that I wasn't going to get caught.

I'd enjoyed the bath. It had been kind of Kit and the guys to let me use their private washing room but given how the rest of the Black Guard felt about me, it had been foolish of me to take them up on their offer, especially when they were out on patrol. One person seeing me without Kit or Payne there to defend me, could have put me in serious trouble.

No matter how much my body ached — and it seemed to ache just as much today as it did yesterday, maybe even more — I needed to remember to not draw attention to myself.

I redressed and splashed water on my face, hoping that would make me feel better, more refreshed, less like I'd overexerted myself and was now paying the consequences.

It didn't. I was still sore and tired.

The footsteps outside my door had quieted, so I risked glancing outside. The hall was empty, but that only meant the men on the first shift were in the great hall having breakfast, as well as those novices who wanted to get an early start on their lieu day and return to Lehyrst.

I was still restricted to the Gray and couldn't go to Lehyrst, but I wasn't sure I wanted to go even if it was permitted.

Mikel and his friends were no doubt planning retaliation for me threatening them even if I was just defending myself, and I doubted any of the guardsmen in Lehyrst would protect me. I doubted Rider, Talon, and Quill went to Lehyrst either... well, I knew for a fact Lord Quill wasn't because I had to meet him in the infirmary at the fifth bell.

Even if one of them was there, it would look suspicious if I hung around them. And really, what would I say to them? Rider clearly didn't like me, and Talon, who I thought might be a possible ally obeyed Lord Rider's orders and could turn on me at any moment.

The only men in the Black Tower I might consider friends were Kit, Payne, and Lewin, and they were in the infirmary.

My stomach growled. If I didn't want to run into anyone in the great hall, I had to wait until after the second shift of the day had eaten breakfast, which meant after the third bell. But there wasn't any guarantee that the men working in the kitchen would still have food out or that they'd let me have any of it.

No, best to join the line and pray I didn't run into Mikel and his friends, and that the other guardsmen ignored me.

CHAPTER 8
Sage

DOWN IN THE GREAT HALL, I joined the line of guardsmen waiting their turn to get breakfast. The man in front of me was a human who was big and bulky like Payne, and the man who stepped up behind me was a fae with a similar build.

I squared my shoulders and resisted the urge to shrink in on myself. Even after a rotation of practicing and learning that I wouldn't be punished for looking a man in the eyes or looking anything other than meek and submissive, the urge was still there.

Father, I hated that I felt that way.

But I couldn't deny years of *training* or the fact that I couldn't trust any of these men. They might push or trip me when I wasn't looking or worse. They'd already proven they didn't think Lord Rider's punishment of stable duty was enough for having gone through the fae ring after dark, and with a new rotation starting tomorrow, I feared they wouldn't think whatever new assignment I'd been given would be enough.

I turned my head slightly so I could look at the man behind me from the corner of my eye. He wasn't looking at me and kept his gaze above my head even when the line shifted forward.

In the kitchen, the men ensuring the platters on the counter were filled with food glanced at me then looked away. I grabbed two slices of bread, some meat, and made a sandwich, then took an orange from the fruit bowl at the end and hurried out of the kitchen and back out of the great hall. No point in sticking around and sitting among men who didn't like me.

I returned to my room to eat then sat on my bed trying to figure out what to do.

Given how sore I was, I should probably move around to stop my muscles from tightening up even more. Yesterday, I'd walked the perimeter of the training ground and no one had bothered me. The library had also been pretty private, with only Tyon there trying to teach himself how to read.

Thinking of Tyon and the library reminded me that I'd originally gone there to look for information about all the things I didn't know enough about like the fae and their culture as well as my magic and even the shadow creatures and the Gray.

I also wanted to check in on Kit, Payne, Lewin, and even Grefin to see how they were doing, although I wasn't sure if Flint would allow me into the infirmary or if they would be up for talking with me.

Only one way to find out: go to the infirmary.

Also, if I waited until after my mandatory talk with Lord Quill about my magic then maybe he'd direct me toward books in the library that would help me.

A shiver swept through me at the thought of Lord Quill. I didn't know how I felt about him. A part of me ached to be near him, to feel his kindness and concern, something I hadn't felt since my mother died. But another part didn't trust that kindness and knew it could vanish the moment Lord Rider gave an order.

But it was still smarter to see if Lord Quill could suggest some books than wandering the library hoping I'd find something useful. Which meant visiting Kit and the others first.

With that decided, I headed to the infirmary.

After a quick walk to the other wing of the Black Tower, I stopped outside the infirmary door and raised my hand to knock, then hesitated.

Should I just walk in? Last night I'd crashed through these doors in a panic, but I'd been trying to save Payne's life.

The memory of barging in made my stomach clench. I hadn't gotten into trouble for it, but that didn't mean I wouldn't if I did it again. I rapped my knuckles against the heavy wood and waited.

No answer.

I knocked again, harder this time, and pressed my ear to the door. Nothing but silence. Maybe Flint was with one of his patients in the patient rooms at the back and couldn't hear me.

After another moment of waiting, I cracked the door open just wide enough to peek through. The main room was empty, the examination tables clean, and morning light streamed through the high windows and across the pale stone floor. There were no signs of blood or chaos or pain like there'd been a few hours ago.

Footsteps echoed from the hall at the back of the large room, and I pushed the door open wider just as Flint emerged, wiping his hands on a clean towel.

"Here to see Kit and his team?" he asked with a smile. He wore his usual black pants and pale blue doublet, and I realized the doublet was the same color as Zinnia's robes. Was blue the color for fae healers?

"Yes," I said, relieved that the healer didn't seem angry at me like all the other guardsmen.

Of course, I did save Payne's life, so hopefully that counted for something. Maybe if word got out about that—

I cut that thought off. I didn't want the entire Black Guard to know I could see the future. That would just make people more interested in me and go against everything I was striving for.

"Kit and Lewin are in the first two rooms," Flint said. "Both asleep or unaware from the large dose of pain draught I gave them. Payne's in Kit's room if you want someone to talk to."

I nodded and headed down the hall that led to the private recovery rooms. The door to the first room stood open and I glanced in. Lewin lay on the bed covered up to his waist with a simple sheet, his bare chest wrapped in thick linen strips. His complexion was pale, but his expression was calm and peaceful, and it didn't look like he was in any pain.

The room was similar, if a little bigger, than my room in the barracks, with a narrow bed against one wall. Instead of a trunk at the foot of the bed, there was a chair, and beside the head of the bed was a low, long bedside table, big enough to hold a tray of medical supplies. Against the wall opposite the bed stood a door, perhaps to a closet?

Lewin wasn't conscious, so I moved to the next door which was also open. Inside the room was an identical mirror image to Lewin's. Kit lay motionless on the bed, his breathing deep and even. His sheet had been pulled up to mid-chest, but I could still see the top half of the thick linens wrapped around his torso as well.

Beside him, Payne sat hunched forward in a chair that had been pulled close, holding Kit's hand — the hand that hadn't been severed — in both of his. Kit's hand almost looked delicate wrapped in Payne's large grip, which meant mine would look child-like in comparison.

Kit's other hand was hidden by the sheet, and for a moment I feared that he'd lost it. Everything had happened so fast last night and then I'd had to deal with Sir West, Lords Quill and Rider and Talon in the Garden, so my memory was fuzzy. But I was sure Flint had reattached it with his magic.

Of course, if his magic was powerful enough to reattach a hand, why were Kit and Lewin still being given medicine for their pain?

Payne glanced up at the sound of my footsteps and offered me a tired smile. His complexion was still a little pale, and the man looked haggard with dark circles under his striking amethyst eyes. He'd probably stayed up all night at Kit's side, worrying.

"Hey," Payne murmured, his voice low and gruff so he didn't wake Kit.

"Have you slept?" I asked, keeping my voice soft as well.

"A little. I'm the next room down." Payne jerked his chin toward the next room in the opposite direction of Lewin's. "I just can't stop worrying."

"But Flint healed him, right?"

"As much as he's allowed," Payne replied. "Healing magic isn't rare, but it isn't common, either. There are only three healers working for the Black Guard and there's only ever one on duty at any given time. Here—"

Payne carefully shifted over to the bed, sitting by Kit's legs, and motioned to the now empty chair.

"Thanks." I sat and studied Kit's face. Like all fae — well all fae except Sir West and maybe Ash if you couldn't look past his scars — he was beautiful with refined features and long thick eyelashes that any woman would kill for.

And yet I didn't feel an attraction to him like I felt with Talon, Lord Quill, Ash, or hell, even Lord Rider.

"Because there's only ever one healer on duty," Payne said, "none of the healers are allowed to do more than the bare minimum to save a life or prevent permanent disability if possible."

Which would explain why many of the older guardsmen had scars. I'd figured they'd been injured in the field and couldn't get to a fae healer in time, but I guess that wasn't the case.

"They have to ration their magic in case more injured guardsmen come in before they can restore their power. So Flint saved Kit's hand, for which I'm grateful," Payne said. "But bone is harder to heal than flesh and muscle, so it's still broken."

"And everything else—" I gestured to the linen wrapped around Kit's chest. "It's been treated without magic or with just enough magic that non-magical treatments will suffice?"

"Exactly," Flint said from the doorway.

The healer held a tray with a bowl of porridge, two slices of bread, and a hank of green grapes. He set the tray on the bedside table, drawing my attention to what I'd thought was a closet door. From my position in the room, I could now see that it was actually a bathing room like the one in Kit's elite team's suite.

"Are you going to wake him?" I asked.

"I could mitigate the effects of the wistellel with my magic, but it's better if he keeps sleeping. No—" Flint gave Payne a hard look. "The food is for this one. If he isn't going to sleep, he needs to eat."

"I'm not hungry."

"You only think that because you're worried about your bonded," Flint said, his expression softening. "But he'd want you to keep your strength up. Sawyer might have saved you by giving you the antivenom, but that only helps your body fight off the poison. It's still inside you, making you weak."

I stood, offering Payne the chair back so it would be easier for him to eat at the table, but he waved me down.

"I can eat off my lap."

Flint handed Payne the tray and the large fae shoved a spoonful of porridge into his mouth.

"There you go," Flint said as if Payne were a stubborn child. "And don't worry, I won't force you up to your suite tomorrow, like I should. As long as I have a free bed, you can stay down here."

Payne ate another spoonful of porridge and Flint left.

With a sigh, Payne's attention drifted back to Kit, the spoon forgotten in his fingers. "I want to thank you. If it wasn't for you, I wouldn't be here arguing with Flint."

I shifted in the chair, uncomfortable with his tone and the reminder that while I'd saved him, I'd also made myself way more interesting than I wanted to be.

"Your shoulders are too small for the weight they're going to carry," he added.

I frowned and he glanced at me.

"The sight is a hard gift, even for a fae." His gaze dipped to his spoon as if he just realized he was still holding it, and he scooped up another mouthful of porridge. "When we're young, all fae are taught about the various types of magic that might be in our spark. The sight was one of the magics that terrified me."

I shuddered at his words. If a fae as strong and confident as Payne was afraid of my magic, maybe I should be too.

Sure, I'd been afraid of what I'd seen, of Sawyer's death and then my own. But the fact that I possessed the power hadn't scared me. Of course, when it had started, it hadn't been visions. It had just been bad feelings.

Now I was seeing things and my premonitions were coming more frequently.

Did that mean at some point I'd be lost within my visions, unaware of the reality around me like Flint said?

I couldn't let that happen... not until I knew Sawyer was safe. After that, maybe it would be best if my mind wasn't with my body. Mikel, Durand, and the others had proven I wasn't even safe in the Gray as a man. I definitely wouldn't be safe as a woman. And even if I left the Black Tower unscathed, I'd be punished by the king of Erellod, or worse sent back to my stepfather, Edred, who'd severely discipline me before selling me off in marriage.

CHAPTER 9

Sage

I SAT with Payne for the rest of the morning, keeping him company and quietly talking about him and Kit. I learned that they'd joined the Black Guard at the same time and had become fast friends during novice training. All the while, his amethyst eyes had sparked with warmth as he gazed lovingly at his mate, making my heart ache with longing.

Would anyone ever look at me like that? Like I was the only person in the world for them?

Like I mattered?

Would Ash?

I shoved that thought aside. It was foolish, and even if it wasn't impossible, it certainly wasn't practical, given my current situation.

"We flirted on and off for years," Payne said, "but it wasn't until two years ago that Kit told me my soul called to his."

Heat crept up Payne's neck and into his cheeks, and I bit back a smile at seeing this enormous fae warrior blush.

"I was so relieved when he confessed," Payne admitted, his voice dropping even lower. "I'd had feelings for him from the moment we first met, but I never said anything. Kit has magic, so he was eligible for a female mate, and I didn't want to..." He shrugged.

"You didn't want to get in the way," I finished softly.

"Yeah, but it turns out no one's soul ever called to him the way mine did."

He chuckled at that and told me stories about their time together as journeymen guardsmen and then when they formed a hunting team with Lewin and Hodge.

His expression darkened at the mention of Hodge, and he didn't go into detail about how the man had died, but if it had been anything like the glimpse I'd gotten of the bear attack, I understood why Payne didn't want to relive that.

We talked until the fourth bell rang and Flint returned with a new tray filled with food for Payne.

My stomach rumbled, reminding me it was lunchtime, but I didn't really want to face all the silent glares from the guardsmen in the great hall. Sure, no one had tried to trip me since I'd threatened to kill Mikel in his sleep, but that didn't mean they weren't waiting for the right time to strike.

"Go on," Flint said. "I don't know if Quill will want to teach you meditation right away, but if he does, you won't be able to concentrate with your stomach making all that noise."

With a sigh, I returned to the great hall. It was the same as breakfast where the guardsmen's eyes would glaze over the moment they noticed me or they'd instantly look away. No one tried to trip me, and I didn't hear any snide comments, whispered or otherwise. It was as if the men had decided my new punishment was that I didn't exist.

And if that was all they were going to do…? Great.

I wanted to be invisible. Being invisible meant less opportunity for me to screw up and someone noticing I wasn't a boy.

Except I couldn't believe that ignoring me was the new plan. It couldn't be. They had to be planning something, and I had to be ready for it.

I made myself another sandwich, pocketed another orange, and headed back to my room to eat. I wasn't sure if Payne wanted more company during lunch, but I didn't want to wear out my welcome. I also didn't know if me showing up too much would bother Flint.

Flint hadn't treated me like the other guardsmen. Technically, he and the other healers in the Black Tower weren't guardsmen and weren't committed to a mandatory period of service like the other fae — or a lifetime of service like the humans. But that didn't mean Flint wasn't a part of the Black Guard *brotherhood*.

And while he might not have shown his dislike of me because of whatever healing vows fae healers took, that didn't mean he approved of me. I couldn't mistake politeness for acceptance.

When I finished my lunch, I stepped back out into

the hall to see a guardsman with a bundle of scrunched up clothes open the narrow door by the stairs and toss his laundry into the bin.

Grefin had said the bedding was only washed every two rotations. Did that mean everyone's bedding, or was there a rotation where some guardsmen were one rotation and the rest were the other rotation so as not to overwhelm the guardsmen doing the laundry?

Given that I'd only been in the Black Tower for a single rotation, it was probably safe to assume I shouldn't strip my bed and expect new bedding from the quartermaster. That said, I needed to stop by his quarters to get my new clean uniforms as well as learn what my morning chore would be for the next rotation.

But first, I had to meet Lord Quill in the infirmary to talk about my fae-touched ability.

The guardsman who'd had the dirty laundry headed down the hall toward the sitting area, thankfully away from me. I slowly closed my door and followed after him, hoping his faster pace and longer legs would put distance between us.

Every muscle in my body hurt, and I prayed to the Father that whatever chore Lord Rider and the quartermaster gave me, it wouldn't be as physically demanding as mucking out the stables.

I returned to the infirmary and slipped inside, not wanting to wait out in the hall. Lord Quill arrived just as the fifth bell started to toll and offered me a tentative smile which confused me until I realized the last time

Lord Quill had seen me, *Sawyer*, I'd collapsed on the running trail and thrown up.

I offered him my own tentative, tight-lipped smile. I needed to be careful and stay focused, so I didn't mix up what I did in the Gray with what I did in the Garden.

"So," Quill said. "Rider tells me your fae-touched ability is the sight."

"Yeah."

One of the guardsmen assigned to helping Flint walked into the infirmary's main room, his eyes narrowing when he saw me. He wasn't one of the men from last night which meant he wasn't supposed to know about my magic, but I couldn't tell from his expression if he knew about it or not.

Quill sighed and gestured to the hall where the private rooms were. "I think there's an empty room in the back. Let's talk there."

"Right."

I followed him down the hall, past Lewin and Kit's room — noticing that Payne was back in the chair at Kit's bedside — past three more doors that were closed and two more that were open then into the second to last room.

It was identical to all the other private rooms in the infirmary with a bed, a low long table, a chair, and a bathroom. My gaze instantly jumped to the bed and my pulse picked up.

No. Nope. Not at all. Not going to think anything about Lord Quill and beds.

Thankfully, Quill sat on the bed instead of giving me

the choice of where to sit — which was good, since I honestly had no idea what I'd have picked. Sitting on the bed felt too exposed, like I was inviting him to join me somehow.

Except *him* sitting on the bed reminded me of how I'd jumped him and ridden his cock the other night in the Garden.

Jeez. What was wrong with me?

"How long have you been able to see things?" he asked as I perched on the edge of the chair, not committing to getting comfortable and forgetting where I was and who I was talking to.

"Not long."

Unease tightened my insides. I'd been keeping my secret for so long that a part of me didn't want to talk about my ability. But another part, a bigger part that was terrified of what would happen, knew Lord Quill needed to know everything if he was going to help me… or at least everything about my magic, not about me being a girl or my current predicament.

"I had my first vision the day—"

I bit the inside of my cheek. I was about to tell him I'd had my first vision that day he'd called Sawyer's name for the lottery, but that risked him realizing my "sister" had acted strange and he might realize the truth.

"The day before my name was drawn in the lottery," I lied.

"And you told your sister."

"I…"

When Lord Quill had arrived at Herstind Keep I'd

acted as if I'd already known who's name he was going to say, but that had very little to do with my ability to sense the future. I'd only had a bad feeling and years of experience living with my stepfather. But I still needed to say something he'd believe.

"I told her I thought something might happen. I didn't know for sure. Before that, I'd only ever gotten a sense that something bad was going to happen."

"Bad, like what?"

"Like the sweating sickness would be worse than usual or that brigands were going to attack or that a nasty storm was coming. Nothing specific, just a sense of dread about some things."

Quill's expression darkened. "So it's getting stronger."

"And more frequent. It used to be every once in a while, and now I've had a—" *Crap, should I say I've had a few close together? Would he want to know what other visions I'd seen?*

Would he be able to save me if I told him about my impending death?

No, if I told him about that vision, he'd want to know why, he'd ask more questions about me, and I just couldn't risk him learning I was a woman. Not until I knew Sawyer was out of the Five Great Kingdoms and safe. Then, maybe. If he'd proven that I could trust him and that he wouldn't just hand me over to Rider to be punished.

"I've now had two close together," I said, hoping he

wouldn't notice the slip of my tongue. "My name being drawn in the lottery and Payne being poisoned."

"It just means your ability is maturing. You're a little young, but you're also human so we shouldn't be surprised if it's early."

"When would a fae get his magic?"

Sadness flickered through Quill's expression so fast I almost missed it. If I hadn't known how much not having magic hurt him, I probably *would have* missed it. My chest tightened and I regretted asking.

"Men usually start manifesting an ability around our twentieth summer."

If fae manifested their magic when they were twenty then I was an early bloomer since I'd been having premonitions for years. Except Lord Quill had said "men" specifically, which implied fae women were different. Not that I was a fae woman.

And not that I could actually ask about the difference between fae men and women without making Quill curious.

If I saw Zinnia I could ask her... although then she might want to know what my magic was, and I wasn't sure if I should tell her.

Yes, I trusted her to tell me the truth about fae society and to keep my sleeping mating marks a secret, but I wasn't sure if I could trust her to keep my magic a secret.

"Your vision last night..." Quill shifted on the bed, the movement pulling my attention back to him. "Can you remember what you saw? Did you see the serpent that bit Payne?"

"No." The images of the enormous, misshapen bears, their maws open, their claws slashing, the guys screaming and gasping and yelling, all caught between sudden flashes of light in the darkness crashed through my mind. "I— It happened so fast."

Quill leaned forward and rested his warm hand on my knee.

A shudder swept through me, a mix of the fear from what I'd seen and desire at his touch.

"I know it's difficult, but I need you to think carefully. How did the bears behave? Did you see anything else? Anything strange?"

That didn't sound good. He'd only be asking questions like that if he thought there was something wrong with the bears. Of course, Payne had been poisoned, and it didn't sound like anyone noticed anything poisonous around them, so...

"I'm sorry. I only caught a glimpse of the shadow bears. It was dark and my vision of the bears only lasted a moment. Then I saw Payne collapse in the infirmary and Flint say that he'd been poisoned."

Quill hummed in thought and sat back, frowning.

Did he think I was lying or not telling the whole truth?

His gaze jumped back to mine and his expression softened. "It's all right. Visions can be unpredictable, especially if you're untrained. It's not surprising you didn't see much."

"But you were hoping I'd seen something?"

"It most certainly would have made things easier."

He offered me a soft smile. "Right. Well... We should get to what we're supposed to be doing in the first place. Meditation."

Right. Learning to meditate so I wouldn't go crazy. Maybe. If I was lucky.

Of course, I'd already foreseen that I'd die in the Gray so worrying about losing my mind probably shouldn't have been my first concern.

"Will it help me control my visions?" If I could control when they came and what I focused on, maybe I could find a way to survive... and then I'd actually need to worry about going crazy.

"Possibly," he said, his expression serious. "It should keep you from getting lost in them, but there isn't any record of a fae with the sight ever having full control over their visions."

Swell. And I didn't like how he'd said *"should"* and not *"would"* keep me from getting lost in my visions.

Except that was the best I was going to get. If I could survive my foreseen death, then keeping myself sane for as long as possible had to be the goal, since I had no idea if the attack would come before Sawyer was safe.

"All right." It was better than nothing.

"Close your eyes and breathe deeply," he said. "Hold for a count of four, then release slowly."

I closed my eyes and was suddenly hyperaware of how small the room was and how close Lord Quill and I were even though I sat in a chair, and he was on the bed.

I sucked in air, determined to focus. One... two... three... four. I slowly released my breath.

"Good." His tone softened and deepened, reminding me of his tone when he'd begged to help me relieve the pressure from my mating marks. "Keep breathing like that and focus on the spark inside you."

I frowned. I didn't have a spark. I was human.

Except I also had magic. So did that mean I *did* have a spark? Was that what made me fae-touched?

"If you... ah... can't sense a spark," he said before I could ask him what a spark was supposed to feel like, "imagine one in the middle of your chest, anchored within your body."

I drew in another breath, held it, and released it slowly while trying to picture a small flame in the center of my chest, and not how the wooden bedframe creaked as Quill shifted positions.

"My spark is like a miniscule star," he murmured, his voice caressing my senses and drawing a highly inappropriate shiver of need through me. "A pinprick of light rooted in the heart of my being, an anchor that tethers my spirit to my body."

My imagined flame shifted to my heart and melted into a shimmering white star the size of my thumbnail, and I couldn't help wondering if I imagined mine bigger than Lord Quill's because I knew he didn't have magic and I did or if something else controlled my imagination.

"Talon, because his magic allows him to control darkness, says his spark is like an eclipsed sun, big and powerful with a black core and a thin red ring around the circumference."

My white star flickered, but didn't change color or shape, and I drew in another breath.

"Focus on the point of connection between you and the spark," he purred. "On how it's locked inside you."

I shuddered softly at the words "inside you," remembering how it had felt to have *him* inside me.

"How it's buried within the core of your being."

A stronger shiver rolled down my spine, bringing soft, sensual desire.

Damn it. Concentrate.

I sucked in a sharp breath, determined to focus and not think about how he sat on the bed, how I'd tackled him and taken my pleasure.

Father, it was harder to think with his husky voice driving me crazy than it had been when I'd been in the actual bedroom where we'd had sex.

"Now slowly send your senses out from the core to the rest of your body. Feel your lungs fill with air every time you breathe in, the tightness in your chest as you hold your breath, and the emptiness as you release it. Feel your muscles and limbs, your fingers and toes. Your skin—"

I felt a heat low in my core and my skin tingling. I felt a warmth pulsing around my neck and down my chest where my impossible mating marks were when I was in the Garden. I felt an aching yearning that I couldn't and shouldn't feel for a love that would never be mine. I felt alone and angry and trapped in my circumstances. I felt too much.

My eyes flew open. Lord Quill had leaned forward,

his face close to mine, and I jerked back, my chair tipping back precariously.

Quill grabbed the chair's arms, catching me before I fell then pulled it back, his face now even closer to mine than before. His emerald eyes locked with mine, and a mix of desire and fear that he'd realize who I was stole my breath.

Concern and confusion filled his expression, and he opened his mouth as if to say something, then dropped his gaze and leaned back giving me space.

"The goal is to make you hyperaware of your physical body and your spark so you always know how to return to it."

I was pretty sure that wasn't what he'd been about to say.

CHAPTER 10

GREAT GODDESS, what was wrong with me? Had I actually been about to kiss him?

"I think that's enough for now," I told Sawyer, my voice gruff. "We should meet during the evening after class every couple of days." And somehow, I'd figure out how to control myself. "But whether we meet or not, you should practice every night before bed."

I didn't know how much the meditation would help, but it was the only thing I could offer him that might let him control his magic.

Sawyer nodded and pushed out of the chair, wincing with the movement, his actions stiff. He headed for the door, and I forced myself to stay sitting on the edge of the bed, my body shaking with the effort.

The door clicked shut behind him, and I collapsed back on the bed with a groan.

The small recovery room felt too quiet, too small. Pale afternoon light filtered through the single window, barely bright enough to compete with the softly glowing fae stone in the ceiling.

I squeezed my eyes shut and pressed my palms against them.

I was losing my mind.

He'd just sat there with his eyes closed, and I couldn't help seeing his sister then the new arrival to the Garden, Sage. The need to protect her— to protect *them,* love them, cherish them was overwhelming.

I'd been drawn to him like a moth to a flame and had been about to kiss him when his eyes had opened. And then I'd fallen into his brown gaze, so similar to the stunned ones I'd gazed into when I'd called his name a rotation ago.

Goddess, I had to know where she was.

He'd said his sister was fine, safe, but I couldn't bring myself to believe that. The urge to find her, to bring her into the fae realm where I could protect her, clawed at my insides. No woman was safe in the human realm.

But I already knew from the last time I'd given in to the need to ensure his sister's safety that he'd clam up and become even more wary of me.

It was only a miracle that I managed to swallow those words and say something else. I just had to trust him and prove to him that I was worthy of his trust in return. Which was going to be even more difficult since I'd been forced to support Rider as the Lord Commander of the Black Guard and leave him trembling and throwing up on the running trail.

I scrubbed my hands down my face and huffed. This

was getting out of hand. I couldn't stop thinking about her — a human woman I'd barely met — and I couldn't stop seeing her in Sawyer and Sage.

And really, I should be worrying about Sage and how she couldn't change her clothes in her spirit form. That most likely meant she couldn't control when she manifested in the Garden or when she left. And with her sleeping mating marks, and my mother's obvious interest in her, not to mention that Crane was still on the lose, she was in as much danger, maybe more, than Sawyer's sister.

I pushed myself off the bed and headed down the hall to Kit's recovery room to check in on him.

Inside the small room, Payne slumped in a chair that was definitely too small for his large frame. He was fast asleep, his head had fallen back at an uncomfortable-appearing angle, and soft snores escaped his lips. Kit was also asleep, lying motionless in the narrow bed, his complexion too pale from blood loss.

I stood in the doorway for a moment, debating if I should enter and wake Payne.

From what I'd heard, the whole team had been through hell last night. Kit and Lewin had almost died from their injuries, and Payne was only alive because Sawyer had foreseen that he'd been poisoned.

Better to let him sleep, even if his neck would be killing him when he woke. Given how seriously injured his bonded had been, I doubt I'd be able to convince him to leave, even if he was just going to sleep in the room next door.

I stepped back quietly, returned to the infirmary's main treatment room. The room was empty, Flint possibly in the greenhouse tending to his medicinal herbs, and the examination tables were clean, their wooden surfaces gleaming under the bright light overhead, while the rolling tables he used to hold medical tools and supplies when he was working on someone had been pushed against the wall near the large wooden cabinet, ready for the next emergency.

What I really needed was to focus on the issues I could actually do something about.

The novice training would resume tomorrow morning, and I'd need to be on the watch for how they treated Sawyer. Should I convince Rider that one of us needed to run the trail with the boy to ensure they didn't attack him again?

I'd like to think that Rider had scared the wrath of the Goddess into them when he'd yelled at them, but some of the advanced human novices this time around seemed stubborn.

Of course, I doubted Rider would agree to that or that it would actually help the boy get along with the other novices.

And how the other novices treated Sawyer wasn't something I could do anything about. I could only reward people for good behavior and punish them for bad. I couldn't actually change how they thought.

No, if I wanted to take action, it would have to be with Sage. There were things I could do to help her that would make a difference for her, which I doubted any of the other guys were thinking about.

The first thing I needed to do was go early to the Garden and discreetly arrange to have clothes waiting for her in her bedroom's wardrobe. I might not be able to get them for tonight, but certainly by tomorrow night.

I doubted the High Priestess would demand Sage make an appearance so soon after being attacked so there were probably a few days before she had to leave the suite, but the sooner I got her clothes the better. You couldn't be too careful, not with my mother and the games she liked to play.

I stepped out into the baily and drew in a deep breath of the Gray's perpetually damp air. Mist curled around my boots, and the overcast sky hung low, threatening a rain that almost never came.

To my left and slightly in front of me stood the glassed-in greenhouse filled with all manner of herbs and some fae magic to help them grow with the realm's limited sunlight. I couldn't see Flint inside, but that didn't mean he wasn't hidden among all that greenery.

Beyond lay the bailey with a dozen guardsmen going about their duties. The novices might have time off along with a few other guardsmen, but no one else did. The Black Guard was ready to defend the Gray and the Gates of the Realms every hour of every day without fail.

With a sigh, I wandered along the bottom of the castle's wall hoping the fresh air would help clear my mind.

West had given his word that he wouldn't say

anything about Sage's sleeping marks, which meant only one of us needed to be with her now, and tonight was Talon's turn.

Which surprised the hell out of me. Talon had spent decades being deliberately rude to women, keeping them at arm's length so he'd never risk bonding with one. He was one of the most handsome fae alive, but with the shadow entity trapped within his shadow magic it was too dangerous for him to be mated. It was too much of a risk to hope that someone would understand that the shadow wasn't evil and wasn't controlling him.

What was worse, was that the shadow fed on sex and exuded an allure that attracted both women and men alike, making it even more difficult for Talon to avoid women looking to form a mating bond with him.

Of course, given how shy Sage was and how she seemed to have accepted Ash and all his scars, I doubted she'd be seduced by Talon's pretty face, but his allure was another story.

Except with how rude Talon had been when they'd first met and how wary she was of men, his allure might not stand a chance. Tonight was probably going to be awkward and uncomfortable for both of them.

I paused mid-step. Maybe I should join them. Just to make sure—

No. I'd agreed when Rider said we should take turns. It made sense. We still had our duties as the leaders of the Black Guard and we couldn't ignore them, not with the state of the Gray or the novices. And most certainly not with the High Priestess watching us.

That, and I'd already arranged to meet my second in command at the White Tower in the Garden. I was already falling behind on my duties because of the novice training, I couldn't afford to let something important slip through the crack. Both the Black and White Towers needed me focused, not distracted by a woman who made me ache for someone and something I couldn't and shouldn't want.

Footsteps approached, and I turned to see Rider striding toward me. He moved with his usual predatory grace, his hair half tied back in a topknot, the shock of white at his left temple standing out against the rest of his dark locks. A few guardsmen near the stables glanced our way before quickly returning to their work.

"How'd the meditation lesson go?" he asked.

I shrugged. "As well as can be expected, I guess. It's hard to tell because it's all on him. I can't see what he sees or tell how well he's concentrating."

"We have to try something or we'll lose him," Rider said.

"Yeah, I don't know how long he has," I replied. "It sounds like his ability is growing in strength. Hopefully it will stabilize."

"Hopefully." Rider's expression darkened. "One of Ash's men informed me that the Order confiscated the artifact that trapped Sage's soul in the Garden."

"Did the Head of Artifacts at the White Tower get to catalogue it first?"

I had no idea if this new information proved or disproved the theory that the High Priestess was involved in Sage's attack. The artifact, an intricately wrought silver bracelet, kept a spirit in the Garden from returning to its body so it most certainly would be a useful tool for the Order, but there was also a chance that examining it might reveal information about who originally possessed it or even created it.

"Yes, but he didn't have it long enough to examine. The Order claims that they want to do their own examination first."

Which didn't surprise me, but that meant the artifact wasn't going to help us figure out everyone who'd been involved in attacking Sage since there was no guarantee that whoever had procured the artifact had also been in the sacred grove... not that I expected it too, but it had been an avenue to investigate.

"Did Ash's man say anything else? About Crane? The others who escaped?" It was still early in the investigation, but I had to hope. The sooner this was resolved, the sooner I could convince myself to keep my distance from Sage.

"Only that no one's mentioned Wells' dagger."

Sage had said it had been engraved and Wells had clearly been using it for ritual magic. It was most likely another artifact, but the fact that neither the White Tower nor the Order indicated that they had it was another mystery.

"Yarrow's keeping the investigation locked down tight," Rider said, his expression hard. "Even Ash's contacts inside the Order can't get details, just that there are no leads."

No leads. One confiscated artifact and another missing, and all four outstanding assailants gone. At least Addax was probably dead in a ditch somewhere from the hole Rider had stabbed in his torso.

A cold, hollow weight settled in my chest. Crane wasn't the type to flee. He was the type to watch, to plan, to strike the moment he felt he could.

And with Sage having killed Wells...

"Do you think they'll try again with the forced bonding?"

"Or revenge," Rider said, voicing what I'd just been thinking. "Either way, she's not safe."

CHAPTER 11

Sage

I BLINKED my eyes open and groaned. I was back in the fancy suite in the Divine Residence, lying on the floor in the same position I always ended up in when my spirit manifested in the Garden.

Swell. I'd hoped practicing the meditation Lord Quill had taught me right before bed would have helped keep my spirit in my body. But obviously not. It either didn't work on controlling my spirit form or I needed a lot more practice.

Sir West stood a few feet away, his massive frame towering over me. He held out his hand in a broody gesture to help me up, and I took it and stood, my gaze darting around the room as I steadied myself.

Someone had cleaned up, putting the furniture back where it belonged and replacing the broken table with a new one.

And there, sitting on the couch, was Talon.

He was as stunningly beautiful as ever with his long

white-silver hair and the earrings in his delicately pointed ears catching the light from the chandelier, and the captivating swirl of pink, purple, blue, and gold in his eyes.

The memory of his allure seeped through me, hot and achy, and in my mind's eye I saw the moment we'd first met, that drop of water trailing down his naked chest to his partially erect—

Heat burned across my cheeks, and I wrenched my gaze away from him to scan the rest of the room. Rider and Quill weren't there.

I frowned and Talon pointed to himself. "Quill and Ash's friend. Talon."

"I remember."

The catch, as always with my life right now, was remembering what I was supposed to know in the Garden and not anything that I'd learned about him in the Gray.

We hadn't really interacted here. Sure, he, along with the others, had saved me from Wells and Crane and those other men, but he hadn't really spoken to me. Not last night, and not much after being attacked.

Our most memorable interaction was when I'd first arrived in the Garden and he'd been rude to me.

Of course, after being attacked by the shadow trapped within him and knowing no one would understand, it made sense for him to put distance between him and everyone else.

Another flash of heated desire sank low within me at how Talon's allure had overwhelmed me and left me gasping.

Talon rose from the couch in one fluid motion and crossed to the chair closest to me, sinking into it with a grace that made my pulse lurch with desire, even though I still stood. He was close. Too close. I could see the individual colors swirling in his eyes — pink bleeding into purple and blue, shot through with gold threads.

"I thought I'd keep you company this evening." His voice dropped, turning warm and intimate. He leaned forward, his gaze drifting down my neck to linger on my mating marks before slowly traveling back up to meet my eyes.

I shrank back, unable to stop the reaction before it happened, suddenly hyperaware that he could see my dull, lifeless marks, and tell that a few of the marks had changed from red to green, indicating that I'd already bonded a mate.

Which I prayed wasn't actually the case and was just a result of Zinnia's magic putting the marks to sleep.

"You look stunning tonight."

Stunning? What the—?

I wasn't stunning. I was too sharp, too severe to be beautiful even as a human. In amongst all his fae beauty, I was plain. So why was he looking at me like that? Like he desired me. He wasn't interested in a mate.

"He doesn't have to stay," West rumbled.

Except if Talon didn't stay, then I'd be alone with West, and I wasn't sure how much I liked that idea... even if Talon was acting strange.

"It's fine." I sank onto the edge of one of the chairs facing Talon, uncomfortable with his presence and uncertain how to talk to him while West moved to stand to my left and slightly behind me, a looming sentinel.

I really wanted to retreat to the bedroom and try to go back to sleep with the hope that I'd return to my body in my room in the Black Tower. But I didn't want to be rude, and I still felt like there were social rules that I didn't know about that I needed to follow.

Maybe if I was polite to him for a little while, I'd be able to excuse myself and retreat to my room.

Talon shifted in his chair, angling toward me, and his hand came to rest on the armrest closest to where I sat. His gaze drifted down to my neck again.

My heart thudded and I fought to keep my expression even. I tried to draw in a steadying breath, but it was ragged, and my cheeks heated with embarrassment.

Talon's lips curved into a soft smile, but it felt fake, practiced.

What was he doing?

"Quill is arranging for clothes," he said. "They'll be waiting in your bedroom tomorrow evening."

"I appreciate that."

"I also wanted to apologize." His tone deepened even more, sending a shiver of need sliding down my spine.

"Apologize?" My mind raced through what he could be apologizing for.

I really wanted him to apologize for abandoning me on the running trail or for his shadow attacking me and embarrassing me in front of Lord Rider, but I knew that wasn't what he was talking about.

"I was short with you when we first met." He

held my gaze, his impossibly colored eyes mesmerizing me. "I was concerned about my duty outside of the Garden, but that's really no excuse to be rude." The lie fell easily off his tongue, and if I hadn't already known the truth, I'd have completely believed him.

But I did know the truth, and this sudden charm wasn't him.

"I understand." I strained to think of something more to say. "Your ah... duty must be very stressful."

I couldn't remember if Ash or Quill had told me that Talon was a captain of the Black Guard but given that we'd only really met the other night and I'd just been attacked, I had to hope he wouldn't think my question strange.

"It can be." His fingers drummed lightly against the armrest, drawing my attention to how close his hand was to mine.

I inched my fingers away, everything within me saying I needed to put distance between us and a small frown flickered through his expression.

"I'm the Captain of the Gold Tower in the human realm." Talon flashed me a soft, charming smile as if he was about to share a secret with me. "But I find I'm thinking about... other things when I'm here." The way he said it, the way he looked at me made my stomach tighten.

This wasn't the Talon I knew in the Gray. This was wrong, so wrong.

Why was he acting like this? Did he think because my

mating marks were asleep that he'd be able to seduce me without any of the consequences?

Was the man currently sitting beside me the real Talon? Not the one I knew in the Black Tower?

Perhaps his shadow needed to feed and that was why he was taking a risk with me.

Except I couldn't feel any of the aching, desperate need inspired from his shadow's magical allure.

I wished Ash were with me instead. I wished he was the one flirting with me and prayed he was doing all right and wasn't—

Wasn't what? Hurting? Lonely? Missing me the way I missed him?

My chest ached at the thought of him. The warmth of his body pressed against mine, his teasing breath washing over me when he whispered in my ear, the things he said that made my skin flush, and the way he'd held me like I was something precious, something worth protecting.

I bit back a huff of frustration. I had no idea what Ash would be doing right now. It wasn't as if I knew anything about him. Hell, I knew more about Talon because I interacted with him as Sawyer than I did about Ash.

And yet my soul ached for Ash in a way it didn't for anyone else.

"What's the human realm like?" I asked Talon, desperate to say something since I wasn't sure I could just retreat to my bedroom without upsetting him.

"I haven't seen much of the realm. I'm restricted to

the Gold Tower and Addur, the capital city of the Kingdom of Erellod where the tower is located. But the area around Addur is rich farmland, very much like our western province."

I nodded, pretending I knew what he was talking about. I'd only been to Addur a few times when my parents had been alive. We'd travelled in a stuffy carriage, so I hadn't gotten a good look of the land outside of the city's walls. That, and I had no idea what the fae's western provinces looked like.

I asked about humans and his duties as a Captain of the Gold Tower, trying to keep him talking about himself so he wouldn't ask any questions about me.

But every answer seemed to circle back to me. Comments about my courage in surviving the attack, suggestions that he could show me more of the Garden, observations about how intriguing I was.

Each compliment made me more uncomfortable, more aware that this wasn't the Talon I knew.

West stood silently at my shoulder, without a doubt scowling at Talon the whole time, until someone knocked at the door. With a grunt, the knight strode over to it and cracked it open.

"My lady, Magister Zinnia is here to see you," West said, his large frame blocking the entrance preventing me from seeing anything in the hall.

Oh, thank the Father!

"Yes, thank you." I gave Talon an apologetic look, hoping he couldn't see how relieved I was. "I should probably talk with her about my... ah...." I brushed my fingers across my collarbone drawing his gaze back to my mating marks, "my condition."

"Of course." He glanced at Sir West who glowered at him then flashed the knight a brilliant smile. "I'll wait here in the sitting room in case you need assistance."

"Magister Zinnia," I said as she stepped inside. "Let's talk in my room."

I gestured to the fancy bedroom, feeling like a complete fraud with my polite speech and fake smile.

"How are you feeling?" she asked as she closed the bedroom door, and we headed to the small seating area by the window.

"I'm managing." I slumped onto the window seat, leaving her the chair.

"I'm sorry I couldn't be here last night," she said. "I had a medical emergency and then wanted to do some research into the strange magic that was affecting you."

"Did you learn anything?"

"Not yet. I've never encountered anything like it before." She reached out her hand. "May I check to see if it's still affecting you?"

I stared at her outstretched fingers. She'd already healed me. If she was going to discover I was really a human she would have figured that out already, and yet, it felt like the more often I let her magic connect with me, the more vulnerable I'd become.

Except there was no other way to determine if the strange magic both she and Magister Aster had sensed within me was gone.

"All right." I placed my palm in hers and her warm, soothing magic seeped up my arm.

I sagged back against the cushions and closed my eyes. As much as I wanted to resist and keep myself closed off and protected, that wouldn't help. The more I relaxed, the faster this would be.

The warmth of her magic spread across my chest and swirled inside me, then, a moment later, it retreated back down my arm.

Zinnia sat back and hummed in thought. "The magic is weaker than it was the other night, but it's still there."

"Could that be why I can't change my spirit form clothes or even control whether I come to the Garden or not?" I asked. "Will that stop once the magic is gone?"

"Maybe. The magic could be interfering with all of that, although your inability to stop yourself from coming to the Garden is probably because of your mating marks."

"But you put them to sleep."

"And that just means you won't be able to form a mating bond." Zinnia's expression softened. "I warned you about the desire spikes, the same could be said for the unconscious compulsion to come to the Garden that we women experience when it's time for us to find our mates."

"So I might be able to control it... *eventually*?"

Damn it. Controlling it right away would make my life so much easier. I didn't want to have to juggle what I knew about Talon, Quill, and Rider in the Gray as well as in the Garden, and I sure as hell didn't want to deal with Sir West.

But it didn't sound as if I had much of a choice.

I closed my eyes, willing myself to relax. Except every shadow in the room felt wrong, every creak of the strange tree-castle or thump of someone in another suite made my heart lurch.

Father, I was exhausted. But my mind wouldn't stop.

Crane was still out there, along with three others who'd helped him.

Would they try again? Drag me back to the sacred pool and finish what they started, or—

The memory of stabbing Wells, over and over again determined to break the forming mating bond rushed through me in a flash of hot then cold.

Or would Crane want revenge instead?

I needed to figure out how to stop manifesting in the Garden, and I needed to do it, now.

CHAPTER 12

Sage

I WOKE tired and achy with my head stuffed with fae court etiquette and worries about the High Priestess demanding I make a public appearance. Zinnia and I had talked for hours before I couldn't stop yawning and she told me to go to bed where I'd tossed and turned, knowing Sir West was staring at me.

Now it was morning, I was back in the Gray, and I needed to shove all that information to the back of my mind and remember who I was pretending to be and what I was doing.

And what I was doing was dreading the day.

My body still hurt from running the trail until I threw up and from where Mikel and his friends — as well as Wells — had hit me, and I was terrified about what they planned for me.

Of course, another part of me, a part that was slowly growing in strength, was angry that I was afraid.

I was stronger than this.

I was stronger than them.

I had to be. Because if I wasn't, my only remaining family member would die in the Gray like our horrible stepfather wanted. And that was unacceptable.

With a groan, I got out of bed and splashed water on my face. I just needed to pay attention to my surroundings and not be caught alone with them.

The memory of them ambushing me just before the log bridge on the running trail shuddered through me and I swallowed back my nausea.

Without a doubt Lord Rider would make us run the trail and I *had* to be ready for another attack.

Father, was this the attack I'd seen? The one where I was dead in the Gray?

I squeezed my eyes shut and tried to remember the vision. There'd been two attackers, I'd heard them, but I'd only partially seen the one...

And his boots had been brown. His pants as well. He hadn't been wearing a Black Guard uniform.

That didn't necessarily mean that Mikel and his friends wouldn't be the ones to kill me, just that they wouldn't be killing me while on duty. It also didn't mean that I'd be safe on the trail, only that I wouldn't die while running it with the other novices.

And there wasn't anything I could do about it.

I couldn't hide in my room and I didn't want to. For however long it lasted, I was Sawyer Herstind. I didn't have to bow to everyone and be meek.

I straightened my fresh uniform — having picked up two new clean ones from the quartermaster's office yesterday afternoon — and stepped out into the hall with the other guardsmen on their way to the great hall for breakfast.

And while I *was* Sawyer Herstind, a man, I also wasn't stupid. I made an easy-to-carry sandwich for breakfast and took it back to my room to eat.

Without allies, mealtime was just awkward and uncomfortable. There was no one to watch my back or glare down anyone who might want to try anything. Sure, no one had even tried to trip me since my first lieu day and the oranges had even come back, but I wasn't foolish enough to assume that was a permanent change.

I also wasn't foolish enough to assume Tyon was an ally. I might have come across him again yesterday afternoon and spent another few hours teaching him to read, but that didn't make us friends. Even if we were, Tyon was probably the weakest of the novices, and I refused to put him in a position where the others would pick on him.

My breakfast done, I headed down to the infirmary. Yesterday, when I'd gone to the quartermaster's office and gotten my clean uniforms for the new rotation — as well as confirmed that I wouldn't receive clean bedding until after the next rotation — I'd learned that my morning duties for the rotation would be in the infirmary... and that Mikel and Durand were on "scrub work," whatever that was, while Bramwell, Hamelin, and Ambrose were on scullery duty.

I was grateful I wasn't back in the stables or assigned to the laundry, but I was also disappointed that none of the men who'd threatened me had been assigned there instead.

But of course, life wasn't fair, and I shouldn't have expected any of them to be punished for what they did, especially since I hadn't told anyone and I doubted any of them had confessed.

At least with being assigned infirmary duty I'd have Payne, as well as Kit and Lewin if they were awake, to keep me company. Flint also had been kind to me compared to everyone else, so with luck, my morning duties would be a relatively calm reprieve to what I expected the rest of my days were going to be, and maybe I'd learn some useful healing skills.

Except when I pushed open the infirmary door, a different fae wearing a pale blue doublet stood in the middle of the room. And unlike Flint, this fae also wore a longsword at his hip.

The man's golden eyes narrowed. "You're as small as everyone says you are."

He didn't sound pleased to see me.

Then his attention shifted to above and behind me and he huffed. "Good. You're both early."

I glanced behind me to see one of the other novices, Garridan, step into the doorway behind me. The man was almost as bad as Tyon when it came to fighting, but from the snippets of conversation I'd overheard that made sense since before his name had been drawn in the lottery, he'd led a relatively sheltered life and had just taken his vows to be a priest of the Great Father.

"I'm Reef," the fae said. "I'm the healer at the Black

Tower for this rotation, but I'm also a guardsman. I completed my fifty-year service and have stayed on as a healer."

Which explained why he had a sword. He'd trained as a warrior as well as a healer.

"Garridan, you're with me. Sawyer—" the fae leveled his hard golden stare on me. "The last room at the end of the patient rooms is a cleaning room. The water has magical cleansing properties. I want you to wipe down every surface in this main room then scrub the floor." His eyes narrowed. "Don't drink the water. It will kill you."

Cleaning duty? Well at least it was better than mucking out stalls and hauling wheelbarrows of soiled hay to a manure pile on the other side of the Tower's walls.

Reef gestured to Garridan to follow him and headed down a second hall, away from the patient rooms. "Do you have any healing knowledge, Garridan?"

"No," Garridan said as he hurried after the fae.

"No worries. We'll get you started on the basics."

My throat tightened and a bitter taste filled my mouth. I knew I shouldn't have been disappointed, but it still stung to know that I was relegated to cleaning duties while the other novice was going to learn a new skill.

Sure, I knew some basic healing, having helped my mother, Udara, and the other maids tend to our family's wounded men when they returned from a bandit hunt, but Reef didn't know that. No one did.

And I knew right away it was foolish to think Reef

would assign Garridan cleaning duties tomorrow and teach me. This was part of my punishment and I had to accept that.

With a sigh, I headed down the hall with the patient rooms. Lewin's door was partially open, but the man was still asleep. Next to him, Kit and Payne were talking quietly with each other and I didn't want to disturb them — there'd be time later, even if it was at the beginning of my lunch break.

The room at the end of the hall was about the same size as the patient rooms without the attached bathing room, and I touched the fae stone by the door to brighten the light inside. Along the right-hand side was a pump and basin like in my room and large counter. Three buckets were neatly stacked beside the counter, and above them was a rack with four rungs holding various sized cloths and towels. To the left were a few shelves with bedding and other supplies, a couple of the rolling tables I'd seen Flint use to hold his medical equipment when he'd worked on Kit, and a collection of dusters, brooms, and mops.

There weren't any medical supplies, so the cloths and towels were probably used exclusively for cleaning, and anything that touched a patient was probably in another room — probably the room Reef was showing Garridan right now.

I half filled one of the buckets with water and stared at the strange shimmering blue glow emanating from the liquid. It also gave off a sharp sour smell that made me wrinkle my nose in disgust.

It was definitely magical and not something I'd want to drink.

How many times had someone tried to drink it before Reef felt it was necessary to include the warning not to consume it? Which meant there were either a number of really stupid men in the guard or that Reef thought I was stupid.

Probably the later.

I grabbed three of the cloths hanging on the rack, hooked them in my belt for when I needed them, and carried the bucket back down the hall to the main room. With my sore muscles, even the half full bucket was almost too heavy for me, but I managed to get it into the room without spilling.

I started in the corner closest to the hall with the patient rooms and got to work wiping down every flat surface and every area where I thought someone might put their hands or fingers. My medical knowledge was pretty basic: keep things clean and bandage tightly. But it made sense that if you wanted to keep wounds clean, you needed to keep your hands clean, and since Reef hadn't given me more detailed instructions than that, I had to hope whatever I was doing met whatever his cleaning standards were.

CHAPTER 13

Sage

For better or worse, Reef didn't criticize my cleaning. He didn't compliment it either. When the fourth bell rang and I was only halfway through scrubbing the floor, he just huffed and told me to go.

I grabbed another sandwich and an orange from the kitchen and ate in my room again before heading to the practice fields.

With my stomach clenched with unease, I walked through the pasture gate and scanned the area for danger. Ahead of me stretched the rocky, uneven practice area and pasture partially shrouded in mist. Men I didn't recognize warmed up near the archery targets while others sparred with practice swords. Their laughter and shouts echoed across the field, jarring against the turmoil churning inside me.

So far, Mikel and his friends weren't here, but neither were Lords Rider, Talon, or Quill. Which meant I could be in danger if my aggressors showed up before the Black Guard leadership.

No. If they were going to do anything, they'd do it on the running trail where Lord Rider or anyone else wouldn't be able to see them. They wouldn't risk getting caught by being out in the open. Even if the other guardsmen didn't stop them, surely—

I huffed. I couldn't count on Lord Rider or Talon. But surely Lord Quill would help me. Wouldn't he?

A shudder swept through me at the memory of Bramwell grabbing me and Durand—

The others had just watched and jeered and I—

I pushed those thoughts as far back in my mind as I could. I couldn't think about it. Not now. Not ever. I wouldn't ever let it happen again.

Except I had no idea how to stop them.

My best bet, I guessed, was to go off the running trail, determine if they were waiting to ambush me, and if they were, cut through the forest to the river. After that, it would be just like if they'd tossed me in at the log bridge where I'd wade through the river and use the ladder cut into the rocks to climb up the other side.

Thankfully Rider— *Lord* Rider I corrected myself. I had to remember when I was in the Gray, he and Quill were lords.

Thankfully he arrived before any of the other novices, the large Lord Commander of the Black Guard carrying the two bags of rocks for those slowest around the running trail.

Hunh. If I did manage to slip past Mikel and his

gang, maybe I wouldn't be the last one off the trail this time.

Lord Rider glanced at me, his expression hard and unreadable as he strode across the practice field toward the two large, jagged boulders marking the beginning of the running trail.

I didn't want to be alone with him, not after I'd seen his fury. The rage I'd seen in his eyes when he'd yelled at me to run the trail until he told me to stop had been more terrifying than Edred's rage.

With Edred, I'd known what to expect and knew I could handle it. With Lord Rider, I'd seen a ferocious, wild monster burning in his eyes, and knew it would tear me to pieces if he ever let it free.

Except I didn't know if I wanted to stay standing by the pasture gate and risk Mikel and Durand being the next through. If it were just Bramwell, Hamelin, or Ambrose I might be all right. They seemed to go along with whatever Mikel wanted and didn't instigate things... although Ambrose had punched me when Durand had tried to undress me.

I brushed my fingers over my still tender cheek. I hoped Ambrose's nose still hurt and that Flint hadn't completely healed it.

Regardless, it was better to face Rider's glare than risk running into someone I didn't want to, so I slowly made my way across the field to the running trail.

The fifth bell rang just as I reached Lord Rider, and I glanced back to see Talon, Lord Quill, and the other novices rush through the pasture gate. The novices hurried over while Talon and Lord Quill set down large sacks by the sparring rings. They were most likely filled with whatever practice weapons we were going to use that day.

Then they turned their attention toward the running trail and my breath caught. Father, why did they have to be so beautiful. Once again, impossible sunshine seemed to halo Quill's head, accentuating his boyish charm which only made Talon look more sexual, as if desire oozed from his pores — which given his shadow, I suppose it did.

It was obvious that here in the Gray both of them were more relaxed, more in their element. Talon most of all. I hadn't realized how on edge and uncomfortable he'd been in the Garden, but watching him move, hell, just watching him breathe, I could tell his posture was calm, confident, and natural.

And that confidence was alluring.

I heaved my attention away from them. I needed to focus on what was important, and that most certainly wasn't a pretty face.

I scanned the group of novices as they approached. Mikel, Durand, Hamelin, and Bramwell were in the middle of the group, while Ambrose — with thick blue-black bruising around both eyes — was a few paces behind him.

I bit back my smirk. *Thank you, Flint, for not fully healing the bastard.*

Talon and Lord Quill took up positions on either side of Lord Rider, and I inched around to the back of the group of novices. I was sure everyone had noticed me, but I didn't want to be anywhere in the group when they all started to run for the trail — I'd already learned that lesson.

"Welcome to your second rotation, novices," Talon said. "I hope you got lots of rest and relaxation in Lehyrst because we're done going easy on you."

Some of the men snickered at the mention of Lehyrst, while others — those who weren't used to the rigors of physical training — groaned.

"Now you have chores in the morning, training in the afternoon, and classes after dinner," Talon said.

"This rotation you'll be divided into two groups. Those with fighting experience and those without." Quill swept his gaze over the novices, and I shifted my attention to the ground, afraid he'd make eye contact with me. "Those with fighting experience will be fast-tracked through training to get you into the regular guard rotation."

"Those with experience will also qualify to enter the competition for an elite position," Talon added.

"We will?" one of the fae novices asked.

"Another hunter team got taken out the other night," someone else said, their voice low, "they need to fill those positions fast."

"But to allow novices—"

"Just means you're here at the right time," Rider growled. "You're not special. And even if you manage to land an elite position, you're still not special. You let your ego affect your work and I'll strip you back to a regular guardsman without a second thought. Are we clear?"

All the novices straightened, their expressions snapping back to serious. "Yes, Lord Commander."

"All right. You know the drill," Rider huffed, and he jerked his chin toward the entrance to the running trail. "The last ones around the trail from each of the groups runs again with the rocks."

The novices took off, running up the hill then disappearing down the other side, while I half walked, half jogged after them, my body complaining with the movement.

"You're going to need to go faster than that if you don't want to be running that extra lap," Rider said, making my pulse lurch.

I opened my mouth to tell him I was pretty sure it wouldn't matter how fast I ran but remembered the look of absolute fury in his eyes the other day and scrambled up the rise then down the other side.

All the muscles in my legs hurt by the time I reached the bottom of the hill, and I swore, when I came last and had to run again with the rocks, I was going to walk the entire way — if I could even walk by then.

I glanced behind me to confirm Lord Rider wasn't following or standing at the top of the hill watching and slowed to a lurching walk-jog that was as fast as I could manage knowing I still had the whole trail to run.

I followed the path around the scraggly trees, jagged outcroppings, and along the narrow ridge with the sharp drop down a shale slope to a fast-moving river until the scrubby side of the ridge rose and I was about to head back into the trees.

A couple hundred yards into the trees, the path would make a sharp turn and open up to the clearing and the log bridge, the place where Mikel and his friends always ambushed me. This was where I needed to go off the trail and sneak past them.

Quietly as I could, I slipped into the underbrush and carefully sneaked toward the clearing. I strained to hear any sign of them, whispers or snickers or anything, but all I could hear was the rustling of dry leaves and the creaking of scraggly tree trunks and branches in the breeze.

I reached the edge of the clearing and sank down behind a bush.

The area was empty.

I scanned the forest on the other side but couldn't see anyone.

I waited.

It had already taken me longer to get here than usual, I doubted Mikel and his friends would hang around for much longer and risk Rider getting suspicious.

A gust of wind swept through the trees sending a flurry of dead leaves swirling through the clearing.

Still nothing.

Did I risk it?

It wouldn't be easy to double back and check out the other side of the path. The ground on that side stayed sharply sloped and it would be harder to sneak up on someone.

I picked up a stone and tossed it into the shrubs on the other side of the path, hoping to startle anyone who might be hiding there.

No reaction.

Had they actually given up on punishing me?

Shadows! There was only one way to find out.

With my hand on the hilt of my sword and my body tense, I stepped onto the path.

No one jumped out at me.

I jerked my gaze around, desperately scanning for the smallest indication that I was in danger. Maybe they *had* given up.

Unless they'd changed where they wanted to ambush me.

Except this clearing was the best place for an ambush. The undergrowth was thick here and there was a sharp turn in the path. Past the log bridge the bushes thinned out, providing less cover for anyone who wanted to hide. Not that Mikel and his friends had been hiding after their first few attacks.

Damn it. What did I do now?

Lord Rider was already going to be pissed that I was taking so long and the thinner groundcover that made laying an ambush more difficult also made it more difficult for me to sneak up on anyone.

CHAPTER 14

Sage

THERE WASN'T anything I could do. I had to carry on and pray an ambush wasn't waiting for me farther up the trail.

The churning in my stomach turned to cold, hard dread. I straddled the log bridge and inched across on my butt, not trusting my sore body to keep my balance while crossing it. Then I hobbled down the path, my gaze darting toward every shadow and every rocky outcropping that could hide a man.

My legs were screaming at me and my nerves shot by the time I reached the steep slope at the end of the trail. I staggered up it, then lurched down the other side to the boulders marking the trail.

All the other novices stood in the field looking bored and not one of them — including Tyon — looked out of breath. Which meant I'd taken far too long.

Lord Rider glared at me and huffed. "Looks like

Sawyer and Tyon are running with the rocks at the end of training."

Talon offered me a sympathetic smile before turning to the rest of the group. "All of the fae, Durand, Bramwell, Hamelin, Ambrose, Aldis, Sawyer, Jokin, and Sivis, you're with Rider. You're the experienced fighter group. The rest are with me and Quill."

We all marched up to the flat area where the large sparring rings had been carved into the stone where Talon and Lord Quill had dropped off the practice weapons.

"Rider's group picks first," Quill said, and the less experienced novices stepped back. "We won't need to pay so close attention to weight and length for a while, and by then they'll have moved on to their regular blades."

I shuddered at the thought. I didn't want Mikel, Durand or anyone swinging a sharp weapon in my direction.

I waited until everyone else in my group had picked their practice blade. Given my size and strength compared to theirs, I doubted any of them would consider the few weapons appropriate for me, so I wasn't worried that they'd be taken, and I was right.

There were three blades I could pick from, and while one of them was closest in size and weight to my actual sword, I picked the lightest of the three. My arms still hurt from a rotation of stable duty, and I had no idea how long I'd be swinging it around today. I doubted this was going to be like the testing last rotation where everyone had a turn and that was it.

"Partner up," Rider said, motioning for our group to move out of the way so the inexperienced fighters could pick their weapons. "We're doing small spars. There's no circle but keep it tight and don't lose track of who's around you."

The nine fae novices glanced at each other, then swept their gazes over the humans, while Mikel and his gang turned toward each other, and Sivis, Aldis, and Jokin did the same. Everyone pointedly ignored me.

"Don't worry about who your partner is," Rider huffed. "You'll be changing a couple of times today and again over the next few days. You won't repeat a partner until you've gone through everyone."

Swell. That meant I couldn't avoid sparring with Mikel or Durand. Or Ambrose — who was probably holding a grudge for the black eyes.

Everyone found a partner, leaving me with Jokin. He was the least skilled of the experienced novices and a few years older than my real age of twenty, not the fifteen I was pretending to be.

He'd been on the town guard of a small town in the north of the Kingdom of Thermalea before his name had been drawn in the lottery, but the town either didn't have skilled instructors or couldn't be bothered with an in-depth education.

"Fine," Jokin huffed. "Let's get this started."

Mikel shot him a dark glare, and his mouth snapped shut, adding to my suspicion that the new plan was to pretend I didn't exist.

Maybe Lord Rider had said something to them. That

was the only explanation for why everyone had changed tactics. No one was trying to put me in my place, bump me out of the way, take away oranges, or ambush me on the running trail.

Now they were proving to me that I was no one. Nothing.

I swallowed back my sigh of relief. They'd probably be pissed knowing I was grateful that they were going to ignore me, and that I *needed* them to ignore me. The longer they did, the longer I could pretend I was Sawyer.

Jokin circled me warily, his practice sword held in a decent guard position. We exchanged a few testing blows, the clang of our blunt, metal practice swords joining the chorus of similar sounds from around us.

I blocked his swing toward my left shoulder, the impact sending a jolt down my already aching arms. My lighter blade ensured my arms wouldn't tire out too early but that was about it.

Jokin pressed forward with two quick strikes, and I managed to sidestep the second one. For the briefest moment, his eyes widened slightly with surprise as if he hadn't expected me to dodge it before his expression hardened again, returning to that deliberate coldness.

We continued trading blows, the steady rhythm of attack and defense making my arms burn as sweat gathered at my temples, under my arms, and between my breasts.

With my aching body, it felt like an hour passed in our steady exchange — when it had likely only been half that time — before Lord Rider's voice cut through the training yard. "Switch partners!"

We broke apart, and Jokin moved away to find his next partner. I stood where I was and watched as everyone paired off again until only Hamelin stood across the practice area, his jaw tight with the realization that he was the only one left.

With a huff, he strode toward me. "Might as well get this over with early."

"That's the spirit," I said, my aching body making me reckless. And, if I was being honest, I wanted to see if I was correct about their new tactic.

He glared at me until Mikel cleared his throat, then, after much difficulty, Hamelin managed to school his expression into blank indifference.

Hamelin took his position, his longsword noticeably heavier and longer than mine giving him more weight behind his attacks and even more reach than his long arms already gave him.

He swung with precise, controlled movements. I blocked his first strike, my arms trembling with the effort. His second blow came harder, forcing me back a step.

Though he kept the strikes within what could be considered acceptable for sparring, each one landed harder than necessary. And given that he'd been a soldier before his name had been drawn in the lottery, I had no doubt he knew exactly how hard he was striking.

My muscles ached with the effort to block him, and as much as I wanted to practice blocking and parrying, I wasn't going to last.

I switched my focus to my footwork and dodging, using my speed as much as possible and slipping past his guard only when I saw clean openings.

I managed to score a few light touches to his arm and shoulder, but my sore muscles made my movements sloppy, and I couldn't follow through on most of my attacks.

We kept at it, the clash of our blades settling into a wary dance as I dodged and weaved around his heavier strikes. Sweat stung my eyes, and my breath came shorter with each exchange.

"Switch partners!" Lord Rider barked again, and we separated.

The pattern continued through several more partners. By the time the seventh bell rang, signaling the end of practice and the dinner hour, every muscle in my body ached.

I waited until everyone else had returned their practice weapons to the pile of practice weapons, before dropping mine on top.

As I turned away from the pile of weapons, I felt eyes on me, and glanced up to find Talon watching me, his pale, multicolored gaze... strange.

Was he concerned about me? Before he'd obeyed Rider to leave me puking on the running trail, I would have thought the strange expression meant he was concerned, but now I wasn't sure.

Or was he thinking something else? I'd spent time with him as a woman in the Garden. Had he noticed a resemblance?

Shadow bled over Talon's mesmerizing gaze, turning it black, and sudden aching desire crashed through me.

I needed him. Needed him now. My body heated, my core throbbed, and everything within me screamed to rip my clothes off and throw myself at him.

Please, take me. Fill me—

"Sawyer!" Lord Rider barked.

I jerked and somehow wrenched my attention to my feet, away from Talon's gaze. My pulse roared in my ears, my cheeks burned, and my breath was too fast.

From the corner of my eye, I saw Talon's feet take a step toward me and I lurched back.

"Round the trail with the rocks," Rider said. "You, too, Tyon."

Right. The rocks. I'd been the last one off the trail from the group of experienced novices. "Yes, Lord Commander."

I turned my back on Talon and half jogged half hobbled as fast as I could across the practice field back to the boulders marking the running trail where the two bags of rocks waited.

Tyon hurried past me, grabbed the strap of one of the bags, and with both hands hauled it up high enough to get it over his head.

I picked up the other bag, the weight making my arms ache, and slung the strap over my head to settle on my shoulder as well.

"Jeez, these are heavy," I huffed. "How do you run with this?"

Tyon shot me a panicked look before wrenching his attention to the trail. "I'm not supposed to talk to you."

Ah. So I was right.

He slowly jogged — more of a brisk walk — up the hill, and I followed, my legs telling me in no uncertain terms that I was *not* going to be running the trail.

"It's all right," I told him.

We crested the rise and staggered down the other side.

"I'm still willing to help you learn to read when no one else is around," I said. "But I also understand if you don't want to risk it."

Tyon shot me a sad, grateful smile. "I don't understand why they have to be assholes about it."

I didn't either. And yet I knew there were horrible, hateful people out there who didn't need a reason to be cruel.

All I could hope was that pretending I didn't exist wasn't just a ploy to get my guard down and that they planned to do something worse.

CHAPTER 15
Talon

Sawyer staggered under the weight of the bag of rocks, hobbling up the hill at the beginning of the running trail, and my shadow writhed under my skin, restless and angry.

Its emotions match my own, along with a deep, seething frustration because I wasn't doing anything. And unless I abandoned my position as a captain of the Black Guard, there wasn't anything I could do.

I knew it would take more than a few days for the boy to recover from running the trail for most of a bell, but it still made me furious to watch him struggle, especially since I knew his punishment hadn't been deserved.

It had been a miracle my shadow had remained hidden within me all through training today — something I hadn't had to worry about before Sawyer Herstind had stumbled into my life — but no matter how hard I fought to concentrate, I'd still been unable to stop looking at him.

Quill had taken the inexperienced novices through sword drills, and I'd barely paid attention, my anger growing as I watched the other experienced novices talk and engage with each other as they sparred until they'd partnered with Sawyer. Then they were cold, no words, no acknowledgment.

And when he'd sparred with Hamelin—

I clenched my jaw as my shadow billowed within me.

Hamelin had been an experienced soldier before he'd become a guardsman, and it had been clear he'd been striking Sawyer harder than necessary. He had to have known better. He'd likely sparred countless times before. Except Rider hadn't said anything, just let the large man bash at the boy who was dodging but was moving with half the speed and grace he usually did.

Not that Rider could say anything without making it look like he was favoring Sawyer, but still— Sawyer had looked so small, so fragile against the larger more experienced swordsman, and everything within me, along with my shadow, had screamed that I needed to protect him.

Except even though I didn't know Sawyer very well, I knew enough that he probably wouldn't have welcomed my interference.

Which only made me angrier.

"Sawyer will be all right," Quill said, his tone placating, setting me even more on edge as he opened one of the sacks for the practice blades and started shoving them in.

Rider huffed. "I don't like the way he's moving."

"You don't, do you?" I snapped before I could stop myself. "And whose fault is that?"

Rider's gaze jumped to mine, his expression dark and filled with just as much frustration — and was that guilt? — as I felt. "It's my fault."

"Hey." Quill shoved the sack of practice blades at me, forcing me to take hold before he turned to the second one. "It couldn't be helped. We had to maintain order, and it hasn't broken his spirit. This will make him stronger."

"It sure as hell could have been helped," I shot back.

Rider winced, confirming the guilt I'd seen in his eyes.

Jeez. What the hell was wrong with me? Rider was already beating himself up for making the boy run for so long. I didn't need to rub it in.

Except I knew what was wrong. I was losing my mind. My shadow was stronger than ever, barely contained under my skin, and there was something about Sawyer that drove it crazy.

My allure had even slipped out, and from the way Sawyer had tensed when he'd glanced in my direction, it had clearly affected him.

My shadow had pulled back the instant it realized what had happened, which was strange, not because my allure had slipped out, but because my shadow's hunger was growing again and it had never pulled back before. Never shown restraint when it was starving.

It had been days since it had last fed. It would need to feed soon.

And it wanted Sawyer again.

On top of that, I had to convince the High Priestess I was courting the new arrival, Sage, while somehow keeping her at enough of a distance that the Goddess didn't bind our souls together before I could figure out how to get out of the forced courtship. And I felt disgusting after my performance last night.

Even though her mating marks were asleep, I didn't trust that the Goddess wouldn't find a way to make us mates, and that couldn't happen.

I also couldn't afford for the High Priestess to kill me or lock me up, but there was a way out of Her Brilliance's demands and there wasn't one out of a mating bond.

So I'd taken a risk. Given what Ash had said about how shy Sage was, I'd guess that if I pulled out all of my charm, she'd be wary instead of attracted. And she had been.

The memory of the suspicion filling her emerald eyes made my stomach churn. I didn't want her to doubt me. I wanted her to trust me, especially since I knew there were so few in the Garden she could trust right now.

But I couldn't have a mate. Ever.

Unless it was Quill.

And that was never going to be, because I'd never force him to give up his dreams of being mated to a woman and having a family.

"I talked with Ash last night," Quill said as he put the rest of the practice weapons into the second sack. "He says the plan is to shun Sawyer. Interact with him as little as possible."

"At least that's better than attacking him every day," I said, my attention jerking back to my anger over the boy.

Rider took the sack from Quill and growled, his wolf so close to the surface I was surprised he wasn't growing fur on his hands and arms. "That won't make him a guardsman."

It wouldn't. Being a guardsman meant being part of a team. Guardsmen needed to rely on each other and work together, or someone died. If the other guardsmen were pretending Sawyer didn't exist, then there was no one watching his back.

"It's only been one rotation," Quill said. "They'll warm up to him eventually."

Except would that "eventually" come before or after someone got seriously hurt?

Rider shifted the sack on his shoulder and fell into step beside me as I headed toward the barracks.

"Still can't believe you volunteered for tonight," I said.

He grunted.

"A hundred years of avoiding women, and now you're volunteering to watch over a stranger." I shook my head. "Bold move."

"She needs protection." The words came out clipped, defensive.

"Right." I let that hang between us, watching the tension creep into his jaw.

He glared at me. "Don't."

"Sure." I raised my hands in surrender but couldn't stop wondering if he felt the same pull to her that I did.

It certainly looked like his wolf was interested given how he'd almost ripped West's throat out for refusing us entry into Sage's suite.

I might not want a mate, but I couldn't deny there was something about her. That and my shadow was determined to protect her.

"Careful," I said. "Keep this up and people might think you've gone soft."

"That so?" His jaw tightened. "Then what's your excuse?"

Well, shit. I'd handed that to him on a platter, and I couldn't even defend myself. No way was I telling him, or anyone, that the High Priestess had ordered me to court Sage. I'd find a way out of that mess soon, and no one needed to know about it.

"So..." Quill cleared his throat. "Any news on the investigation?"

Rider's jaw tightened. "Still nothing."

Which meant Sage was still in danger, and the only thing we could do was wait by her side and hope one of us along with West would be enough... if we could even trust West.

CHAPTER 16
Rider

My wolf snarled inside me as I strode down the Divine Residence's hallway toward Sage's suite.

Tonight was my turn to watch her, and my wolf was too damn eager.

I clenched my jaw. I didn't want to be here, didn't want to spend hours near a woman who made my wolf howl with need every time I caught her scent. But she was surrounded by people she couldn't trust after being attacked by a bunch of assholes, and she needed someone to protect her.

That, and I knew she was stuck somewhere in the human realm, most likely a slave, and I was going to get her out.

I just had to earn her trust first since I wasn't supposed to know about her human-realm situation.

I huffed.

Easier said than done since I didn't *do feelings* and

always said the worst possible thing when I was around a woman.

I'd rather face a pack of ravenous shadows than make small talk. With shadows, I knew what to do. With women...

My thoughts jumped to Isemay, my mate — my *only* mate. I hadn't been an idiot around her, hadn't felt I had to say anything if I hadn't wanted to.

But that part of me was long dead with her, with our unborn child, with the man I thought I'd be.

My wolf heaved under my skin. It didn't understand what the problem was. It had claimed Isemay, now it was claiming Sage, and thought my emotions in the topic were pointless. Sage was his and it protected what belonged to him.

Mine.

Not. Mine, I growled back at it as if that, somehow, could convince it against what it had already decided.

And it didn't really matter. Not now. I had to protect Sage, and I had to earn her trust, so she'd let me save her. Even if my wolf hadn't claimed her, I wouldn't have been able to turn my back on her. I—

Everything within me froze, my wolf suddenly alert.

I'd reached the door to Sage's suite, but something was wrong. Yes, the hall was empty, and I didn't hear anything, but—

My nose twitched, catching a musky, cloying scent, and my pulse leaped, my claws surging from my fingers.

That scent—

A growl rumbled in my throat. It was one of the scents from the sacred pool after Sage had been attacked. One of the two scents I hadn't been able to match with a person.

One of those assholes had been here, right outside her fucking door.

Everything inside me went cold. Then hot. Then murderous.

Had they gotten inside? Had they gotten to *her*?

West would protect her… if West wasn't involved in the whole thing.

I lunged for the door and kicked it in, the wood exploding inward with a crack that echoed down the hall. I was through before it finished swinging, claws out, wolf surging toward the surface.

The sitting room spread before me with its intricately carved furniture, enormous marble fireplace, tapestries and heavy rugs.

No sign of Sage.

West slammed into me before I could take another step.

The knight's massive form drove me backward, his forearm crushing into my throat as he pinned me against the doorframe beside the splintered door. A dagger tip pressed against my gut, the blade just under the bottom of my leather armor, angled up to slice through my bowels and give me an agonizing death.

"Give me one reason why I shouldn't gut you," he hissed, his voice low, his expression deadly.

My wolf snarled, claws flexing, but I forced myself not to fight back. West wasn't the threat right now.

"Someone," I growled past the pressure on my throat. "Outside her door. One of the men from the pool."

West's arm didn't ease. His eyes searched my face, looking for the lie.

"I can smell him," I said. "The scent is fresh. Less than an hour."

His gaze flicked to the ruined door behind me, then back.

I held still. My wolf wanted to lunge past him and check on Sage, determine if she'd already manifested and was being held captive in the bedroom, but I couldn't scent the assailant past the doorway, which meant whoever it was hadn't been in the suite.

West's eyes narrowed, but he stepped back, his dagger still pointed at me but thankfully no longer digging into my gut.

"Show me."

"It's a scent." How the hell was I supposed to show him a scent?

He quirked an eyebrow, just a flicker of movement before his face returned to its usual grim expression.

Fine. I shifted to the side, unable to completely put West at my back, and took a few quick sniffs. The assailant's scent was strongest at the door, concentrated near the frame and the lock.

"Here." I dropped into a crouch, pressing closer to the floor. "He stood here. Recently. Less than an hour."

West crouched beside me, his gaze running along the

wood grain, and his nostrils flared as if he, too, could scent like a wolf.

I hadn't thought his magic went beyond physical enhancements, but maybe I was wrong and West could enhance more than just his strength, speed, and durability.

If that was the case, we needed to be careful what we said around him. If he could enhance his sense of smell, he could enhance his hearing as well.

West frowned and turned back to the suite. "Inside as well?"

Guess there was a limit to his enhancement. Either that, or he was testing me.

My wolf huffed at that. We had the keenest sense of smell in the realm. West couldn't be better than us and only looked like a fool if he was actually testing us.

"No. The scent stops at the threshold," I growled. "He didn't enter."

West stood and sheathed his dagger, but his hand jumped to the hilt of his sword.

I rose and faced him across the doorway. My throat throbbed where his arm had crushed into me, and from the hard set of his jaw, he still wanted to gut me.

The feeling was mutual.

But we had a bigger problem. One of the men who'd attacked Sage had been right outside her door. Watching. Waiting.

"I found eight scents at the sacred pool," I said. "I told the Order about it when they interviewed me, Talon, Ash, and Quill."

Something flickered in West's gaze. My best guess was frustration that the Order hadn't mentioned anything about the scents to him. But since the expression happened so fast, it was hard to tell.

"Two of the scents didn't match the dead or the men I already recognized. This is one of them," I finished.

His grip on his sword's hilt tightened. "You're certain?"

Did he think I was an inexperienced idiot?

West's gaze jumped back to the doorway, and my wolf heaved inside me, determined, ferocious.

I didn't trust West. I didn't know whose side he was really on, or if he'd follow orders regardless of what was right.

But right now, he was the only ally I and the others had standing between Sage and whoever had been lurking outside her door, and there was always a chance we wouldn't get to Sage before she manifested in the Garden. If that happened, it was just her and West until I, Talon, or Quill could get to her.

"The door needs to be replaced," West said, his voice a low rumble.

He stepped into the doorway and jerked his chin toward the summon stone by the fireplace, his message clear: *I* had to summon the servant.

I bit back a snarl. As the Lord Commander of the Black Guard, I outranked him, and *I* needed to protect Sage. But given how obstinate he was about his duty, I doubted he'd step away from the doorway until the door was replaced.

I stormed to the stone and activated it with a touch of my fingers. A matching stone would light up in the servants' quarters and the servant assigned to Sage's suite would rush up.

"So Yarrow is in charge of the investigation," I said, turning back to him and trying not to make it obvious that I was desperately trying to read his expression.

The muscles in West's jaw flexed and his eyes narrowed a fraction.

Best guess: he wasn't a fan of Yarrow, either.

But was it because Yarrow was an arrogant asshole who probably liked to remind West that he wasn't pretty like every other fae, or because he didn't trust the Order's investigator.

"And now one of them is bold enough to come to her door," I said.

"He didn't enter," West said, his voice low.

"This time." My wolf heaved inside me, desperate to ensure Sage's safety even though she clearly hadn't manifested yet. "Whoever he is, he's not afraid of the Order and he's not afraid to be in the Divine Residence. He's either confident we won't catch him, or he knows the investigation won't touch him."

The fire popped and something flickered in West's eyes. He'd already thought of that.

Good. I'd thought the bastard wasn't stupid. It was nice to have proof.

Footsteps sounded down the hall and I stilled. A moment later, someone gasped and a young male servant rushed into sight, staring at the splintered door.

"The door needs to be replaced," West rumbled.

The man, who might not have even been old enough to manifest in the Garden and was likely physically present in the Divine Residence, paled at West's glare, wildly bobbed his head, and scurried away.

My wolf snarled and heaved inside me, desperate to take action. Except there wasn't anything we could do. We had to wait until Sage manifested and then I needed to convince her to trust me.

The door would be fixed, eventually, and until Crane and the remaining assholes made a move, I had to wait and protect.

Fuck, I hated waiting.

CHAPTER 17

Sage

I OPENED my eyes to once again find myself lying on the floor of my Garden suite, Sir West's enormous frame looming above me.

Lord Quill's meditation hadn't worked this time, either. Not that I'd expected it to. I'd only been meditating for two nights now, but a girl could hope.

The novices' evening class about the Gray and the shadow monsters had taken longer than my half shift in the stables had during the previous rotation, and I'd made a point to practice my meditation afterward, forcing me to stay up later than usual. But even the exhaustion of trying to sit still in a classroom and listen to a lecture and then going to bed late hadn't helped.

Father, all I wanted was to sleep.

But I wasn't and there wasn't anything I could do about it right now.

With a sigh, I pushed myself to my feet, wondering who my chaperone for this evening would be.

I swept my gaze around the room. For some strange reason I wasn't in the middle of the room like I usually was. I was beside the... broken door? With Sir West standing guard at the entrance.

What the hell had happened now?

Sir West had his hand on the hilt of his sword but didn't look worried — if the man ever looked anything other than grim — instead he looked more on guard. So either whatever had happened wasn't serious, or it was over.

The rest of the sitting room looked the same with the soft golden glow from the elegant chandeliers and the fire in the hearth illuminating the ornate furniture, the tapestries, the various ornaments dotting tables and the mantle. The balcony doors were open, and the pale glowing flowers ringing the balcony railing trembled in the night breeze.

And there by the balcony doors, partially hidden in shadows, stood Lord Rider, his back rigid and his gaze firmly fixed on a point somewhere just over my head.

I'd thought he'd just been here the other night to support Lord Quill and Talon and that he didn't actually care about me.

Except if that were the case, it didn't make sense he'd be here... now.

Regardless, I knew without a doubt that Rider wanted a mate as much as Talon did, so tonight was going to be uncomfortable and awkward. I could only pray he wasn't going to try to pretend to flirt with me like Talon had.

Rider shifted from one foot to the other, his discomfort clear, making me wonder why he'd volunteered to take a shift watching over me to begin with.

The last time we'd been alone in the Garden, he'd literally disappeared into thin air. Now he was voluntarily in my suite.

Through the open balcony doorway beside him, I could see the distant lights from other rooms in the Divine Residence and the soft glow of flowers in the Garden below.

The muscles in Lord Rider's jaw flexed and he shifted his weight again.

The silence stretched between us.

Rider's fingers tapped against his thigh, then stilled. His jaw worked as if he wanted to say something but couldn't find the words.

I curled my fingers into the gauzy fabric of my dress, seeking something to do besides just stand there and stare at him.

Maybe I should sit.

Maybe I should retreat to my bedroom and leave him with Lord-Even-Less-Chatty, Sir West. The two of them could glare at each other all night.

Except that wasn't fair to him.

I might not like Rider or trust him to have anything but his own interest in mind, but he was here, giving up his evening, to ensure I was safe. Perhaps I should be more cordial.

Quill was nice to me.

Maybe Rider wanted to be friends, too.

He didn't know I was the annoying novice in the Gray. Here, I was just some woman who'd been attacked that he knew nothing about.

"So," I said. "Have you ah... Have you been waiting long?"

Rider's silver eyes flickered to mine for a brief moment before darting away.

"Yes," he replied, his voice gruff.

Well. So much for conversation.

His eyes widened as if he just realized what he'd said.

"But I don't mind," he added in a rush. "We agreed to take turns and tonight's my turn."

Which confirmed my suspicion that he didn't really want to be here.

"You're ah... safe here. With us, I mean. With me." The words came out stilted, awkward.

Outside, laughter and music from the courtyard drifted up through the night air. Inside, the only sound was Rider's measured breathing, deliberately controlled as if he were forcing himself to remain calm. I shifted my weight, the soft rustle of my dress unnaturally loud in the quiet room.

"I—" Rider cleared his throat. "There are clothes."

I raised my eyebrows in question. "Clothes?"

"Yes, Quill arranged for them. He had them delivered because you can't—" His gaze slid down my body, his pupils dilating, and a hint of a feral look flashed through his expression.

A traitorous sliver of desire raced down my spine before his attention jumped back up to my cleavage...

which wasn't overly impressive because of my slight frame and—

Right. My mating marks. He was looking at my mating marks, not my figure.

And jeez, why did I even care what he thought of me? I wasn't interested in him. I didn't want him as a mate. I didn't want anyone as a mate. It made no sense that my feelings would be hurt because I'd confirmed he believed being here was his duty and nothing more.

I crossed my arms, suddenly feeling exposed and embarrassed to think that Rider would look at me with desire, or that I'd even want him to.

He jerked his gaze back up to my eyes. "He didn't tell anyone why you wanted them. Only that you did," he added, as if that was what had made me uncomfortable. "They're in the wardrobe. In the bedroom."

He gestured to the opulent bedroom that everyone assumed was mine even though the smaller bed in the other bedroom was too small for Sir West.

I hurried inside, and Rider and West followed as if I couldn't figure out where the wardrobe was or how to change my clothes by myself.

Heat bled across my cheeks.

Were they going to stand there and watch me change?

"Quill thought you might want options," Rider said, as he stepped past me to the large, intricately carved wardrobe that stood against the far wall and pulled open its doors.

Inside hung at least a dozen dresses in different

colors. I stepped closer and reached out, brushing my fingers over the different fabrics.

Most were made of a combination of the same gauzy, lacy material as my current dress, but a few were less lace and gauze and more silk.

There were a variety of styles, but all of them had high collars and necklines that would completely cover my dormant mating marks. To make up for the less than revealing front, all of them were backless or had high slits up the sides, revealing almost the same amount of skin as my original barely-there dress just in different places.

"You should try them on," Rider said, his voice gruff.

"Of course."

"Quill thought the green one might look nice on you."

There were two green dresses, one a bright emerald the color of Lord Quill's eyes, the other a softer, paler shade of green.

"Well, I'll—" He jerked his chin toward the door.

"Right."

He turned, his broad shoulders blocking the doorway. "If you need anything, you can ask. I mean, you can ask me." The words came out in a rush and he hurried out.

What was with him tonight? Lord Rider was gruff and awkward, but tonight he'd been... strange. Stranger than the last time we'd talked in the Garden. Was it something to do with the broken door? Or was something else going on?

Sir West gave me a tight nod then left as well, leaving

the bedroom door open a crack, and I bit back a sigh. I supposed if I really wanted to guarantee my privacy, I could haul all the dresses to the bathing room.

Except I couldn't help wondering if Sir West would insist I leave that door open a crack as well since I was alone.

I turned back to the wardrobe, running my fingers over the fabrics. There were deep blues and rich purples, the two different greens and a warm gold. The material slipped between my fingers, impossibly soft and worth more than anything I'd ever worn in my life.

Even before my father had died and my mother had remarried Edred, our family hadn't wasted our wealth on lavish clothing. We hadn't wasted it on anything lavish. It had been more important to ensure we had a well-equipped guard to protect our lands against brigands.

I pulled out the emerald dress. It had gold threads woven through it that caught the light and would probably look good on me with my green eyes and bright red hair. But if I wore it, I'd match Lord Quill.

Would that be considered a sign that I was aligning myself with him? That seemed like something the fae court might do... although I hadn't seen many fae wearing white, the same color as the High Priestess.

I thought back, trying to remember if I'd seen anyone in white, but I couldn't recall either way.

There weren't any white dresses in the wardrobe, so it might be best to assume white was reserved for the High Priestess herself and perhaps those closest to Her Brilliance.

Which still didn't answer the question of whether wearing a dress that matched someone's usual clothes indicated a relationship of some kind like it did in human courts.

And I was probably making this more complicated than it needed to be. I was already wearing a red dress. It was probably safest to wear a different red dress, then no one could make any kind of assumptions about my change of clothing. The last thing I needed was to accidentally signal an alliance I didn't understand to people who played games I didn't know the rules to.

CHAPTER 18

Ash

I PRESSED my back against cold stone and reached for the next handhold. I was four and a half floors up the wall of the north wing where the Order of the Sacred Grove housed their garrison and offices, and almost at my destination.

Unfortunately, the north wing was all function with uniform square blocks that blended naturally into the Great Tree's supporting branches. It barely had any of the ornamental bullshit like the rest of the Divine Residence, and that made climbing it that much more difficult.

My fingers found purchase on a narrow ledge barely wide enough to hold onto with nothing but empty air below. If I fell... well, I'd send my spirit back into my body, jolt awake with a massive headache that would last for days, and have to start climbing from the bottom again since there was magic preventing anyone but the

Lord Commander of the Order and his captains from manifesting inside the north wing.

And I really didn't want to start this climb all over again.

The decorative edge was worn smooth by centuries of rain and wind and time, and I hauled myself higher as the familiar burn spread through my arms and shoulders.

Good. That was something to focus on besides the churning in my gut, a way to concentrate on my mission, because I couldn't think about her.

Red. Sage.

Goddess. She was in her suite in the opposite wing of the Residence — if she was still manifesting into the Garden at this hour — safe and protected by one of my brothers-in-arms while I was clinging to a wall.

According to Rider, they'd worked out a rotation so someone was always in her suite when she manifested. Even Talon had volunteered, which just spoke to how compelling the stunning, shy, redhead really was, since he couldn't afford to be anywhere near her.

If she accidentally bonded with him and found out about his shadow it was all over. No one would understand the truth about his shadow.

Except someone had.

A too-small novice who'd made one hell of a mistake when he first entered the Gray. Talon's shadow had attacked him and he'd understood the entity wasn't evil.

It had taken years for me to accept the truth and stop being wary of Talon, and I'd known and trusted Talon for over a century.

The memory of Sage looking at me with kindness, desire, and not a hint of fear despite my hideous appearance flashed through my mind's eye.

If anyone else could accept him, it would be Sage.

Except that desire she'd had for me had been because of her marks, not because she knew or cared about me. I had to keep reminding myself of that. I couldn't forget the truth of my reality.

My chest ached at the thought, and I hung on the wall for a moment, letting the wind cut across my face, reminding me of who I was and what I did.

She was perfection and compassion and strength and everything I'd ever yearned for in a woman, and Wells and Crane had tried to break her. If Sage hadn't killed Wells, I would have. I would have protected her.

Except I'd already failed her in that respect. Crane, Addax, Thunder, and one other had escaped and the only way I could protect her now was breaking into Yarrow's office and learning everything I could about his investigation.

I found my next grip and pulled, my muscles straining. Yarrow's office was still another floor up, and Sage, on the other side of the Residence, was even higher.

For a stupid, ridiculous moment I thought about climbing to her suite, embracing her, and ensuring with my own eyes that she was safe.

But that was a fool's dream. The guest suites in the south wing were on some of the higher branches, and a fae with magic that could manipulate trees had ensured that no one could climb that high.

Not that it mattered. Even if I could reach her, I shouldn't.

The irony made me want to laugh. I was barred from the Divine Residence because of my scars, and yet here I was, scaling its walls anyway. Just not the part that mattered.

I gritted my teeth and focused on the climb.

The Garden meetings with others had been tense lately, and not just because one of the guys was always missing and a constant reminder that they got to be with Sage. Things in the Gray hadn't eased up, and I had no idea when we were going to be shown a reprieve.

Kit's team was off the roster for at least four rotations unless Reef had any extra magic he was willing to donate when his rotation ended, and the attack only made it more obvious that something was wrong with the shadows. They weren't behaving the way they used to, and I shuddered to think what that might mean.

On top of that, things with Sawyer were still uncertain. Sure, Mikel had convinced Durand and the others that the best way to teach the boy his lessons was to isolate him. It drove him crazy that Kit and Payne were still talking with him, but he couldn't do anything about that, and all the other guardsmen had agreed with the next tactic.

Thank the Goddess for that at least, since ignoring him ensured no one was trying to kill him.

I reached the window ledge to Yarrow's office and hauled myself up the last few feet. The office beyond the clear glass was dark, everything still and silent.

Mindful of my balance, I examined the latch. It was pretty basic, nothing a slim stiletto couldn't tip open, and conveniently in my spirit form I could manifest one with a thought.

With a flick of my wrist, I released the latch then pushed the window open.

In the dim moonlight, I scanned Yarrow's severely organized office. Everything lay in precise place, not a paper out of alignment nor a book unshelved. The desk sat centered a few steps from the window and the chair was pushed in. Even the inkwell sat in what I suspected was a measured position.

With no personal effects, no paintings, no mementos or trophies, the room told me everything I needed to know about my cousin if I hadn't already known him all my life. He despised anything that wasn't ordered or controlled.

I slipped inside, easing the window shut behind me, and letting the night settle around me, comfortable in a way I never was in daylight. Here, my scars didn't matter. Here, I was just another patch of shadow.

I crossed the two steps to the desk and brushed my fingers across its bare surface, studying the drawer just under the desktop and the three stacked drawers on the righthand side. Yarrow's investigation notes would be here somewhere. He was too methodical to keep them anywhere else, and he'd never take them home, that went against protocol.

The first narrow drawer under the desktop probably had quills, charcoal sticks for quick notes, and other miscellaneous stuff, that and — unless Yarrow had suddenly become lazy — his notebook would be too thick for that drawer, so...

I turned my attention to the first of the stacked drawers on the right. It was locked, but the lock was almost an insult and easily picked with a materialized lockpick.

With a soft click of the lock and a gentle pull, I slid the drawer open, and there, on top of a pile of folders lay Yarrow's leatherbound folio where he kept all his notes for his current investigation.

Carefully, I untied the leather thong securing the pages and opened it.

Somewhere in these pages was a name, a witness, something that would lead me to Crane and the others who'd escaped. Something that would let me protect her the only way I could right now.

Goddess! All I wanted was to hold her again, to feel her warmth against me and know with my own eyes and body that she was safe.

Instead, I was alone in the dark, searching my cousin's notes for scraps.

The first few pages were his observations about the sacred pool's chamber and what he knew about the attack. The next pages were his interviews with Rider, Talon, and Quill, a note with each of them indicating that Wells had had a dagger but no dagger had been found.

I hadn't been interviewed because I wasn't considered noteworthy despite having been there and being a Captain of the Black Guard.

I quickly flipped through those pages, already familiar with the information, until I reached his notes on the magical artifact, the bracelet, that had trapped Sage's spirit in the Garden.

The first few pages were a list of every measurement taken, every detail about the craftsmanship, and every failed attempt to determine how its magic worked and trace its origin.

At least the Order's magisters had examined it, even if the magisters at the White Tower hadn't.

Except they hadn't found anything and they weren't as studied as the Head of Artifacts at the White Tower.

I turned the page. This one had Yarrow's thoughts.

Bracelet. Enslaving magic.
Construction seems familiar.

My pulse lurched.

He recognized it?

He had a good memory, and his magically enhanced gaze meant he noticed details others didn't.

Checked archive.
Found a note about a similar item documented twenty years prior with a number of other unusual artifacts secured during an investigation.
Requested ledger.
Case ledger missing.

No record of checkout. No transfer. No destruction order.

Well, shit.

If the bracelet indeed belonged to the group of artifacts secured by the Order, that had far-reaching implications, not to mention the fact that the case ledger about the twenty-year-old case was missing.

I read through the rest of the pages, committing them to memory while keeping their order intact. Yarrow's handwriting shifted subtly as the pages progressed. Heavier pressure on certain words. Shorter sentences toward the end. He wasn't used to dead ends. He didn't like being blocked.

Sure, there was a chance the twenty-year-old ledger had just gone missing, but neither Yarrow, nor I liked coincidences, and this felt too much like a coincidence.

I closed the folio, replaced it exactly as I'd found it, and double checked the drawer to ensure I'd left no indication that I'd been there. Then I returned to the window, opened it, and stepped on the ledge.

Yarrow's notes raised more questions than they answered.

He held pride in his role as the Order's top investigator, so he wouldn't lie in his notes. If he'd known anything about the bracelet beforehand, he wouldn't have mentioned the missing file, which meant he wasn't directly involved in Sage's attack. But I'd already known that.

That didn't mean he wouldn't bury his notes or at the end of his investigation file a case ledger conveniently missing all suggestion that the Order might have originally had the bracelet in their possession if he was ordered to by the Lord Commander of the Order of the High Priestess. But right now, Yarrow's notes were complete.

And those notes made it clear that someone with access to the Order's archives had removed the case ledger from a previous case. Which strongly implied that the bracelet from that case was the bracelet that had trapped Sage's spirit in the Garden.

Did that mean the High Priestess was involved or just an Order clerk?

Whatever it was, I would learn the truth, and I would ensure Sage's safety. I had to.

CHAPTER 19
Sage

I PUSHED through the infirmary doors into the morning light streaming across the main room. It was halfway through the rotation and so far every morning had been the same. Reef told me to do the cleaning while he taught Garridan basic healing arts, sometimes even letting Garridan help him treat minor injuries.

But I didn't want to complain. Cleaning the infirmary was easier than mucking out the stables and didn't strain my already aching muscles.

I'd also learned that if the injury looked minor, Reef didn't use his magic to determine its severity or to heal it. Payne hadn't lied — not that I'd expected him to — when he'd said the Black Guard healers conserved their magic as much as possible, but it was nice to get confirmation.

And that meant so long as the injury was small, perhaps only requiring a few stitches at most, I could probably get away with receiving medical attention instead of dealing with any injuries myself and hoping no one noticed.

Of course, there was no guarantee that Flint or any of the other healers in the Black Guard were as stingy with their healing magic as Reef was. For all I knew Reef didn't have a lot of magic power to begin with and had to be particularly circumspect with it.

And really, it was best to avoid getting injured at all.

This morning, Reef stood at one of the patient tables in the middle of the room tending to a man with a bleeding arm. The injury didn't look too bad, and Reef must have thought the same because he'd pulled one of the rolling tables close and was stitching the wound together instead of closing his eyes and releasing his power.

The healer glanced up as I strode past him, but I didn't bother asking if I was going to be doing anything different today. He'd seemed upset the day before yesterday that I'd bothered asking, as if talking to me was too much work.

Which, now that I thought about it, might not have been because he thought it was too much work just that he was supposed to be going along with everyone else and pretending I didn't exist — something he couldn't actually do because he was in charge of me for my morning chores.

I headed straight to the hall with the patient rooms and the cleaning closet at the end.

Behind me, I heard the infirmary doors open, then

Reef greet Garridan and tell him to come closer to watch how he sewed the stitches.

I reached the cleaning room and started filling one of the buckets with the magical cleansing water, the sharp sour smell stinging my nose.

"You know both novices are supposed to do the cleaning so it's done in half the time," Payne said from behind me, startling me and making me slosh water out of the bucket. "You're both supposed to get training in basic healing."

I shrugged and went back to filling the bucket. "It's fine."

"No, it isn't."

"Stop bothering my novice," Reef said, his voice sharp as he approached from down the hall.

"Your novice? Could have fooled me," Payne huffed. "An infirmary rotation is supposed to be half cleaning and half basic healing. Sawyer's been on scrub work for five days straight. I've been thinking of informing the quartermaster that he must have been misassigned."

Reef's eyes narrowed. "How I run my infirmary is my business. Not yours, the quartermaster's, or anyone else's."

"It'll become everyone's business once the boy is in the field and needs to know how to bind a wound."

Thankfully I already knew how to bind wounds, but I also knew speaking up right now would just draw unwanted attention, not to mention undermine Payne's argument. And while I felt it was unnecessary, I didn't want Payne to think I wasn't grateful for the time and consideration he'd given me.

"It doesn't matter if the runt can bind a wound or not," Reef said. "No one trusts him. He can learn basic healing the next time he's assigned infirmary duty."

"Don't be an idiot," Payne huffed. "If he can't be useful in the field, he won't gain any trust. With his size, no one's going to put him on the front line. Basic healing is the field skill he should be focusing on."

"Well, he'll just have to prove all of us wrong," Reef shot back.

Now it was Payne's turn to narrow his eyes. "What's that supposed to mean?"

"We're shorthanded," Reef said with a dismissive wave before turning his attention to me. "Put the bucket away, we're going to the ring to meet a merchant with medical supplies and escort him back to the Tower.

"*You're* going to escort him?" Payne asked

Reef's hand dropped to the hilt of the longsword at his hip. "It might have been before your time, but I served my fifty years as a guardsman before I came back as a healer."

"Then you know no one goes beyond the wall by themselves," Payne said.

"I'll have the runt and Garridan," Reef said. "The area's patrolled and it's daytime. It's safe enough."

Safe enough. I didn't like the sound of that.

"Two *novices* don't count," Payne shot back.

Maybe Reef was an exceptional fighter, and it

wouldn't matter that while *I* might be able to hold my own against a small shadow monster, Garridan didn't stand a chance. He wasn't one of the novices experienced with fighting and the glimpses I'd gotten of his skills over the last couple of days made my brother — who could have tripped over his own feet while standing still — look like an adequate swordsman.

"And safe enough, isn't safe at all," Payne growled.

"Then find someone to back me up?" Reef spat. "You can't, can you? Because there's no one else right now. I checked."

"I'll go."

Reef's eyes widened with surprise. "Your team is still on medical leave. We both know as soon as Kit and Lewin are given the go ahead you'll be put back on light duty and you won't see lieu time for days."

"Still going." Payne shrugged. "I could use some exercise."

"Fine." Reef jerked around and stormed back toward the infirmary's main room. "Garridan, grab your sword and let's go. We're going to the gate."

"What a fucking moron," Payne hissed under his breath. "And did he just tell that novice to get his sword? He's supposed to be wearing it at all times."

"He says it gets in his way." And it wasn't my place to correct him. "He's never had one before, so he's still getting used to it."

"That's no excuse, and Reef should know better and correct him," Payne said.

But Garridan was Reef's favorite novice at the moment. I had no doubt if I set my sword aside, Reef would reprimand me without a second thought.

CHAPTER 20
Sage

I FOLLOWED Reef and Garridan out the infirmary's side door into the bailey. My gaze caught on the greenhouse with its enormous sheets of glass that still amazed me every time I saw them. Before arriving in the Gray, I'd never seen a window that size before, and while it was cloudy like a lot of windows in the human realm, I knew from the clear enormous glass windows above the doors in the Black Tower's great hall, that the glass didn't have to be that way.

Near the stables, a fae guardsmen maneuvered a wheelbarrow full of manure toward the outer wall as if it didn't weigh anything. Except I knew for a fact just how heavy the load had to be, and I was grateful I hadn't been assigned stable duty again for my second rotation.

It had been days, and my body was just starting to feel normal again. Even without having been forced to run on the trail until I'd collapsed, I doubt I would have survived another full rotation hauling manure.

Payne fell into step beside me as we crossed toward the gatehouse. Ahead of us, Reef walked with his hand on the hilt of his sword, his posture more like a guardsman than a healer despite his pale blue doublet, while Garridan looked nervous.

I couldn't blame the other novice. It had been made perfectly clear in our evening classes that while the practice yards and the running trail were protected by magical wards that prevented shadow monsters from attacking us, nowhere else — and that included the road to the fae ring — was protected.

We marched straight to the Tower's gatehouse, a thick structure built from the same massive stone blocks as the rest of the fortification that framed the large arched entrance. The heavy wooden gates stood open just wide enough for a pair of riders or a wagon to ride through.

The two guardsmen manning the gate watched us approach with wary expressions, and one muttered something under his breath that sounded a lot like a curse.

Yeah. Payne wasn't the only one who thought taking two novices beyond the Tower's walls was a bad idea.

We stepped through the enormous doors and onto the main road. The bricked path stretched out ahead of us before dipping down and curling around a large stone outcropping, and mist swirled around my feet. Overhead, the sky pressed low with gray clouds.

To my left, the massive Shadow Gate towered above the mist, ominous and threatening, the whole purpose for the Black Guard. A shiver ran down my spine with a mix of fear that the seal keeping the gate shut would fail and the Gray would be overrun with shadow monsters, along with the terror that my envisioned death would come true.

I glanced at Payne beside me. The enormous fae looked powerful and strong as if he hadn't been poisoned six days ago.

He was walking proof that I could change what I saw, that I had reached him in time and made a difference when all the other times I'd failed to protect the people I cared about.

I had to hold on to that hope. It was possible. I could survive.

As we walked down the slope and around the outcropping, the road began to climb, and I could finally see the fae ring at the top of the hill.

It was farther away than I'd expected. Of course, the only other time I'd been down this road was when I'd been slung over the front of Rider's saddle like a sack of grain. It had been dark, and I hadn't gotten a good look at anything.

Not that I'd wanted a better look at what I now knew were shadow hounds. The glimpses I'd gotten in the dark were more than enough.

We reached the fae ring at the top of the hill, which was also the end of the road. The large silver and bronze circle sat partially buried in the ground with mist swirling around its bottom, and the same swirly fae writing found on all the rings traced up one side almost too high for someone as short as me to reach.

As we approached, some of the symbols lit up, and a

moment later, a white light blossomed in the center, a small white flower that slowly unfurled and grew until the entire ring was filled with brilliant, shimmering magic.

Out of the light plodded a brown donkey, pulling a covered wagon with a canvas canopy tall enough that I could probably stand up inside it even if none of the other men could. A heavyset man with graying hair sat on the wagon's bench, the reins held loosely in his weathered hands.

"Reef!" the heavyset man called out as the back of the wagon cleared the ring and the light went out. "I'm surprised to see they let you out of the infirmary."

"I wanted to check the quality of the cleaning spirits. The potency of the last batch was low, Iztal, and there's no point in hauling the barrels to the Tower if I'm just going to turn around and send them back," Reef replied, not revealing that we were actually shorthanded and didn't have the guardsmen to spare to escort the merchant to the Tower.

The man, Iztal, frowned. I guess Reef wanting to check the quality of whatever was being delivered right here at the ring was unusual. Or perhaps Iztal was insulted that Reef suspected the quality of his wares.

But the frown only lasted a moment and his smile returned.

"Of course, of course." The merchant hopped off the bench and sauntered to the back of his wagon.

Payne shifted beside me, his gaze darting over the rocky terrain. He still looked calm, like a warrior just doing his job, but I couldn't ignore the tension building inside me.

Just because Reef thought everything would be fine didn't mean it would be. Sure, the shadow hounds had attacked me at night when shadow monsters were supposed to be more active, but I'd also been attacked by a shadow dragon in the middle of the day. Nowhere in the Gray was safe.

"We should probably do this in the bailey, not out in the open," Payne said.

But Reef waved him off like he was being ridiculous and followed Iztal to the back.

"Come on, Garridan. The barrels are heavy." Reef shot me a disgusted look. "And that one won't be any help."

The merchant unhooked and dropped the tailboard, revealing wooden barrels packed on either side, leaving a narrow passage between them up to the bench at the front of the wagon.

Garridan grabbed one side of the closest barrel, Iztal grabbed the other, and they hauled it out and set it on the bricked road.

The barrel came up to my waist, was dark wood, bound with iron bands around it, and a brass handle set into the lid. Reef grabbed the handle, twisted it, and opened the barrel.

Inside, bright blue shimmering liquid gave off the same sharp sour smell as the water from the infirmary's cleaning room. Only this liquid was brighter and had a stronger scent.

Reef dipped a finger into the liquid and closed his eyes. The shimmer in the water intensified. He had to be using his magic to test it, but I didn't know how healing magic could be used that way. Perhaps the same ability that helped him examine a body to determine where someone was injured let him determine the qualities of the liquid.

And guessing was as close to the truth as I was going to get, since I doubted Reef would tell me anything even if I asked.

"Good," he said as he opened his eyes and wiped his fingers on his pantleg. "It's high potency."

"All the barrels are from the same batch," Iztal assured him.

Payne's hands dropped to the hilts of his paired large swords. "Great, now let's get moving."

"Fine, fine," Reef huffed and jerked his chin at the barrel indicating Garridan and the merchant should load it back onto the wagon.

Behind Reef, just out of the corner of my eye, something moved among the uneven landscape... or had that just been the fog undulating with the breeze?

I squinted at a scrubby bush maybe fifty feet away pressed against a rocky outcropping.

The bush shivered as if struck by a sudden gust of wind, but I didn't feel the rush of air on my skin and the fog didn't swirl faster. Which meant—

My pulse lurched. "Look out!"

With a bone-chilling screech, a shadow monster

bounded out of the bush, crossing the distance in the blink of an eye.

It was a hound, the same kind of monster that had attacked me the last time I was at the fae ring. But unlike before, now it was daytime and I could see it in full, horrific detail.

Smoke swirled around its mottled white and gray body, bleeding from the spikes jutting from its misshapen form, and black saliva dripped from its open maw. A maw filled with far too many sharp teeth.

It dove right past Reef and latched onto Iztal's thigh, snarling and wrenching its head to tear through the man's clothing and flesh.

Blood sprayed across the barrel and the front of Garridan's pants, and Iztal screamed. He fell, dropping his side of the barrel and sending it crashing onto the bricked road. The wood cracked and the shimmering blue liquid flooded around him, our feet, and mixed with the growing pool of the man's blood.

"Fuck!" Payne drew his sword and sliced through the creature's neck in a powerful stroke. "Get him in the wagon."

Garridan stood frozen, his wide-eyed gaze locked on the blood pouring from Iztal's leg.

More hounds bounded toward us, moving fast. One leaped straight at Garridan, but his focus was entirely on Iztal, his face pale and his breaths short and shallow.

I slashed at the monster, my blade cutting deep into its side making it bleed viscous black blood instead of just slicing off a few spikes like I'd done the last time.

With a snarl, it jerked away, and one of Payne's massive swords swept down and decapitated the hound before it could strike again.

Before I could even think to say thank you, Payne turned and killed another hound, this one large and all black.

Reef's sword flashed through the air, killing one that was almost all white, but for every creature they killed, two more appeared, and they were at a disadvantage trying to defend themselves while also trying to protect me, Garridan, and the merchant.

We— or at least me, Garridan, and Iztal needed to get into a more defensible position. And Iztal needed medical assistance or he was going to bleed out on the road.

CHAPTER 21

Sage

One of the shadow hounds threw its head back and screeched and the two closest to it screeched as well. Then more screeches sounded, sharp and shrill, echoing all around us, four, six, ten? How many hounds were there?

We couldn't stay where we were. We had to get to cover and the closest cover was the wagon. I grabbed Iztal's arm and tried to tug him to his feet, but he was too heavy.

"Get up!" I urged, pulling harder. "Please, you have to move."

But he just kept screaming as he clutched his leg, his body rocking back and forth, blood pouring between his fingers.

I whirled toward Garridan. "Help me!"

The idiot didn't move, completely frozen in his shock, his wide-eyed gaze locked on the merchant's bleeding leg, his face pale and his breaths desperate gasps.

This wasn't going to work. The man— hell, most men were too big for me to move by myself, and the merchant was larger than normal. I needed help.

"Garridan."

No reaction.

"Garridan!" I snapped.

The novice didn't even flinch at the tone in my voice. He just kept staring at the blood.

Shit.

Shit shit shit.

I grabbed the front of Garridan's jerkin and yanked him forward, and his attention finally jumped to me. "Help. Me."

He blinked as if he hadn't understood what I was saying.

For the love of—!

"We need to get the merchant in the wagon," I said, enunciating my words. "Now."

I pulled him closer to Iztal and crouched on the man's other side.

Garridan frowned, but he did grab the arm closest to him — thank the Father! — and together we hauled Iztal to his feet. The merchant howled in agony with the movement, and his weight sagged between us.

Fuck.

I wasn't going to be able to hold on.

"Come on," I hissed through clenched teeth. "You just need to get into the wagon."

Panting and gasping, Garridan and I hoisted Iztal

into the back of the wagon then climbed in after him, squeezing into the narrow space between the barrels.

It wasn't great, but at least we had the semblance of walls on either side of us even if they were just canvas. Any amount of cover had to be better than just standing out in the open on that road.

I glanced down the narrow aisle between the barrels to the front of the wagon. The canvas opened to the bench, and I could see the donkey. Its posture was stiff, its ears flicking this way and that, its tail slashing side to side as if it were about to bolt but couldn't figure which direction to go.

I yanked my attention back to Garridan who stood awkwardly beside Iztal, once again transfixed by the blood.

What the hell was wrong with him?

Except I knew what was wrong with him. He'd led a sheltered life as an orphan in a temple to the Great Father and when he'd been old enough, he'd taken his vows as a priest. Obviously, the man hadn't seen any kind of violence or serious injury before, and just moving Iztal hadn't been enough to startle him into action.

Except Iztal's breathing was getting shallower, and all that blood pooling around him meant he didn't have much time.

I had to stop the bleeding, and the best way was to use a rope or belt and secure it around his leg above the wound.

Except my belt wouldn't work. It was the only thing keeping my too-large pants up, and I couldn't afford to be tripping over my clothes in the middle of a life and death fight.

I grabbed the front of Garridan's belt.

With a yelp, he jerked back, his hands flying out to stop me. "What are you doing?"

"Saving that man's life."

I batted his hands away, unhooked the catch, and yanked his belt free in one quick movement.

"You're what?" he squeaked.

I dropped to my knees beside the merchant, wrapped the belt around his thigh and yanked it tight.

The man screamed and all the color drained from his face.

I gritted my teeth against the urge to apologize and secured the belt. Sometimes you had to hurt someone to heal them. It wasn't like I was a fae healer and could use magic — and I wasn't going to bother the fae with the healing magic standing a few feet away because he and Payne were the only reason we were all still alive.

Iztal's eyes grew glassy, the shock of his injuries starting to overwhelm him, and I grabbed the front of Garridan's jerkin again and yanked him to his knees—something I could only do because he was already crouching forward with the low canvas top.

"Apply pressure." I shoved his hands against the merchant's bleeding leg and prayed that when I let go Garridan would stay put.

Given all the attention Reef had given him, the other novice should have already known basic healing. Even if he didn't know he could tie off a limb to slow bleeding, he should at least know about applying pressure and be able to do that.

But Garridan was completely stunned, and I wasn't going to bet on him remembering anything.

Payne grunted and I glanced back out at the fight. His massive swords swept through the air, decapitating another hound, and he was rushing toward a third or fourth... or who-knew-how-many without pausing. Beside him, Reef struck down a smaller one, his blade moving fast, proving he was a skilled guardsman and not just a healer.

But more kept coming, bounding forward as if birthed from the rocky terrain and mist around us.

All around us, shadow hounds screeched, sending frozen fear lancing through my heart and stealing my breath. How many more were there?

Quill had said in the first evening class for the novices that shadow hound packs usually consisted of eight to twelve hounds, but I could already count six dead hounds on the ground, five more live ones around Payne and Reef, and a few more creeping closer.

There were too many. Certainly too many for Payne and Reef to handle by themselves.

I wrenched my attention back to the front of the wagon.

I'd never driven a horse-drawn — or in this case donkey-drawn — wagon before, but if Payne decided we needed to make a run for it, someone needed to be on the bench, ready to get that donkey moving. And the only someone available right now, was me.

I stepped into the narrow passage between the barrels and headed toward the bench and the donkey's reins.

But before I'd even gotten halfway, a massive, black shadow hound leaped onto the donkey and wrenched it down

The wagon jerked, jostling me, and the donkey brayed, the sound sharp, desperate, and suddenly cut off.

My pulse lurched, my thoughts spinning unable to comprehend what I'd just seen. It had happened so fast. The donkey hadn't stood a chance, hadn't even had the opportunity to kick or bite the hound.

The shadow monster's head bobbed up, blood and black saliva dripping from his partially open maw, and its black, soulless eyes locked on me.

Frozen fear crackled across my chest and arms, and I tightened my grip on my sword, the metal tip tapping against the wooden barrels crowded around me as I trembled.

Except the weapon was going to be useless in the tight confines of the wagon. There wasn't enough room to properly swing it, and my arms weren't long enough to stab the monster without being within reach of its claws.

I needed space. I couldn't get trapped in the wagon.

I lunged toward the front of the wagon, but the hound moved faster, jumping onto the bench and shoving its head inside the covered area.

Oh, crap.

I wrenched back, wildly swinging my sword in a desperate attempt to keep it from coming any closer.

The monster jerked back with a surprised snarl, but I doubted the thin piece of metal in my hand was going to hold it off for long. One swipe of its massive paw and there wasn't anywhere for me to dodge.

What I needed was something to block its strikes.

My gaze landed on the barrel beside me and the brass handle in the lid.

This was a stupid idea.

But it was the only idea I had.

I grabbed the handle and twisted. The lid popped free just as the shadow hound swiped at me with its wickedly sharp claws.

I wrenched up my makeshift shield, blocking the strike. The impact reverberated up my arm and woodchips flew into the air.

My pulse roared, and instinct drove my sword arm forward, stabbing at the monster.

My blade nicked one of the spikes, sending a gust of whirling black smoke rushing around the hound, but the creature's black blood didn't drip or splatter onto the barrels.

The shadow hound swiped again, harder and faster, and my fingers started to slip on the brass handle.

Crap. This wasn't working.

I already knew my arms were too short to properly stab the thing, there wasn't enough room to swing, and there was nowhere to dodge. The whole area eliminated any advantage I, as a small, nimble fighter, had in a fight, and there was no way I was going to kill it. Someone else was going to have to do it. The only thing I could do was hold out until that happened.

I dropped my sword and used both hands to hold up the shield.

The shadow monster bashed away at it. My muscles screamed with the agony of holding my ground, but I kept standing. I had to protect the merchant and Garridan. I just had to hold on until someone could help me.

A yell sounded ahead of me, but I couldn't see past the shadow hound filling the front of the wagon. The hound screeched and jerked to face whoever was behind it. A sword stabbed into its side and sliced it open with a rush of viscous black blood. A second sword cut into the hound's neck, drawing more blood, and the hound collapsed, falling off the wagon.

Grefin and one of the fae guardsman from the gatehouse looked inside the wagon. I stood there panting while they stared at me, their expressions a mix of anger, worry, and surprise.

Oh, thank the Father!

"Nice shield," Grefin said.

"Thanks." I dropped the barrel lid and collapsed to my knees.

"What the fuck is going on here?" Rider roared, from the other side of the canvas top, and I flinched.

I was just following orders, but with my luck I had a sinking feeling that somehow this mess was going to be my fault.

CHAPTER 22

Rider

Reef was a fucking idiot.

My horse shifted underneath me, nervous around all the blood and dead shadow hounds scattered across the road.

I tightened my grip on the reins as my wolf heaved inside me, furious and desperate to tear something apart.

Moments ago, Slate had run into my office saying Reef had taken his novices beyond the Tower's protective wards, and I'd instantly thought he was wrong. Nobody was that stupid.

But Slate wasn't a liar, and Grefin and Payne had already reported that Reef wasn't doing his duty with regards to Sawyer, assigning him all the cleaning duties while mentoring Garridan, so I shouldn't have been surprised that Reef thought an outing with novices who hadn't even completed two rotations was a good idea.

The only saving grace was that Payne had gone with them. And without a doubt Payne hadn't gone along out of the goodness of his heart. He'd gone because he cared about the boy and knew Reef was a fucking idiot.

I let my gaze drift over the mess of Reef's reckless decision. The donkey that had been pulling the wagon was dead, its throat ripped out, and blood pooled around its body, soaking into the bricked road. At the back of the wagon, a dozen dead shadow hounds lay scattered across the ground, and Payne and Reef stood with their swords drawn, sweat and grime streaking their faces.

In the back of the wagon, Garridan knelt, pale and wide-eyed, his hands pressed against the leg of our usual cleaning spirits merchant, Iztal, who gasped and panted, his face gray with blood loss, while Sawyer knelt in the middle of the wagon, squeezed between the barrels, his head hanging down making it impossible to tell if he was injured or not.

I could have lost two novices today. Before they'd even become guardsmen.

My wolf snarled and churned inside me.

"Get the wagon to the Tower," I barked.

Slate and Grefin unhitched the dead donkey, hauled it off the road, and hitched one of their horses to the wagon instead.

I jerked my chin at the back of the wagon. "Reef. Get in and heal the merchant."

Reef frowned at me and I glared at him. His eyes widened and he scrambled up, squeezing into what little space was available between Iztal, Garridan, and the barrels.

There wasn't enough room in the back for Payne

with everyone else and the barrels crammed in there, so he strode to the front of the wagon and climbed onto the bench next to Grefin.

The human guardsman gave Payne a tight nod and a knowing look, a wordless understanding passing between them.

I bit back a growl. Grefin worked well with Kit, Payne, and Lewin. The silent communication between the two of them proved he was a perfect match for their team, and I'd been hoping he'd enter the competition for an elite position so I could promote him. But Grefin had been overly cautious when he'd first joined the Guard, and without a doubt, the shadow bear attack had made him revert to his old ways. Which meant I was going to have to find someone else to put Kit's team back together.

We hurried back to the Tower, drawing as close to the infirmary doors as possible.

Reef and Slate helped Iztal out of the wagon and into the infirmary. Garridan still sat in the wagon, staring at his bloody hands like he'd never seen blood before, which I knew wasn't true because Payne had reported that Reef had let Garridan assist with basic healing during his infirmary shift.

Sawyer climbed out the front, his shoulders hunched forward like he was trying to make himself smaller.

My chest tightened at his posture. It was too much like how he'd looked when he'd first arrived in the Gray. Too much like a wide-eyed, red-haired beauty I knew in the Garden.

And now that I knew Sawyer's behavior came from getting beaten, it was obvious he was afraid of me and thought he was going to get punished for Reef's mistake.

The growl I'd managed to swallow back earlier strained against my throat.

I didn't want the boy afraid of me. I didn't want him afraid of anyone. But I'd fucked up for punishing him for defending himself, and with his history, he assumed all blame for all things would fall to him.

The growl slipped free, making Sawyer flinch, and I wrenched my attention away from him.

The only way he'd stop being afraid was for me to prove he could trust me, and building trust took time.

I needed to be goddess-damned patient.

Which, as an animal shifter, wasn't one of my strong traits.

My gaze landed on the barrels still crowded in the wagon.

Focus on command, making sure the things that were supposed to happen happened. That was what I was good at. Others, like Talon and Quill, could deal with the emotional shit.

So. What needed to happen right now? Someone needed to get the barrels out of the wagon, and someone needed to look after the novices. For now, the barrels could wait until the afternoon shift came on duty. Given Garridan's current state, he'd probably drop his side of the barrel, and Sawyer was too small to help lift them.

"Everyone. In the infirmary," I barked.

Sawyer flinched again, then squared his shoulders as

if reminding himself he could stand his ground now when he couldn't before. He hurried through the infirmary doors, while Garridan continued to stare at his hands.

With a sigh, Grefin grabbed the novice's arm, and gently urged him to hop out of the wagon and go inside. The novice moved like a sleepwalker, his body functioning but his mind somewhere else, and the need to fight, tear, and maim someone surged up inside me.

I needed to hunt tonight. I had to. It was supposed to be my turn guarding Sage, but I wasn't going to be able to sit there struggling with pleasantries... or even just sit there and glare at West after she'd retreated to her room since West was worse with pleasantries than I was.

No, if I saw her tonight, I'd grab her and demand to know where she was in the human realm, which humans were keeping her as a slave, and who I needed to kill to avenge her.

But that would just terrify her. She was keeping her situation a secret so she could protect herself and a human boy, and if I couldn't prove to her that she could trust me, she wouldn't risk telling me anything.

I stormed inside the infirmary with Payne right behind me. Iztal lay unconscious on the first of the three tables in the center of the room, and Reef stood beside him, his eyes closed and both hands pressed against the man's torn flesh. To his left, Slate had pulled over one of the rolling tables and opened a stitching kit.

"All right," Reef said as he opened his eyes and held out his hand for Slate to hand him a threaded needle.

"Slate can sew him up," I said, my voice gruff and dark with my anger and frustration. "I want you to check the novices."

Reef huffed but headed to the pump and basin at the back of the room to wash the blood from his hands.

"I'm sure we'd know if they were injured," he said under his breath, low enough that only me with my enhanced wolf's hearing could hear him.

He went to Garridan first, who sat in one of the two chairs by the infirmary door, still looking stunned. I was starting to worry that he'd taken a blow to the head, but the only blood on him was on his hands, his jerkin, and soaked into the knees of his pants.

The novice continued to stare at nothing as Reef placed a hand against his neck, closed his eyes, and checked his medical condition.

"He's fine," Reef said with a frown as he captured Garridan's cheeks between his palms and forced him to make eye contact. "Aren't you?"

Garridan blinked slowly.

"Guardsman," Reef said, his tone softening and surprising me.

As much as Reef was a healer, he was often brusque and abrupt. He dealt with the body, not the mind or the soul, and didn't care to learn about anything else.

Garridan blinked again and swallowed, some of the shock melting from his expression. He wasn't perfect — it would take a while for him to overcome the terror of his first battle with shadow monsters — but he was better than a moment ago.

"Now Sawyer."

Sawyer jerked at the sound of his name, his eyes widening. "I-I'm fine."

I narrowed my eyes at him.

"Really." He held out his arms showing me his clothes. They were bloody but I couldn't see any tears on them. "Not a scratch."

He wasn't holding himself as if he were injured, either.

Except it seemed strange that he wouldn't want Reef to check. Did he think Reef's magic hurt? It couldn't be because he didn't want to waste Reef's time since it only took a moment for him to check someone's condition.

No, the boy was jumpy and smart. He knew Reef shouldn't have taken them beyond the Tower's wards, and now he didn't trust Reef... if he ever had to begin with. Very few humans knew how fae magic worked, and for all I knew, Sawyer thought Reef could learn about his magic and use that knowledge to make his life in the Black Tower more difficult than it already was.

And there wasn't anything I could do about that right now.

"Fine."

Reef raised his eyebrows at me, his surprise clear that I hadn't pushed Sawyer to accept being tested.

I glared back at the healer and he backed off, smart enough to know when not to press the situation, but clearly not smart enough to know he shouldn't have made this whole mess in the first place.

And *that* needed to be addressed. Now.

My wolf heaved inside me, and the backs of my hands tingled, the precursor to sprouting fur.

"Grefin," I barked, making Sawyer flinch again. "Take Garridan to the baths to clean up. Payne, take Sawyer to his room to change his clothes."

Sawyer opened his mouth as if he were going to argue with me, probably about not needing an escort to the other side of the Tower, but his gaze jumped from me to Reef and back again. His mouth snapped shut, a flickering of knowing flashing through his expression and he turned to leave.

Yep. Smart.

He figured out Reef and I were going to have a *conversation,* and it would be better if he wasn't present.

And for some goddess-damned reason all of the other novices and most of my guardsmen couldn't figure out the kind of asset he was going to be once he actually became a man.

Payne gave me a tight nod, having seen what I'd just seen in the boy, and followed him out.

"Come on," Grefin said, taking Garridan by the arm and leading him out as well.

The infirmary door swung shut, and I turned on Reef, my wolf surging forward, straining to break my control.

"What the fuck were you thinking?" I snarled. "They're in their second rotation. They're not ready to go beyond the wards. And I didn't give you permission to take them."

"I was thinking we're short-handed," Reef said with a

huff, his attention back to Slate stitching up Iztal's wound. "Someone needed to escort the cleaning spirits from the ring."

This time fur did sprout from the back of my hands. "The team assigned to that area was going to swing by and pick him up."

"Then where were they?"

Which was the big question.

Vyell and Jalnar had been on the morning sweep in the area. They'd arrived to the fight at the same time Grefin, Slate, and I had, which meant they would have been late meeting Iztal at the ring.

I was going to have a conversation with them as well to find out what happened, but regardless, Reef shouldn't have done what he did.

Of course, the question that really bothered me was would the shadow hounds have attacked if Sawyer hadn't been there?

It was uncommon for shadows to attack in the day, especially so close to the Black Tower, but not unheard of.

And yet, this was another shadow attack the boy had been a part of.

"Besides, it worked out," Reef said. "I'm impressed with the runt."

I snarled, jerking his attention back to me. My fingernails extended into claws and fur rolled from the backs of my hands up my forearms.

"I meant Sawyer. *Sawyer*," Reef rushed to say, his gaze locking on my hands. "The boy did well. Garridan was useless. He completely froze up." He turned his attention back to Slate and Iztal and hummed in thought. "But Sawyer fought off a hound, got Garridan and Iztal into the wagon, did basic field medicine, then fought off another hound."

My canines sharpened and the bones in my face stretched, on the verge of breaking and shifting into a snout.

He better not have taken Sawyer out there on purpose to test him. That was my job. If he wanted to know how well the boy handled himself in a fight he should have asked me, Talon, or Quill, not taken it into his own hands.

What the hell was wrong with my men?

Was I not commanding enough?

I didn't want to change how I led the Black Guard, but I'd have to if my men kept behaving like idiots.

"He hasn't complained once about cleaning duty this rotation either," Reef added, his posture becoming even more relaxed, clearly having forgotten how close my wolf was to making a violent appearance.

"You endangered two novices," I growled, grabbing Reef's shoulder and wrenching him back to face me. "And you haven't been training Sawyer like you're supposed to."

"I couldn't trust him," Reef stammered.

"That's not for you to decide." Red washed across my vision, and I strained to hold back my wolf.

I couldn't tear into him like my wolf wanted. Hell, I couldn't even punish him like a regular guardsman. He was a healer. Even if he'd been a guardsman before, he wasn't one now, and I couldn't put him on a shit duty or restrict his lieu time.

I couldn't even afford to suspend him because we didn't have enough healers in the first place. Too few were willing to work for the Black Guard.

"You took training into your own hands, and you endangered two novices and a human merchant who might decide not to do business with us again," I snarled. "I'm docking you four rotations of pay."

"You can't do that!"

"Be happy that's all I'm doing," my wolf growled, my voice barely recognizable as fae.

Reef jerked back, panic flooding his expression. "R-Right. Of course, Rider."

My wolf's growl deepened.

"Lord Commander," Reef corrected. "The boy will be afforded the same considerations as every guardsman."

"Good."

Now I just needed everyone else to do the same.

CHAPTER 23
Sage

AFTER ASSURING Payne I was fine, I returned to the infirmary. Thankfully, both Lord Rider and Slate were gone, and Reef made no indication that the Lord Commander of the Black Guard wanted to discipline me. There was still time remaining before the fourth bell and I hadn't had a chance to start any of my assigned cleaning, so I headed toward the hall with the patient rooms and the cleaning closet.

"Not that way," Reef said. "I think you've moved on from basic cleaning."

He jerked his chin, indicating I should follow him, and led me to the hall at the back of the infirmary, the one Garridan had been taken to, but not me.

This hall was a little narrower than the patient hall with only three doors in it. The first door was open and led to a room filled with shelves packed with thick leather-bound books and a lone desk sitting in the middle. The next door was to a suite with a small sitting room and another open door inside leading to a bedroom. I couldn't see it, but given how the other rooms in the infirmary and the elite wing of the Tower were set up, the suite most likely had a private bathing room as well. The last door in the hall led to a large supply room that was packed with bandages, medicines, tinctures, salves, and medical tools.

He gave me the tour of the supply room, then told me to gather a replacement stitching kit and bandages to restock the main room.

After that, he gave a lecture about basic healing in the field, almost, but not quite praising my quick thinking for tying off the merchant's leg before he bled to death and getting Garridan to apply pressure.

Garridan never returned to the infirmary, and I couldn't help wondering if his inability to react during the fight had made Lord Rider reassign him to a different morning chore or if the man was still too shocked to do anything other than follow basic instructions.

Which made me wonder how I, a woman, had kept fighting when Garridan, a man, had completely frozen up? Everything I'd been taught— everything *Edred* had beaten into me was that women were weak. We weren't capable of taking care of ourselves, we weren't responsible enough to manage property.

And yet when it came down to it, I acted. I always acted.

I'd saved Sawyer by taking his place, I'd saved Payne by revealing my fae-touched ability, and I'd kept Garridan and the merchant alive.

When my morning duties ended, I checked in with Kit and Payne. Kit looked up from where he sat propped up in bed beside Payne as I stepped into the doorway to his room.

"Heard about the shadow hounds," Kit said.

Given how fast rumors flew through the Tower, it wouldn't have surprised me if everyone had heard about the hounds by now.

Of course, it also wouldn't have surprised me if what actually happened shifted to put me in a negative light or if no one believed I'd actually fought off the hounds.

Payne's expression darkened. "At least you kept your head. Slate couldn't believe you thought to use a barrel lid like a shield."

I shrugged, uncertain what to say to that. I hadn't had much choice and just done what I'd needed to survive.

"You know," Kit said. "When Rider opens up the competition for an elite position, I think you should compete."

I what—?

"Why would you say that?"

No one liked or trusted me. There was no way Lord Rider would let someone like me take an elite position in the Black Guard when there were so many other stronger, more experienced guardsmen around.

"Lord Rider would never—" I began.

"Of course he would," Kit said. "Right now, you have more experience fighting shadows than any other novice."

"That doesn't mean I'd make a good hunter."

"There are more than just hunter positions available." Kit offered a soft smile. "You were a lord so I'm assuming you can read, which puts you ahead of many guardsmen for a position at the White or Gold Towers."

"And you stayed calm during that fight. You knew enough to get Iztal and Garridan into the wagon and you improvised a shield when you realized your sword was going to be useless in that tight space." Payne leveled a hard look at me and raised his eyebrows in question. "That's why you dropped your sword isn't it?"

"I wasn't going to get close enough to stab it and my grip had been slipping on the lid." I'd had to make a choice and while I'd known it was foolish to drop my weapon, I'd had to do it.

"And that's why any hunter team should be happy to have you," Payne said, flashing me a brilliant smile.

Except hunter teams hunted shadow monsters and I'd barely managed to injure one. There was no way I'd be good enough to do what Payne and Reef had done today.

"The competition is at least a few rotations away. You'll have more novice training and then there's special training for the competition," Kit said as if he could read my mind and knew how ridiculous I thought their suggestion was. "Being a powerful warrior is a benefit for a hunter but so is being observant and staying calm."

I doubted any of the hunter teams would like observant, calm me, over someone with skill like Mikel, Durand, Hamelin, Bramwell, or Ambrose. They were all more experienced than me with fighting and were probably just as observant and calm in a battle. Probably more so since while I might have seemed calm, I'd been terrified.

"Just think about it," Kit said with a soft smile. "Go on now. I doubt you've been excused from this afternoon's training so you should probably get something to eat."

"Right."

With my gaze focused forward and ignoring everyone around me because I didn't want to know if they were gossiping about me or not, I grabbed a sandwich from the kitchen and hurried to my room.

Inside, I dropped to the edge of my bed and raised my sandwich to take a bite, but my hands shook. In fact, all of me shook.

Father, how had I survived that?

It had been terrifying. It didn't matter that I'd foreseen my death and it hadn't looked anything like what had happened this morning. I'd already proven I could change what I'd seen by saving Payne's life, and there was nothing that said other events couldn't also change my future.

Shadows! And Kit and Payne thought I should compete for a position on a hunter team and do that every night?

I could have died or been horribly maimed or even injured enough that Lord Rider would have insisted Reef heal me and then everyone would know I wasn't really Sawyer.

My pulse roared in my ears. I hadn't been in the Gray

anywhere long enough to ensure his safety, and I had no idea how I was going to keep hiding the truth.

At some point, the novices were going to go shadow hunting, and I feared that was going to happen sooner rather than later, and I couldn't trust the other novices to protect me like Payne and Reef had.

I squeezed my eyes shut and fought to draw in long, slow breaths.

I could do this. I had to do this. It didn't have to be forever. It just had to be long enough for Sawyer to get out of the Five Great Kingdoms.

And hey, as much as I expected it, Rider hadn't yelled at me.

He'd been furious but hadn't stuck around to lay the blame on me. Which fit with what I'd learned about him during the few awkward evenings we'd spent together. He might be brusque and hard, but he was fair.

I still couldn't completely believe he wouldn't punish me later, but a traitorous part of me, the part who saw the awkward, gruff man in the Garden wanted to believe I could trust him.

And really, I shouldn't be worrying about that. I'd drawn more attention to myself, and the guardsmen were back to gossiping about me, the exact opposite of what I'd wanted to have happened.

I didn't care that Reef made me clean the infirmary every day or that the other guardsmen pretended I didn't exist. My goal had always been to be just another guardsman, someone who faded into the background, and it seemed like every other day something happened that made everyone notice me all over again.

Competing for an elite position would only make everyone notice me more. Scrawny Sawyer thinking he was good enough to be a Black Guard elite?

I huffed a bitter laugh.

Even if the idea didn't terrify me, no one would accept me. Kit and Payne were crazy if they thought me competing was a good idea.

Although...

Something soft and bittersweet twisted in my chest.

They *had* suggested it. Two experienced guardsmen thought that maybe I, a woman, could be an elite. Sure, they didn't know I was a woman, they thought I was a boy, almost a man, but still— It seemed incredible, impossible, my wildest dream.

Maybe in another life.

Maybe once I knew Sawyer was safe.

Would it be even worth the risk to try?

No.

Stop it.

I was being foolish. I shouldn't even daydream of it because it was never going to happen.

CHAPTER 24

Sage

I FINISHED my sandwich and pulled myself together. I needed to focus on my most immediate problems: not being discovered, figuring out how to stop manifesting in the Garden and avoiding the dangers there, and surviving my impending death. And the best way to do that — or at least deal with the Gray related problems — was carry on as usual and use the other guardsmen as a means to improve my fighting.

All but one of my opponents this afternoon were fae, and the human was Ambrose who was almost as good as a fae. Sure, there wasn't going to be any comradery between us, but the pride of the few fae I'd already sparred with, as well as Mikel and the rest of his followers, wouldn't let them lose to a runt. Which meant they never held back, and I could use the sessions to improve my reaction time, my dodging, and my ability to determine if I had an opportunity to score a hit.

With my thoughts focused on that, I left my room,

took the side stairwell down to the bailey, staying as far away from the great hall as possible, and stepped through the pasture gate.

"Hey," Talon said, startling me.

He leaned against the tall wall, arms crossed. A gentle breeze tugged at the strands of his long white-silver hair, and my attention swept up the locks to the delicate gold earrings in his pointed ear, his sculpted cheek and then his mesmerizing eyes, as if compelled by magic.

I looked at him and couldn't look away.

Heat flooded my cheeks, and my breath caught, trembling between inhaling and exhaling, my body reacting before my mind could catch up.

Father, why did he have to be so beautiful? Why did I have to be stunned by him almost every time I saw him?

The breathlessness only lasted a moment and then my mind took over, but there was always that first initial reaction that always overwhelmed me.

I wrenched my gaze to the large boulders marking the edge of the running trail on the other side of the practice yard.

"My lor—" I bit the inside of my cheek.

Talon didn't want to be called a lord, but even though it had been days since he'd abandoned me on the running trail, I still had no idea where I stood with him. Before the incident with the running trail, I would have happily called him Talon like he wanted but now calling him by his name felt too familiar. "Captain."

Out of the corner of my eye, I watched one of his

silver eyebrows rise in question to my formality, but he didn't correct me.

"You had an exciting morning," he said. "How are you feeling?"

"I'm—" I didn't want to think about it. I'd just managed to focus on what really mattered and push down the fear I had from seeing those monsters close up in daylight. I didn't want to talk to Talon about my feelings. For all I knew, he'd report everything back to Lord Rider, which meant I needed to be careful what I said to him. "I'm fine."

"I see." The words came out flat, like he didn't believe me, and he studied my face for a moment, then looked away.

The silence stretched between us, the mist sitting in the lowest levels of the practice yard undulating like miniature lakes.

I pursed my lips, feeling like I should say something but not knowing what. This was so awkward. Painfully awkward. It had been so much easier before I'd known the truth: that he'd obey Rider and abandon me if commanded.

And really! I didn't understand why that bothered me so much. We hadn't been friends. He was my superior in the Black Guard. And yet I'd thought I could trust him.

But that day had proven I couldn't trust anyone, and I had to keep remembering that.

"I heard you fought them off with a barrel lid," he said with a soft chuckle.

A hint of something soft and warm unfurled inside my chest at the sound before it shivered down into my stomach.

"Well, I..." My gaze dropped to my feet and I yanked it back up. "I had to do something."

"That was definitely something."

His lips curled into a soft smile and the warmth in my stomach grew, seeping deeper into my core with a soft, achy need, and I fought the urge to stare at him again. Was that his allure? Or was I just mesmerized by a handsome fae?

Rider stepped through the pasture gate, the bags of rocks slung over his shoulder. This close, he towered over me, his broad muscular body making me feel — and most likely look — like the child everyone thought I was. His silver eyes locked on me, sharp and assessing, and my chest tightened. I still had no idea if he was angry at me for what had happened at the fae ring.

I took a step back, giving him more room to pass between me and Talon, even as another shiver of desire rushed down my spine.

With a grunt, his gaze shifted to Talon, who gave him a tight nod. Male communication at its finest. Together, they strode across the practice grounds toward the running trail together, leaving me to wonder what they'd silently communicated — and I knew without a doubt they'd communicated something, and that something was about me.

Three of the fae novices hurried through the pasture gate after them, barely giving me a first look let alone a second one. At least they weren't all staring and laughing over the fact that I'd had to use a barrel lid to defend myself.

I followed the three fae novices at a distance as they made their way across the practice grounds toward the running trail. A few minutes later, the fifth bell rang, and the rest of the novices hurried through the pasture gate, joining us at the boulders.

Lord Rider's hard gaze swept over the group, his silver eyes sliding over me, making that whisper of desire flare a little stronger, then he jerked his chin.

We all knew what to do. We'd been doing it for one and a half rotations now.

The fastest novices took off, their boots pounding against the rocky path as they disappeared over the first hill. I shoved down the desire starting to simmer in my core and hurried up the rise at the back of the group so no one could trip me. Then I maintained my position ahead of the slowest inexperienced novices but the last of the experienced ones.

Mikel and his friends hadn't ambushed me since this rotation started, but I didn't want to press my luck by being faster than any of the other experienced novices. Hopefully ensuring that I was always the one doing the extra lap with the bag of rocks at the end of training was enough for everyone to keep thinking I knew my place and they wouldn't need to remind me again.

As expected, no one ambushed me, and just like the last three days of my new running plan, no one commented that I was faster than some of the inexperienced guardsmen once I'd crested the final hill and jogged back out onto the practice grounds.

The other experienced guardsmen were already picking their practice swords, and, as usual, I waited until they'd all selected.

Today, I picked the sword that best matched my own sword in length and weight. Even after the terrifying fight with the shadow hounds, my body was almost feeling as well as it had before I'd first entered the Gray. I was still a little achy, but it wasn't close to what I'd felt after a few days of stable duty and certainly nowhere near to what I'd felt for the first few days after my grueling run on the trail at the end of my first rotation.

In reality, I should have picked a sword that was heavier than mine to help build up my strength and stamina in preparation for the fight of my life that I knew was coming, but given that I didn't know what my duties would be in my third rotation and the fact that I'd barely recovered from my first, I didn't want to press my luck.

Being too tired and sore to lift my sword when I needed it the most was suicide. And I sure as hell wasn't going to just lie down and make it easy for whoever was going to attack me.

The three fae who I still had to spar with all exchanged glances, a quick, silent exchange passing among them, before the shortest of them — a man with short brown hair and red-orange eyes — sighed and stepped toward me.

We circled each other with our practice swords

raised, and I watched his footwork, waiting for the telltale shift of weight before he struck.

Heat crawled up the back of my neck, making me frown. What was that?

It felt like someone was watching me — which I was sure people were but this felt... more.

The fae lunged and I dodged, swinging at him as I moved, but he parried my strike and countered with a lightning-fast jab. I barely twisted out of the way in time and was grateful the man didn't press his attack while I was off balance.

The heat on my neck turned into an ache of awareness, and the need in my core that I thought I'd burned away with the exertion of my run around the trail, pulsed, sudden and strong.

The fae struck again and I sidestepped, his blade still brushing against my sleeve. Damn it. I was too slow. If our weapons had been sharp, that would have ripped my shirt, and that was way too close for comfort.

I sucked in a sharp breath and refocused on his stance, straining to catch that miniscule movement that happened just before he attacked. I needed to concentrate, damn it. I couldn't afford to let anything distract me.

Except the ache in my core grew hotter and seeped deeper.

Was that Talon's allure? Or was I imagining it?

The fae novice's next strike came fast and, with no hope of dodging it, I barely got my sword up in time to block it. The impact jarred up my arm before I managed to redirect the blade to the side and step out of the way.

Shit. Concentrate. I couldn't afford to be seriously hurt and with this guy's hard strikes, a misstep could send me to the infirmary.

"Switch," Rider barked.

I released a heavy breath of relief only to choke on air on the following inhale as Ambrose strode over to me. His expression was tight and annoyed, and he raised his practice sword without any kind of acknowledgement, which wasn't unexpected. I'd just been certain he would have waited until the last possible moment before stepping up to spar with me.

The blue-black bruising around both his eyes had faded into an ugly yellow-green, but even just the glimpse of it still sent a satisfying thrill through me.

Was it unladylike? Absolutely. But the part of me that felt freer bound to the Black Tower than I'd ever felt as a woman didn't care.

And even though the growth was small and slow, I could tell that part of me was growing stronger.

Would I ever be so foolish enough to think I could do what a man could?

I'd already proven I could stay calm in the face of a shadow hound attack when Garridan couldn't, and much to the frustration of Aldis, Jokin, Sivis, Bramwell, and Hamelin, I'd proven I could score more points on them than they could on me.

I raised my sword and waited. Ambrose was fast, and I didn't trust I was faster than him and could score a point before he countered. Best to wait and see what he did first.

The tingle of heat on my neck burned hotter. Someone was definitely watching me.

I fought to focus on the angle of Ambrose's blade, on the tension in his shoulders before he struck, but the ache in my core flared into a throbbing, desperate need.

Ambrose lunged, and I dodged, countering with a strike that he easily blocked.

We reset and circled again, but my pulse was jumping and the heat was growing stronger and stronger.

I gritted my teeth. What the hell was wrong with me? I had to focus.

Concentrate on the fight, on reading his tells, on anything except the growing ache.

But the achy need and the sensation of being watched was driving me crazy.

Unable to help myself, I glanced over my shoulder. My gaze instantly locked with Talon's and desire roared through me, wild and overwhelming.

Oh, shit. Talon. That was what was wrong with me.

From this distance he looked perfectly normal with no hint of shadowy smoke billowing around him, but the desire threatening to overwhelm me had to be the allure from the shadow trapped inside him.

Ambrose's practice sword slammed against my side. Pain flared across my ribs, and I stumbled, somehow managing to stagger backwards, away from my opponent, and not toward him.

His eyes flashed wide with surprise, and he jerked

back a step, before his expression quickly returned to annoyed indifference.

I sucked in a breath and raised my sword again, forcing my feet back into position and my body back into the rhythm of the fight.

This was a nightmare. I'd been fine since the beginning of the rotation — since Zinnia had put my mating marks to sleep. Why was Talon's allure affecting me now? Why couldn't he control it?

CHAPTER 25
Sage

It was the end of the day, and I hurried into my room, threw the door shut, and pressed my back against it. Aching need twisted through me, hot and desperate, and I couldn't catch my breath, couldn't think past the throbbing heat that refused to fade.

It was a miracle I'd made it through the evening without turning into a complete mess in front of everyone. Father! Why was it so bad now?

I'd thought everything was fine. I'd somehow struggled through the sparring session without embarrassing myself then grabbed the bag of rocks and ran the trail with Tyon. During the run, Talon's allure had faded, and I'd foolishly thought because Talon couldn't see me or I couldn't see him or we weren't anywhere near each other, his allure wouldn't affect me anymore.

But during the evening class, the achy need had flared again, sudden and overwhelming, sinking deeper into my core, making it impossible to sit still and concentrate even though Talon hadn't been anywhere in sight. I doubt he'd even been anywhere near the lesson room.

With trembling fingers, I unbuckled my sword belt and tossed my sword onto the bed. My too-large pants sagged, hanging low on my hips, and I slipped my hand down the front of them, and dipped my fingers straight to where I needed them most.

Sensation shot through me at the first brushing touch against my sensitive nub, and I tipped my head back against the door, biting my lip to hold back a groan.

Damn Talon and his allure. Damn how beautiful he was. Damn that traitorous drop of water trailing down his naked chest that lived forever branded inside my mind.

My breath hitched and I shoved that thought as far back as I could. I didn't want to desire Talon. I didn't trust him, not as he was in the Gray and most certainly not as whoever he was pretending to be in the Garden.

I pressed my fingers harder, circling my nub, and heat spread through my core. My hips rocked forward, my body seeking a release I'd been denying since this afternoon. Father, I felt as desperate — maybe more desperate — than I did before Wells' and Crane's spell sent my mating marks into a frenzy.

My thoughts slipped back to Talon and the magnificent view of his chest, his abs, his—

No. Stop thinking about him. Think of someone, anyone, else.

Fantasy Man. Ash. Think about him.

He was the only one I could trust. He made me feel

safe. And he'd brought me more pleasure than I'd ever experienced in my life.

My desire jerked, as if thinking about Ash made my yearning stronger. I ached for his touch, for his fingers against my sensitive skin instead of mine, teasing me, brushing achingly close to where I wanted him most then pulling away.

He'd slide a finger inside me while his tongue worked my nub, licking and sucking until I couldn't breathe. He'd build me to the edge again and again then ease back, his fingers pushing in and out and curling just right while his mouth tortured me. Quick sudden flicks of his tongue, then long, slow, powerful ones that surged heated need through my entire body and stole my breath.

Father, I could almost hear his low masculine groan of satisfaction when he finally came inside me, his cock pulsing hard.

The heat inside me swirled brighter, stronger, building, expanding, overflowing.

My thoughts spun and the memories of him flooded me. Ash filling me. Ash trembling just like me, both of us panting with need. He'd gripped my hips, holding me steady while he pushed inside with that incredible slick pressure. His cock had stretched me, filled me completely. He'd moved slowly at first, giving my body time to adjust, then harder and faster, his fingers digging into my flesh. The groans that had rumbled from his chest, as shivers of bliss had washed through me.

My fingers moved faster, my breath turned ragged,

and my legs trembled. I was close. So close. I needed this, needed the release. Needed him.

I pressed harder against my nub, my hips rocking in rhythm with my hand as my need spiraled tighter. Heat burned in my core, flaring hotter and hotter until pleasure crashed over me.

I bit down hard on my lip to keep from crying out and stars exploded behind my lids. My muscles clenched tight, straining and trembling, and I couldn't breathe, couldn't think, could only ride the waves pulsing through me.

With a strangled moan, my legs gave out, and I sagged to the floor, breathing hard.

The memory of Ash kissing me face to face in that conception room after the attack rose to the front of my mind. That first brush of our lips had been soft and tender, and my heart had ached at his fear over his scarred face.

My throat tightened. He'd thought he was hideous, thought I'd be afraid of him.

How could I possibly be afraid of him?

He'd comforted me, protected me, satisfied me from the very moment I'd entered the Garden and hadn't asked for anything in return. He'd made me feel precious, something I hadn't felt in a very, very long time, not since before my parents had died.

My eyes burned with tears of frustration and heartache. I wanted Ash back, wanted the safety of his embrace, wanted the surety that he wasn't trying to manipulate me.

Father, why couldn't he be the man waiting for me in the Garden instead of the others?

But he wouldn't be because the fae's High Priestess was mean and manipulative.

No, the only way I'd be able to be with him again was if Crane and the others were brought to justice. Then I'd be safe and able to leave the Divine Residence.

I released a shaky sigh. The desperation burning inside me had eased — a bit — but Talon's allure still hummed under my skin, a yearning I could only hope would fade by morning. And there wasn't anything I could do about my heartache for Ash other than endure and wait. Surely Crane would be caught. Surely I'd be free to do what I wanted after that.

My eyes burned and I closed them, fighting back my tears.

If Rider, Quill, and Talon kept to their schedule, my best guess was that Rider would be waiting for me tonight.

Which was the best of three bad options. I was still attracted to him, but he wasn't heartbreakingly tender and attentive like Quill, and he didn't have Talon's frustrating allure and even more frustrating flirting.

With luck, he'd let me retreat to my bedroom in the suite and I'd spend the night tossing and turning trying to ignore the fact that West was staring at me through the crack in the door.

With a groan, I crawled onto my bed and pressed my palms against my eyes. Meditation. I should probably try meditating. Maybe if I practiced enough, I'd stop manifesting in the Garden, and the ache of missing Ash and Talon's allure would go away completely.

I sucked in a slow breath and released it, then another, and another. I had to focus on the spark in my chest, feel my lungs fill with air, hold it, then release slowly. Just like Lord Quill had taught me.

Once.

Twice.

The darkness behind my eyelids should have been calming. Father, I desperately wanted it to be. But my pulse kept jumping and my thoughts wouldn't settle. Please, not tonight. Not when I was already fighting the damn allure. If I could just make it through one night without manifesting, maybe the allure would fade. Maybe I could get back some control.

Someone cleared their throat, the sound deep and masculine.

Shit.

I was back in the Garden. I had to be since I hadn't heard my bedroom door open, and my mattress had gotten as hard as a floor.

Groaning, I dropped my hands. This time I hadn't even realized I'd fallen asleep.

Wonderful.

Above me, Sir West glared down at me, his expression hard, emotionless verging on angry, the same as it always was every time I opened my eyes in the Garden and looked up, up, up at him.

"The High Priestess has summoned you," he said, his voice flat with no hint about how he felt about that.

My pulse lurched, and my stomach twisted tight, making it hard to breathe.

The throne room flashed through my mind with all those courtiers staring at me, whispering about me. Their hungry, curious gazes weighing on me, boxing me in, making everything within me scream to get smaller, as small as possible.

And that woman! I didn't want to see her again, didn't want her bestowing me with that fake smile, amused by my stammering. I didn't want her to even remember I existed.

But I was her new toy and had known a summons was inevitable.

My throat tightened. I needed more time to recover before facing her games again. The few days I'd been hiding in my suite hadn't been nearly enough.

And of course, she'd had to make the summons when I was once again struggling with my desire. It was as if she'd known.

Except I knew that was impossible. There was no way the High Priestess could have known Talon's allure had overwhelmed me that afternoon. Even if she'd somehow figured out I was a human pretending to be a fae, she couldn't have known I was also a woman pretending to be a man in the Gray.

Could she?

Oh, Father!

No. I couldn't think that. This was a coincidence. I'd clearly been hiding in my room, and I'd been told that she'd summon me eventually. Tonight just happened to be the night. If I was lucky, she'd make it quick, and I could get back to the suite and try to return to my body.

The thought was so ridiculous I almost laughed. Or cried. I wasn't sure which.

Even in the brief experience I'd had with her, the High Priestess didn't strike me as anyone who did anything quickly. Our previous interaction had been calculated, drawn out, and designed to make me squirm. This wouldn't be different and I wasn't in a position to refuse.

I sucked in a steadying breath that did little to actually steady the uncertainty and ache whirling inside me and took Sir West's outstretched hand. My legs shook as I stood and I locked my knees to keep from swaying.

Everything would be all right. Rider would be here, and he'd keep back and out of the way like he had before. He wouldn't draw more attention to me than I'd already drawn to myself or what the High Priestess drew to me.

I glanced over to the couch... where Talon sat.

No.

No no no no.

For a heartbeat, the expression on his breathtakingly beautiful face was unreadable as if he knew what I was thinking. Then his lips curled into a wickedly flirtatious smile.

His allure flared with a hot, achy spike that flushed through my entire body before it sank low in my belly, pulsing and throbbing.

For the love of—

Worst. Day. Ever.

CHAPTER 26
Sage

I SWALLOWED back a gasp and fought to hide the trembling need now thrumming through me, my hands clenched at my sides.

"I thought Lord Rider was supposed to be my companion tonight," I forced out through gritted teeth.

"Rider had business he needed to take care of, so we switched nights." Talon's smile deepened and he leaned forward in exaggerated interest, a move he'd done many times before that made my stomach twist in disgust.

And while my insides churned and my skin crawled, his allure burned hotter.

Why did it have to be him? Why couldn't it have been Rider or Quill or even— I didn't know. Anyone else. Someone whose magic didn't make my body betray me, someone who clearly didn't have some kind of agenda.

I tore my gaze away from him and hurried into my bedroom to change into the red dress that hid all of my sleeping mating marks. I didn't want to potentially color-match with someone, especially not Talon and especially not in the High Priestess's throne room, so I continued to keep my choice of color to the same one I manifested in even though Lord Quill had provided me with a rainbow of choices.

Father! Talon was right there. In the sitting room. And the allure was already making it hard to breathe normally again. How was I supposed to get through an entire evening without giving myself away? Without doing something embarrassing or—

Stop. Just stop.

"Her Brilliance's servants arrived a while ago," Talon called from the sitting room. "I recommend being quick."

My stomach twisted tighter. I didn't want to think about how the High Priestess might be waiting on me and how angry that would make her. I had no way of knowing she wanted to see me until I manifested.

Except I couldn't stop my hands from shaking as I dressed, or the shiver of trepidation and need that race down my spine as I stepped back into the sitting room determined not to look at Talon.

Don't look at him.

Do. Not.

Except I couldn't help it.

My gaze jerked to the couch. Talon sat there, that wickedly flirtatious smile already on his face, and his allure hit hard and hot and heavy. Heat flushed through me and sank low in my belly, throbbing and achy and I fought to breathe.

The afternoon had been bad enough with trying to spar while desire pulsed through me. Now I had to sit through a summons to the High Priestess with this burning under my skin, getting worse the longer I was near him.

Did he even know he was affecting me?

I tore my gaze away and focused on Sir West's back as he moved toward the door.

Don't look at Talon. Don't think about him. Just follow West and get through this.

But the ache grew hotter, and I clenched my hands at my sides to stop them from shaking. I had to hide this, had to get through the evening without my body giving me away.

And I sure as hell couldn't keep the High Priestess waiting any longer.

West turned and strode from the suite without a word. I forced myself to follow, my legs unsteady, my pulse racing as a new horrible thought hit me.

I hadn't heard anything about the investigation into the attack, nothing from whoever was supposed to be investigating it or Rider, Talon, Quill, or West. I wasn't sure if Her Brilliance would bother to inform me that the remaining men who'd escaped had been apprehended or not, but I had to assume no news meant they were still out there.

Which meant being in my suite was the safest place for me. Sure, I could assume that Crane and the other men couldn't enter the Divine Residence, or that they'd given up in their quest to force mating bonds on me, but I had no guarantee of that.

From the corner of my eye, I saw Talon rise from the couch and march toward me, catching up just as I stepped into the hall.

"This way, my lady," he said, offering me his arm in a courtly gesture.

A burning shiver raced down my spine. I stared at his forearm, the sculpted muscles hidden behind soft fabric, and at his calloused hand. My own hand wouldn't move. If I touched him, the yearning would get worse, much worse than if I didn't touch him.

Talon frowned.

Heat crept up my neck. Crap. I'd stared at his arm too long and now looked ridiculous, frozen in place like I'd never been offered a gentleman's escort before.

Fighting the urge to steel my nerves with a sharp breath, I rested my hand on his arm. His warmth blazed through the fabric of his shirt straight into my palm. The heat spread up my arm and pooled low in my belly.

His thumb brushed across my knuckles, a deliberate, teasing stroke, before he led me down the hall with West's heavy footsteps following behind us.

As we walked, I became aware of Talon's attention. Not just his arm beneath my hand or the warmth radiating from his body, but his gaze, as if he couldn't stop looking at me. It was like a physical presence, blazing across my cheek, making my pulse pick up.

The ache between my thighs throbbed hotter with

every step. Each brush of my legs together sent another wave of need rippling through me, and I had to fight to keep my breathing steady. If Talon noticed, if he said something, I didn't know what I'd do.

The hall opened into a wider corridor, although not nearly as wide as the main hall leading to the throne room. Polished wood gleamed under crystal chandeliers, and fae stones embedded in the fixtures cast steady light across walls where stone blended seamlessly with living wood. Intricate patterns swirled through the walls, and flowering vines curled along the edges of arched doorways, their white and pink blooms glowing with a soft light.

My gaze slid over it all without really seeing any of it. The beauty didn't matter. Nothing mattered except the building fever inside me.

Two fae women in flowing silk and lace gowns passed us. Their gazes landed on Talon first — of course they did — then slid to me. One woman's eyes narrowed, her expression cooling as she took in my hand on his arm, while the other woman's attention jumped up to West behind me.

I ducked my head, acutely aware of how I must look — flushed and clinging to Talon's arm like I couldn't stand on my own. Which, at the moment, I wasn't entirely sure I could.

My breathing turned shallow, my chest tight with the effort of holding myself together.

We passed two knights in gleaming armor. They nodded at West, and I barely noticed.

A tremor ran through me, and I tightened my grip on Talon's arm to steady myself.

"Sage?" Talon murmured, his tone soft and filled with concern.

Words stuck in my throat. Everything in me was focused on not doing something stupid—not pressing closer to him, not making a sound that would give away exactly how much his touch affected me. The desire burned through every nerve, making my skin too tight, too hot.

What was wrong with me? The ache had been manageable in the suite... more or less. Annoying, but manageable. Now it consumed everything and I was just walking beside him. Was it his allure? Was it raging out of control?

Talon abruptly stopped and I stumbled to a halt beside him, my legs weak.

His frown deepened, then his pale eyes widened with realization. "Shit."

He grabbed my arm and yanked me sideways into an alcove, pressing my back against the cool stone and pinning me with his hard body.

The hunger that had been building exploded, overwhelming me with lust, and I gasped, the sound too loud and too desperate in the small space.

No. This couldn't be happening. Not here. I could hold myself together if he'd just give me space.

My hands came up between us, pressing flat against his chest. I should push him away. I knew I should. But my fingers curled into the fabric of his shirt instead, and I gazed into the mesmerizing swirl of his eyes.

They were clear and perfect and beautiful. There wasn't a hint of darkness billowing in them or around him, not a whisper of smoky tendrils reaching for me.

It was just me and Talon, squeezed into the alcove, and the teasing, flirtatious man from moments ago had vanished.

In his place was someone sharp and serious, his gaze searching my face filled with a concern that I wanted — desperately wanted — to believe was true.

"Something's wrong," he stated as if he didn't know his magic was driving me crazy.

Except was it?

I didn't know if I'd be able to see his shadow like I did the last time if it was only giving off its allure and not... what? Actively seeking me out? But surely Talon would know his magic was turning me on. He wouldn't need to say something was wrong.

I opened my mouth, but I still couldn't force the words out. I couldn't accuse him of using his allure on me because I wasn't supposed to know about it.

But something was clearly happening and I could tell from the set of his jaw and the hard look in his eyes that he wasn't going to let it go. I had to say something.

And the only something I could logically talk about were my desire spikes. Hell, for all I knew his allure had set one off this afternoon, and I was now finally facing the consequences of it. Surely Lord Quill had told him what had happened in the bedroom, how I'd jumped him overwhelmed with lust, and he'd understand.

"I ah— it's a desire spike." Father, this was embarrassing.

His frown deepened. "A desire spike?"

"Magister Zinnia warned me this might happen when she put my marks to sleep. She said I might experience... surges. You know, like what I experience the other night with Quill."

Talon's eyes went wide, his surprise written in every sculpted slope stating clearly that Quill hadn't said anything.

Embarrassment burned across my cheeks and down my neck.

"You and—?" Talon asked.

Sir West grunted a confirmation, drawing my attention, and I realized he stood at the entrance to the alcove, his broad back mostly blocking us from view of anything walking past. Except he couldn't completely cover everything and anyone really looking would see everything... and my body desperately wanted *everything* from Talon at the moment.

Father, please kill me now.

"I need... relief." The heat in my face burned hotter, almost as hot as the hunger blazing in my core, leaving only a small, desperate voice screaming in my head that I didn't have time for this. The High Priestess was waiting for me, and I couldn't afford to pay the price of upsetting her.

"All right," Talon murmured as he pressed closer.

His hand trailed up my arm, fingers light but deliberate. Even that simple touch made my core burn, my body begging for more. Nothing about this felt like the flirtatious gestures in my suite. The teasing smile had vanished. His jaw was tight, movements precise, like someone performing a task they'd done a hundred times before not because they wanted to, but because they had to.

Because his shadow needed to.

West shifted his weight, the soft scrape of his boots and clink of his armor reminding me that he was right there. He'd hear everything. Every gasp. Every moan. Every desperate sound I couldn't hold back. Every shameful proof of how much I needed this.

My stomach twisted, and I wanted to shrink into the stone, disappear entirely, but there was nowhere to go and my body didn't care about shame, only relief.

CHAPTER 27

Sage

TALON CUPPED my face and tilted it up, and our gazes locked. His eyes held that mesmerizing swirl of colors, but they were cool, assessing. Even Quill when he'd help me relieve the pressure of my desire spike had looked like he'd cared.

His attention dipped to my lips, and he inched closer, his breath mingling with mine, the promise of a kiss hanging in the fraction of space between our mouths before he jerked his head back and slipped his other hand through the high slit in my skirt.

The brush of his fingers against my bare thigh sent a shock of heat rushing through me and forced me to bite back a moan. I was already so wound up, already aching, and he'd barely touched me. He slid higher, and I stopped breathing entirely, my whole body frozen in anticipation, before he paused, just at the cusp of where I wanted him.

My heart hammered not just from his touch and the

yearning burning inside me but from fear. The alcove was too exposed. Anyone could walk past. Anyone could see West standing guard and wonder what he was guarding. And a part of me didn't care, a part that screamed inside me hungry and demanding. I needed him to touch me more, needed relief so badly my whole body shook.

My throat tightened and I wanted to tell Talon to stop, that we should go back to my suite to deal with this. Except there wasn't time. I couldn't keep the High Priestess waiting any longer than absolutely necessary, and he knew it.

Talon released my face, and his mouth moved to my neck, nipping softly, the sharp sensation shooting straight to my core, making me gasp and arch into him. When his fingers finally dipped into my wetness, I had to press my fist against my mouth to muffle the sound that threatened to escape.

I was so slick, so ready, and I couldn't stop the way my hips rolled forward seeking more. Shame burned through me, knowing West could hear every gasp and moan, but I couldn't make myself stop.

Talon stroked me, circling my nub with a rhythm that sent heat spiraling through my core. My breaths came in short, desperate gasps I couldn't control. One finger slid inside me and a hint of relief flooded through me at the intrusion, the sensation so intense I nearly sobbed. Then he slid in a second finger, curling them just right, finding that spot that made stars flicker behind my lids.

His movements were deliberate, practiced, speaking

to years and years of knowing exactly what to do to bring a woman to the edge, but he watched me like he was gauging the effect, not sharing it.

My throat tightened. This should have felt good — it did feel good — but the emptiness twisted inside me anyway. He was here, touching me, but I felt alone, disconnected from him in a way I'd never felt with Ash or even Lord Quill.

Father, I wish Ash were here instead. My chest ached with how much I wanted to be with him again, wanted someone to want me. How could someone who literally oozed sex be so cold and calculating?

Talon shifted, bracing his free hand against the wall beside my head, caging me in while his fingers moved faster inside me, pumping in and out, his thumb pressing circles on my nub. The pleasure built too fast, too intense, my body coiled so tight I couldn't think, couldn't breathe, could only feel the spiraling climb toward release.

My hips moved, grinding against his hand, chasing more, needing more, and I didn't care how it looked or sounded anymore. The fabric of my skirt whispered against us, the sound of his fingers squelching in and out of me obscene in the quiet alcove.

My core spasmed around his fingers, my body teetering on the edge of release and my breathing turned ragged, but Talon's eyes stayed cool even as his own breathing picked up.

A lump formed in my throat.

I knew he had to keep himself separate and in control

so I wouldn't notice his shadow — I couldn't even tell if it was feeding off my release like I knew it needed — but I didn't expect his distance to hurt so much.

Which was ridiculous because I didn't care about Talon and certainly didn't want Talon to care about me. I couldn't afford the complications.

My gaze darted past Talon's shoulder. West still blocked the alcove, his back to us. Father, this was mortifying.

Then my body clenched hard around his fingers, violent and sudden, and I had to muffle my cry against Talon's chest while the release screamed through me. Blazing heat flooded my core, radiating outward until my legs shook so badly Talon had to press me harder against the wall to keep me upright.

Relief washed through me, the frantic clawing lust easing. I could breathe again, think again, forget I ever had this moment with Talon in an alcove where anyone could see—

A sharp, consuming hunger exploded inside me, aching and demanding, worse than before.

No. Please no.

My core clenched around nothing, the emptiness suddenly overwhelming. A sob caught in my throat and my eyes burned.

It hadn't been enough. The desire spike was still there, still burning, and now my body knew relief was possible but incomplete. The desperation clawed at me worse than ever.

Why did my body demand more when I didn't want

to give it? Not to Talon, not when I couldn't even be sure he wanted me in return. Why couldn't this be happening with Ash instead?

Talon eased his hand away carefully. His gaze met mine and something flickered there. Satisfaction, maybe. A job completed successfully. But no warmth. His frown deepened. "Are you—?"

He knew. I could see it in the way his eyes searched my face. I was still shaking, still aching, the urgency worse than when we'd started.

"What do you need?"

More embarrassment burned my cheeks — I hadn't thought it possible for them to get hotter — and I looked away, unable to meet his eyes.

"I ah..." I swallowed hard. I didn't want to say it. "I don't think the spike—" I had to force the words out past the humiliation of admitting it. "The one before wouldn't ease up until Quill was actually inside me."

A heartbreaking softness flickered through Talon's expression, and a part of me wanted to scream at the injustice of it. Neither of us wanted to be in this situation, but he was going to help me anyway, because this, right here, was the real Talon. A man who had to keep his distance but who ultimately cared even about someone he didn't really care about.

With a soft nod, as if he were confirming to himself what he needed to do, he reached for his belt, his fingers working fast at the buckle. Every second felt like forever, my body screaming for relief, and I wanted to grab his hands and make him move faster, but I knew that would only slow him down.

He opened his pants and freed himself. He lifted my leg, hooking it around his hip, and gripped his beautiful cock, already hard and flushed, the tip glistening. I'd fantasized about what it would feel like to have him press inside me, how it would feel to make love with Talon, but being compelled by his allure and a desire spike hadn't been a part of the fantasy.

My insides churned, a tangle of want and yearning and confusing emotions, because I'd trusted Talon, thought I knew who he was, and then he'd proven me wrong.

And now here we were and he was exactly who I first thought him to be. I didn't want to doubt him, didn't want to need him in this moment, didn't want to lose the sense of friendship I'd thought we'd been developing in the Gray before the running trail, didn't want... a whole bunch of overwhelming things I had no control over.

The first press of his length against my entrance made me gasp and then he pushed inside, hard and fast. My breath stuttered out of me. The force and sensation flooded my body, so intense my vision went white at the edges. He filled me completely, the stretch burning and perfect, and I grabbed his shoulders to steady myself.

Oh, yes. Yes yes yes. This was what I needed.

He pulled out and thrust back in, deeper, harder, and I bit my lip to keep from crying out. My core clenched around him, desperate for more, and he gave it to me as if sensing just how deep the ache went.

His hips snapped forward again, fast and fierce, each thrust sending lust spiraling through me. Sweat dampened my skin and I moaned. His hands gripped my waist hard enough to bruise but I didn't care. I needed this, needed him to fuck me harder, faster, needed relief so badly I couldn't think past it.

Darkness billowed through the mesmerizing swirls in his eyes, there and gone, and a hint of smoke curled around his forearms so fast I wasn't certain I saw it. But the whisper of cold seeping into my skin where he held me confirmed his shadow was rising to the surface.

The pace quickened, his thrusts coming harder, deeper. I gasped and clung to his shoulders and pleasure coiled tighter and tighter in my belly. The desire spike drove me to meet each thrust, my hips rolling forward. West's armor clinked nearby, a reminder he was still there, still listening, but the ache for relief drowned out shame and everything else now.

Talon's control started to slip, his rhythm turning rougher, more urgent, and darkness bled back into his eyes, staying this time.

"Fuck," Talon groaned, his hips jerking forward, his length plunging deep inside me, his muscles tense with his release.

My core clenched around his cock, whisps of darkness and icy cold caressed my flesh, and I shattered. The orgasm tore through me, fierce, splintering, ripping a strangled cry from my throat. My inner walls spasmed, gripping him hard, and heat exploded through my belly, radiating outward in waves that made my legs shake. My body convulsed with the force and relief finally — finally! — flooded through me, the desire spike draining away and leaving me boneless.

Talon stilled with a sharp gasp, his release pulsing hot inside me. For a brief moment his forehead rested against mine, the gesture achingly tender, as if for just one second he'd forgotten to maintain his emotional distance.

My chest tightened. His breath washed warm against my lips, and I wanted to close the space between us, wanted him to actually kiss me. I craved something more than this clinical relief.

Then he pulled away, withdrawing carefully and tucking himself back into his pants before fastening them with quick, practiced movements. He straightened my dress, smoothing the fabric with detached care, making sure I looked presentable before stepping back.

My legs wouldn't stop shaking. My face was still flushed, my breath still uneven, and there wasn't a damn thing I could do about it.

The High Priestess was waiting.

CHAPTER 28

Sage

I GATHERED what little dignity I could despite Talon's release slowly seeping down the insides of my thighs, squared my shoulders, and stepped out of the alcove into the hall.

Sir West's expression remained grim as if he hadn't just heard me having sex with Talon and it wasn't a big deal that we'd done it in public where anyone could have seen.

Embarrassed heat flashed through me followed by terrified cold.

I'd had sex with Talon. West had listened to everything, and I'd been too desperate to notice anything beyond Talon and what we were doing.

At least the desire spike or allure or whatever it had been affecting me was satisfied, no longer burning up my insides with a desperate hunger making it impossible to think.

And thinking clearly was what I really needed to do if I was going to face the High Priestess.

Except being able to think clearly meant I knew how horribly that could have gone. Talon could have refused me. Someone could have walked past.

I could have bonded with Talon.

No. I bit the inside of my cheek, desperate to stop my whirling thoughts. Zinnia had put my marks to sleep. Even if I wasn't human, I couldn't form a mating bond with anyone. Zinnia had promised.

And I wasn't going to think about the few marks that had turned green. They weren't real. Me looking like a fae wasn't real. It was impossible, a quirk of magic, a strange waking dream.

I bit back a bitter huff. More like a nightmare. Even if I couldn't naturally form a mating bond, Crane and the other men who'd escaped were out there and I had no doubt their magically induced bonding spell would work on me.

Talon cleared his throat and offered me the crook of his arm.

Right. The High Priestess.

My pulse picked up as we turned a corner into the wide main hall and approached the end where the two heavy doors leading to the throne room stood.

Don't say much. Keep your expression neutral. Get through this.

I had experience with this. The High Priestess would play her games, but she wouldn't hurt me like Edred used to… at least I hoped she wouldn't.

We reached the intricately carved doors with the two guards in gleaming armor standing on either side, their uniforms the green, gold, and white that I now knew indicated they were Knights of the Order of the Sacred Grove.

The guards nodded as we approached and pushed open the doors revealing the massive throne room inside.

The crowd standing before the dais at the front of the room seemed even larger than when I'd first stepped into the throne room… or was that just because I'd been so stunned and confused when I'd first been presented to the High Priestess that I hadn't noticed just how many courtiers attended Her Brilliance's court.

There had to be over a hundred nobles — although I wasn't sure if they were nobles in the sense of human nobility since I knew next to nothing about the political makeup of the fae realm — and they immediately fell silent the second I stepped into the room even though I was certain they couldn't see me clearly from that distance.

Talon gave me a look, but his expression was strange and I couldn't tell if he was trying to encourage me or warn me or something else. Then he stepped away into the shadows at the edges of the room, and my chest tightened.

Swell.

He was abandoning me to the powerful, capricious ruler of the fae realm when I needed support the most. Except from the last time, I knew he couldn't really associate with me because the High Priestess had already been upset about the leaders of the Black Guard spending time with me. She'd essentially told them to focus on their jobs and not me, and I was sure they were already risking her ire by ensuring at least one of them was always with me when I was in my suite alone with Sir West.

I sucked in a steadying breath, focused on what was in front of me, and strode forward. The throne room was massive with half-stone, half-wood walls, a gleaming marble floor, and massive pillars and tree trunks holding up the soaring ceiling. Large arched stained-glass windows depicted fae women with multiple mates, and flowering vines framed each window, their blooms pulsing with soft magical light.

I walked down the long central aisle, West's heavy footsteps behind me loud in the hush. Like last time, all the men — as well as the very few women in the crowd — all wore fine clothes and flashy jewelry that caught the light from the many chandeliers illuminating the massive space. And just like last time, they all stared at me, their gazes hungry, judging, curious, boring into me from all sides.

The urge to hide squeezed my insides. I didn't belong here. I was really a human, but I was terrified if I said something I'd be imprisoned and punished, and I couldn't afford to risk my plan to keep Sawyer safe.

Instead, I kept my pace steady, praying they couldn't tell how nervous I was.

"—was she really attacked or—"

"—look at her dress, it covers all her marks—"

"—hair isn't even styled properly—"

"—Talon is never with a woman—"

I focused my attention on the front of the room with its recessed area with the high dais, the spectacular stained-glass starburst window glowing with brilliant light behind it even though it was night. Beneath it sat the throne, shaped like a starburst as well with golden strips of various lengths protruding from the back, and flowering vines trailing around its base and curling over its arms.

Sitting on that throne, exactly as she'd been the last time, was the High Priestess in her shimmering white gown, her impossibly pale eyes already fixed on me.

This time, she only had two of her mates standing on either side and slightly behind her, the largest one who wore a variation of the knight's armor except with bare arms to expose the radiant white bands ringing his biceps, and the slimmer one who wore the green and gold tunic.

I stopped in the same spot where Lord Rider had stopped the last time, about ten feet from the base of the stairs of the dais, and knelt with a lot more grace than before.

Zinnia had confirmed, kneeling and bowing low was proper protocol when presented to the High Priestess as opposed to the humans' custom of curtseying.

I bowed my head and tried to watch the High Priestess through my lashes, not wanting to be caught unaware. Given how Her Brilliance behaved the last time, I wouldn't put anything past her.

Just answer her questions as concisely as possible. Don't give her extra information. Keep your expression neutral.

The High Priestess stared at me. That gleam I'd seen in her eyes the last time we'd met flashed across her expression, and I fought to keep my breathing steady while I waited.

And waited.

And waited some more.

The silence stretched through the throne room, even the crowd seemed to hold their breath.

Was she going to acknowledge me? She was looking straight at me. Zinnia had said I couldn't say anything to her unless she spoke directly to me.

Stay calm. Just stay calm.

This was just part of her game.

Besides, if I could submit to Edred, I could submit to the High Priestess.

The silence continued to stretch, longer and longer, until my insides squirmed with uncertainty.

"So, Lady Sage," she finally said, her tone sharp. "You've kept me waiting."

She sounded angry, which was entirely unreasonable given that I'd only just arrived in the Garden and had come as soon as Sir West had told me… well—

Heat flashed across my face at the memory of what Talon and I had done in the alcove, and I was grateful she hadn't told me to raise my head yet. I'd needed to handle the desire spike before I could face her, but had someone told her about that? Was that why she was angry? Or was this just part of her game?

Whispers and soft laughter rippled through the courtiers, and I couldn't tell if they knew what Talon and I had done or not.

"Oh, child," she said in a singsong. "You may raise your head."

I looked up and met those colorless eyes. Her lips twisted into a smug smile, wicked delight flashing through her expression for a heartbeat.

She knew. Father above, she knew.

Mortification twisted inside me even as I tried to remind myself that the fae didn't care about nudity and public sex. The things I'd seen in the Garden were proof of that... unless it wasn't supposed to happen in the Divine Residence.

No. I couldn't let my thoughts wander. I had to focus on Her Brilliance right now. So she knew. Was she going to say something?

The High Priestess's expression shifted to something that looked disappointed, and my pulse lurched. She *was* going to say something.

"I'm told you've been... *resting* in your chambers," she said, making "resting" sound like an accusation.

More murmurs rippled through the crowd.

"—to ignore Her Brilliance—"

"—ungrateful—"

"—shameful—"

"—how could she?"

The High Priestess made no indication that she heard, and her expression shifted to false concern. "Have you recovered from your ordeal?"

My mind whirled. I had to say something that wouldn't make this worse.

Except I had no idea what that would be and there wasn't any excuse I could make. "Yes, Your Brilliance."

"And my invitation to attend my court?" The sharp edge returned to her expression. "Have you met my courtiers? Found options for advantageous matches?"

My pulse picked up. "No, Your Brilliance."

The High Priestess tilted her head, feigned confusion softening her features. "Why haven't you? What could possibly prevent you from enjoying the hospitality I've extended?"

Because I wanted nothing to do with her and her court. I couldn't bond a mate, and I didn't want one in the first place. Because I was human. And I didn't trust her!

The words bubbled in my throat, desperate and frustrated, and angry, and I swallowed them back.

I couldn't say that. I had to play the game, had to stay as uninteresting and boring as possible given the circumstances.

"My healer advised prudence, Your Brilliance," I said. Zinnia had implied hitting my head had given me amnesia. Maybe if I reminded the High Priestess of that she'd stop pressing. "Because of my head injury, I didn't want to risk large groups of—"

"Oh nonsense." The High Priestess waved a dismissive hand. "Zinnia is overly cautious. My gardens host small, intimate gatherings, hardly the overwhelming crowds you seem to fear."

"I simply feel I need more time—" *Come on. Please. Just let me hide in my room until I can figure out how to stop manifesting in the Garden.*

"Time." The High Priestess's pale eyes narrowed. "Time for what, exactly? To hide in your chambers while my court whispers about your behavior? To make yourself appear... difficult?"

My stomach twisted tighter and I struggled to keep my breathing even.

The High Priestess sat back, that gleam flashing in her eyes again. "Let me be clear, Lady Sage. You're recovered. You've been given adequate time. I've provided you with one of my most skilled knights for your protection. My courtiers have shown you patience and respect by allowing you space."

She wasn't going to let me escape. Not even with the excuse of having injured my mind.

"Therefore," she continued, her voice turning to an unsettling purr, "you will begin participating in court life. Tonight, my private garden awaits, where I've personally selected a small group of men for you to meet. And in four days... a ball to properly introduce you to my court. Surely you wouldn't refuse such consideration?"

Maybe I could delay it. I was sure if I could figure out Lord Quill's meditation, I'd stop manifesting in the Garden. "Your Brilliance, I—"

A darkness filled her expression that sent shivers down my spine.

"This is not a request," she snapped. "You've been

given privilege and protection. It's time you showed proper gratitude."

My pulse lurched, her tone perfectly clear. If I refused, she'd punish me, to hell with her thinking my spark would be powerful or advantageous or anything else.

"Yes, of course, Your Brilliance," I said, bowing forward and pressing my forehead to the marble floor.

"Excellent," she purred. "Rise, Lady Sage. You have men to meet."

CHAPTER 29

Sage

HER BRILLIANCE GESTURED to the servant by the door beside the dais. It was the same door through which I'd exited the last time I was in the throne room, but this time I wasn't going back to my suite no matter how much I wanted to. At least I had Talon with me. He might be hiding in the shadows of the enormous room, but I was sure he wouldn't let me face these strangers alone.

"A word, Captain Talon," the High Priestess said, and my stomach bottomed out.

No. I needed him. I couldn't face how ever many men by myself. Especially when they hoped I'd make them my mate, and I wanted nothing to do with any of them.

But even if Zinnia hadn't explicitly told me, I knew enough about how things worked that the High Priestess's word was the law and saying anything against her would draw unwanted attention from her and everyone else.

I swallowed hard and stood, my knees aching from having knelt for so long. I could do this. I could face these men alone.

I'd survived worse. I'd survived Wells and Crane, and I could survive meeting a few suitors even if I had no idea what to say or how to act around them. They wanted me to like them, which meant they'd be on their best behavior.

At least this was a semi-private audience. The ball the High Priestess had mentioned would be so much worse — hundreds of eyes watching, nowhere to hide, everyone scrutinizing the newcomer who'd already been attacked.

I forced myself to move, keeping my pace steady even though everything within me screamed to run, hide, pretend I didn't keep showing up in the Garden every time I fell asleep.

Sir West's heavy footsteps fell into step behind me, reminding me that I wasn't alone, that I couldn't ever be alone in the Garden now.

Except meeting these men was the High Priestess's wish and Sir West was sworn into her service. If I asked—hell, even if I begged, I doubted he'd whisk me away.

The servant led us through opulent halls, and I fought to think of a plan, figure out what to do once we got to wherever we were going.

I had no idea what to say to these men, and everything Zinnia had told me about how I should act went against everything I'd been taught growing up.

And while I desperately wanted to break away from the meek, submissive woman I was supposed to be—

No. I *would* break away. I could do this.

The servant stopped at an archway where the stone walls gave way to climbing vines and the open air of a private garden and gestured me through. I stepped into the garden and clasped my hands in front of me, desperate to hide their shaking.

Nine beautiful fae men waited inside, some standing near a fountain in the center of the garden, others seated on the cushioned benches arranged around it. All of them turned to look at me the moment I entered and stood.

The space was small, intimate, enclosed by stone walls covered in climbing vines and those glowing white and pink flowers that grew everywhere in the Garden. Fae lanterns cast warm golden light, and a statue of the goddess waited in an alcove near a second, outside entrance. It felt like a beautiful trap with only two ways in or out and nowhere to hide.

My chest tightened and the splash and rush of the fountain sounded louder, ringing in my ears, reminding me of the last time I was surrounded by men, my hands tied, my body aching, Wells pressing me against jagged rocks. My breathing picked up and the edges of my vision darkened.

No. I wouldn't think about it. Crane and the others were on the run. They had to be. They wouldn't be foolish enough to come after me in the Divine Residence surrounded by Her Brilliance's handpicked courtiers.

I shoved all thoughts of them as deep into my mind as I could. Wells was dead, the Order of the Sacred Grove were hunting the men who Rider, Talon, Quill, and Ash hadn't outright killed. I was safe. I was fine. I could do this.

I forced myself to take a step into the private garden, focusing on the men and not the fountain.

They were all tall, all muscular, and all stunning like every fae man I'd seen so far — with the exception of Sir West — and they all looked at me with varying degrees of desire that made my stomach churn.

I wanted to yell at them, tell them I wasn't a thing, a prize to be won, that I thought fae men were supposed to be different from humans, but I swallowed back the words. In their culture, women *were* a prize to be fought over and won. We were rare, only a quarter of the population, and from what I'd glimpsed of female behavior, they liked and expected this kind of attention.

We were supposed to be powerful, in charge, and able to demand what we wanted, but I certainly didn't feel like that right now. I felt like prey. Just like the last few times I'd been surrounded by fae men.

West positioned himself near the archway back into the Divine Residence and the servant withdrew, leaving me with the nine men who all thought this was their chance to win a mate.

As a wave, all the men moved toward me, and I strained to stay where I was despite being desperate to run away, not sure what I should do or where I should go even if I didn't.

Should I sit? That felt even more vulnerable than standing here with them towering over me.

A man with long black hair half braided up in traditional fae style that reminded me too much of Wells' hair reached me first. He captured both my hands in his much larger ones and raised my knuckles to his lips, his breath hot against my skin. His pale pink eyes were sharp and calculating as they met mine, and something about the way he looked at me made my stomach twist.

"Lady Sage." His voice was warm and practiced and made the hair on the back of my neck rise in warning. "We've heard so much about you."

I cringed at that. The only things he could have possibly heard were that I'd been attacked and that I'd been hiding in my room. Which meant anything else was pure rumor.

I forced a smile. Did I even want to know what the courtiers in the High Priestess's court were saying about me?

Before I could think of a response, another man stepped close on my left, his bright turquoise eyes watching me with an intensity that made me want to make myself as small as possible.

"A pleasure," he purred with a slight incline of his head. He seemed familiar. Where had I seen him before? When I'd been on the balcony and Ash was trying to get me to pick someone to join us or—?

My breath caught in my throat. Or did I recognize him from when I'd been trussed up in the sacred chamber and Wells had tried to force a mating bond on me?

I strained to remember, but I'd been in shock when I'd woken from what Crane had done to me with his magic and aside from a few of the men, the rest were all a blur.

A man with hair so short it made the delicate points of his ears stand out in sharp contrast crowded my right side. "Is it true you were attacked? That must have been terrifying, are you all right, do you need anything, because we heard what happened and it's awful, just awful, and Her Brilliance said we should make you comfortable—"

"I'm fine, thank you," I said, cutting him off before he could keep going, but I wasn't sure he heard me.

The man with black hair still held my hands, his thumb stroking across my knuckles in a way that was probably meant to be soothing but only made my skin crawl. "I'm Cobalt, my lady. And this—" He jerked his chin at the rambling man on my right, "—is Pine."

"It's nice to meet you both." The words came out stiff and formal.

I winced at how awkward I sounded but I didn't know what else to say. I wasn't the confident woman Zinnia said I was supposed to be, and it was much harder to pretend I was than I wanted it to be.

"Come sit with us," Pine said, already moving toward the benches near the fountain. "You must be tired after everything—"

"This way, Lady Sage." Cobalt's hand closed around

my elbow before I could decide if I wanted to sit, and he guided me toward a group of cushioned benches with a grip that didn't leave room for refusal.

I let him lead me because what else could I do? Yank my arm away and run? I didn't even know where I'd go, and causing a scene would only draw more attention. Maybe sitting would make this easier. Maybe if I just got through the next few minutes, I could find an excuse to leave.

Cobalt sat me in the middle of the bench and gracefully sank down beside me. Pine dropped onto the bench on my other side with his thigh pressed against mine through the fabric of our clothes. I shifted away but he shifted with me, closing the gap, almost pinning me between him and Cobalt.

In front of me, the fountain burbled with that constant rush of water that made my chest tighten, while the rest of the men arranged themselves on the nearby benches, drew benches closer to sit on, or just stood around me.

Nine of them. Two exits. And not a single man I trusted among them.

CHAPTER 30
Sage

"Tell us about yourself, Lady Sage," Cobalt said, and I realized all nine men were watching me, waiting for me to say something interesting or charming or whatever it was fae women said in situations like this.

My mind went blank. I couldn't talk about my family. I couldn't talk about most things.

"I'm ah... still getting used to the Garden." Yes, that was a safe thing to say.

"Your family must be proud," Cobalt said. "A new arrival the whole court is already talking about."

My throat tightened. "Ah... yes."

"The attack must have been so frightening," another man said from across the circle, his voice dripping with sympathy that didn't reach his eyes. "Were you badly hurt?"

I didn't want to talk about the attack, didn't want to remember any of it, didn't want to think about how similar being surrounded by these men felt to it.

"I'm recovering," I forced out.

"And what do you look for in mates?" the turquoise-eyed one asked. I think someone had called him Raven.

My stomach dropped. "I... I haven't given it much thought, to be honest."

"Surely you have some idea," Cobalt said, and his hand settled on my forearm.

My muscles tensed, my body locking up. I should pull away, demand he let me go, but I couldn't do it. Everything Edred had beaten in to me screamed to stay small, stay quiet, stay demure.

Zinnia had told me I could demand what I wanted, that fae women were in control, but I wasn't in control. I had no choice but to be in this garden with these men, I couldn't run away or I'd face the High Priestess's wrath, and I couldn't stop thinking of the look on Wells' face... on the look on all the faces of the men who'd thought they could force a mating bond on me. Hungry, certain, entitled.

Just like the expressions on the men surrounding me.

Why did I have to be here? Why couldn't I be back in my suite or with Ash.

Father, I missed him so much. I hadn't wanted to have sex with Talon, I'd wanted Ash and I wasn't sure how I was going to survive the High Priestess's suitors without him.

Cobalt's grip on my wrist tightened, his fingers pressing into my skin, and I couldn't tell if he was trying to hold me still or keep me from jumping to my feet and running away.

"Do you like music?" Pine asked, leaning closer. "I heard there's going to be a concert next week in the central garden, or maybe you prefer dancing—"

"Your marks are covered," someone behind me interrupted. "I heard they were stunning."

"I ah..."

Someone grabbed a strand of my hair, not pulling, just holding it between their fingers. Pine pressed even closer on my other side. The sound of the fountain kept rushing and rushing and rushing, filling my head.

I bit the inside of my cheek. I'd survived worse. I *had*. I just had to get through this.

"You're so beautiful, my lady," Pine said. "Your hair is amazing. Red this shade is rare."

Cobalt leaned closer, his breath warm against my ear. "Relax, my lady." But his voice was too smooth, too practiced. I didn't trust him.

A palm pressed flat against my back. Another hand closed around my other wrist. Pine's hand settled on my waist. My skin crawled everywhere they touched. I couldn't get enough air. The garden tilted, the men's faces blurring together, and all I could hear was water pouring from the fountain.

Pull it together. Get through this. You can *get through this.*

But I couldn't breathe, couldn't think past the hands touching me, the bodies pressing close, the sound of the water.

I tried to look for West, but Pine shifted and blocked my view of the archway.

"Where are you going?" he asked, and I realized I'd started to lean away from them.

The hand on my back slid lower. Someone's fingers pressed into the side of my neck near my collar. More bodies crowded close, blocking the light, and my chest got tighter and tighter until I couldn't pull in enough air.

Please, Father. Please.

My gaze jumped from crack to crack between their bodies, desperate to see past them, to find something, anything—

There, a lone figure standing near the statue of the goddess by the second entrance.

Everything within me froze.

He had white hair and yellow eyes and the same smirk he'd worn when he and Wells had cornered me in the secret nook.

Crane.

Oh, Father!

He was here. He was watching. Why wasn't anyone stopping him? Hadn't Sir West noticed him? Was this all part of the High Priestess's plan?

I wrenched my gaze to the man with the turquoise eyes, desperate to figure out if he'd been one of the men in the sacred chamber.

But I couldn't ignore the press of the men's bodies, their hands all over me. I couldn't think, couldn't breathe, couldn't—

I lurched to my feet. "I need to go."

My voice cracked and I hated it, hated how weak I sounded.

"My lady?" Pine frowned, confused and clearly oblivious to the turmoil raging inside me.

Cobalt seized my wrist, his grip hard enough to hurt. "Her Brilliance wanted you to get to know us."

I tugged against his hold, but he didn't let go. The men on the benches closest to me stood, blocking the way back to the exit, and all I could see was Crane's yellow eyes watching from across the garden.

"Please—" The word came out strangled, barely a whisper.

My vision narrowed, darkness at the edges threatening to smother me. My chest heaved and tears pricked my eyes but I fought to keep them back. I wouldn't cry in front of Crane.

I. Would. Not.

But Father, please.

Then a shadow fell over us and Pine was shoved out of the way. Before I could fully register what was happening, enormous, glaring Sir West had grabbed me. He picked me up and cradled me in his arms as he stormed across the garden back into the Divine Residence.

"Sir West, the High Priestess decreed—" someone yelled.

Fear shivered down my spine that Sir West would stop. The High Priestess had commanded this gathering after all. But Sir West didn't slow down, didn't even glance back at the men.

I clutched at the top of his metal chest plate, needing something to hold onto, and squeezed my eyes shut, unable to stop myself from shaking.

Had Crane actually been in the garden or had I just imagined it? And why had Sir West rescued me? He'd agreed not to tell the High Priestess about my mating marks, but I thought that decision had been more because Lord Rider and the others had threatened him.

But pulling me out of the forced social engagement went against the High Priestess's wishes. Did that mean I could actually trust him?

Or was this all part of Her Brilliance's game to get me to fall in love with Sir West.

I glanced up at him, but he wore the same, hard, grim expression he always did, giving no hint as to what he felt or thought.

Whatever it was, he'd gotten me out of there, and I was grateful.

CHAPTER 31
Talon

I HURRIED through the corridors of the Divine Residence toward the High Priestess's private garden, my shadow writhing beneath my skin, jerking and twisting. Leaving Sage alone with those suitors hadn't been the plan, but refusing a direct command from the High Priestess wasn't an option. Not if I wanted to keep breathing.

When we'd first entered the throne room, I'd given Sage a look, tried to reassure her with it, but I hadn't known what the High Priestess wanted and I didn't want Sage to not be on guard.

Except from Sage's confused and hurt expression, I hadn't accomplished anything with that look. And while I'd really wanted to stay by her side, I knew that would have drawn more attention to her, something I wanted to avoid at all costs.

It was bad enough I'd been so distracted by having

sex with her that I didn't think about standing back when we'd arrived at the throne room doors.

That would have been the smart thing to do.

My shadow heaved with fury and frustration, intensifying my own feelings of inadequacy. What a fucking mess. I'd wanted to reassure her, but I also wanted to keep her at a distance. If I didn't figure my shit out, she was only going to get more confused and hurt, and she didn't deserve that.

Up until a few moments ago when I'd broken down and fucked her in that alcove, everything had been going to plan. I'd been overly flirtatious and she'd reacted exactly as I'd expected with hesitation and wariness. She hadn't wanted me and certainly didn't trust me.

But tonight, she'd been desperate and she hadn't been able to hide it. Hell, even the slightly too-wide-eyed look from West had confirmed something was wrong, and I hadn't been able to let her face the High Priestess like that.

Except helping her, seeing her that vulnerable with someone she wasn't sure she trusted, twisted my insides. She was sweet and shy, the kind of woman Quill would love with his whole heart, the kind of woman I'd wanted to protect before I'd become infected with my shadow.

But I couldn't. Not now, not ever. And it had torn me to shreds to see the pain in her expression when she realized I couldn't give her the emotional support she needed.

All I was good for was a good fuck. And if her

mating marks hadn't been put to sleep I wouldn't have even been good for that.

As it was, Her Brilliance had been pleased when I'd arrived with Sage.

Sure, the High Priestess had acted as if she were pleasantly surprised, but she'd made her pleasure *quite* clear after she'd dismissed Sage to face what I was sure the shy woman thought of as a gauntlet of men.

The whole "*interview*" after Sage had left had been a drama staged for her courtiers, but I couldn't figure out to what end.

She'd been angry Rider and Quill hadn't obeyed her command to focus on the Black Guard and had been attending to Sage in her suite — and I wasn't sure if she'd gotten that information from West or not.

She'd also played up my accompanying Sage, implying that I was finally interested in mating, giving no indication — of course — that she'd ordered me to court the new redhaired arrival. That news would go through court like wildfire, and I had no doubt Sage would soon face the ire of the other women still looking for their mates.

And I still hadn't found a way out of the High Priestess's command to mate her. I'd hunted for a loophole, a weakness in her wording, a plan that would get me out of forming a bond, but the best I had was to ensure Sage didn't like me and we never bonded.

Except that solution, in the eyes of Her Brilliance, would look like failure, and I feared I wasn't useful enough to survive her disappointment.

My shadow twisted and jerked, desperate to escape the High Priestess's trap as I was, desperate to protect her from that horrible woman's machinations.

I reached the archway leading to the High Priestess's private garden. Inside were nine men, some standing, some pacing, some sitting, all displaying frustrated, angry body language. But no West and no Sage.

I pulled back into the corridor, out of sight. Where the hell were they?

"—barely said anything. Just sat there," one of the men huffed.

"She was too quiet," another voice cut in. "I want a woman who'll actually talk to me, not one who looks ready to run."

"She wasn't just quiet," a third man said. "She was shaking. Pale. Could barely catch her breath. She was nervous."

"I thought she might faint," someone else added.

"Nervous?" Someone else barked a hard laugh. "I don't have time for a woman who can't handle a simple conversation."

"She was attacked a few days ago," another voice replied, quieter than the others. "In the Sacred Grove. Give her some time."

"Attacked or not, she could've at least tried," the insulted voice shot back. "We're here because Her Brilliance invited us. The least she could do is make an effort."

"Right. We were hand chosen by Her Brilliance." That voice was tight and angry. "We deserve respect."

"Especially from that knight," another voice huffed. "He just grabbed her and ran. Didn't even listen to us."

"He can't just ignore us like that!"

"Apparently he can," the quiet voice said. "He was assigned to protect her."

"But from us?"

A pause, then someone sighed

"I'm done. She's not worth the effort."

"Her Brilliance seems to think she is."

"Which is the only reason I'm still interested," another replied. "If the High Priestess wants her matched, there must be something valuable about her."

My shadow heaved at that, swirling and sharp inside me. What a bunch of idiots. Women were rare. They should have been bending over backwards to figure Sage out and give her what she needed. But half of them were insulted she hadn't played the typical female flirtatious games for them, and the other half were only interested because the High Priestess was.

Sage had been attacked in the Sacred Grove. And instead of letting her recover in her own time, the High Priestess had thrown her into a room full of strangers.

Shaking, pale, and couldn't breathe was more than just nerves. I'd seen her nervous. Hell, she was always nervous with me, but not to the point of fainting. That was panic, and clearly West had thought the same if he'd pulled her out of there. He knew as well as everyone else that the High Priestess wanted Sage mated, and he wasn't a man who overreacted.

Something had happened, and I needed to figure out what.

I pushed off the wall and hurried back through the corridors of the Divine Residence and up the stairs to the guest suites, my shadow's anger bleeding black across my vision. If West had carried Sage out of that garden, he'd have taken her back to the suite. That was the most secure place for her in the Divine Residence.

I knocked on the suite door and waited.

Was she even all right? West wouldn't have let her get hurt, but that didn't mean something hadn't happened. Something had rattled her enough to make her leave that garden in West's arms.

Heavy footsteps approached, then the door cracked open.

My shadow wrenched tight, suddenly becoming as small as possible, and my vision cleared. West filled the doorway, his sapphire eyes hard, the muscles in his jaw tight, and his posture giving no indication that he was going to let me in.

"I know something happened," I said, keeping my voice low so no one could overhear us.

West's eyes narrowed, clearly considering if he should let me in or not, then he stepped back and opened the door wider.

I stepped past him into the suite, and he closed the door behind me with a soft click, the lock sliding into place. My gaze jumped to Sage who stood close to the hearth, the fire stoked and blazing. She shivered as if she couldn't get warm, her complexion pale, and her arms wrapped tight around herself.

My shadow twisted tighter, furious and desperate to not reveal itself. What the hell had happened?

Whatever it was, it hadn't been nerves. She was terrified.

"What happened?" I asked.

My first instinct was to charm away that fear. A few flirtatious comments, maybe tease her into forgetting whatever had upset her. It worked with most women. But I already knew Sage wasn't like most women. And after having sex with her in the alcove, seeing her vulnerable and desperate, she'd probably think I was an insensitive asshole or panic further, and I didn't want either.

"Nothing." Her gaze dropped to the floor. "It was nothing."

Yeah, that was the posture of someone who believed it was nothing. Just more proof that Sage wasn't like most women. If she were, she'd have told me exactly what the problem was and demanded I fix it... although perhaps a typical woman wouldn't have been upset in the first place.

Except Sage wasn't just upset. She was scared.

And both my shadow and I needed to know why.

But she wasn't going to tell me. I'd screwed that up with my plan to flirt with her and make her wary of me. Now she didn't trust me and I was the only one here who could help.

And I *needed* to help.

Goddess, how did I convince her? She trusted me enough to ease her desire spike, maybe it was in how I phrased it.

"If you can't tell me, then tell West. I'll leave if you want me to."

Her gaze lifted, met mine, and held it. Like she was weighing my words, deciding if I meant them or if this was just another game. The fire crackled loudly in the silence, a log shifting and sending sparks up the chimney. West still stood by the door, arms crossed, his face carved from stone. Then something shifted in Sage's expression. Not quite surrender. More like... resigned acceptance, and she drew in a breath.

"I thought I saw Crane."

"Crane?"

Blinding rage roared through me, my shadow's overwhelming fury that she hadn't been safe, stealing my breath, and sending fear freezing through my veins that it was going to reveal itself to her.

Shadow shit. I was going to lose control. I had to stop reacting and start thinking.

But the core of its essence coiled even tighter, its anger still bleeding through, but its writhing smoke fully contained.

"You saw Crane?" I forced out, my voice dark and raw.

I thought he'd be smart, leave the fae realm and avoid the Garden. The Order of the Sacred Grove was searching for him so why would he risk sneaking into the High Priestess's private garden?

If Sage had seen him then he'd gotten close, too close. The edges of the High Priestess's private garden fell into deep shadows at night, but that garden wasn't that large. That was a serious risk he'd taken which meant he had more plans for Sage or whoever was the mastermind behind her attack wasn't finished with her — because neither of us had ruled out someone else above Crane being responsible for targeting Sage.

"But I don't know if he was really there or if I just..." Her voice dropped lower. "Or if I just..." She looked away, her jaw tight. Like she thought I wouldn't believe her. Like admitting she might have been wrong was somehow worse than staying quiet.

I turned to West. "Did you see him?"

"No."

Sage shrank in on herself, her arms tightening around her body as her gaze dropped back to the floor.

Did she think she'd imagined him? That her fear had played tricks on her? And now she was convincing herself she was wrong, that she hadn't seen him.

It didn't matter if she had or not. The safest assumption for her, was that Crane had been there.

"Just because West didn't see him, doesn't mean he wasn't there." I glanced at West. "The garden was crowded, right? You couldn't see everyone?"

West's gaze shifted to Sage. "The garden *was* crowded."

I raised my eyebrows at him, willing him to not be an asshole and reassure her that we didn't think she was crazy and we believed her.

"There were shadows near the other entrance," he said, his voice gruff.

She pursed her lips, but I couldn't tell if she was trying to keep in words or tears or both. It was as if she couldn't bring herself to trust that West or I would believe her.

Which only made me wonder more who she was and where she came from.

"And I believe you. I believe you saw him and we should take precautions," I said.

"Agreed," West grunted.

"Except I can't just hide in my suite." A stray tear broke loose, trailing down her cheek, and she furiously brushed it away with the back of her hand. "The High Priestess won't let me."

She wasn't wrong. The High Priestess wanted to see Sage mated, whether for the good of the fae, Sage, or just to entertain herself. She would parade Sage in front of those men again and she wouldn't be able to say no.

My shadow's rage turned frigid, chilling my insides so deeply I feared the next time I breathed out everyone would be able to see my breath.

"I'm going to have to figure out a way to see Her Brilliance's suitors without being surrounded." She drew in a breath, her shoulders relaxing a bit. "I don't want so many of them in the room at once. And I don't want them to touch me."

Pride warmed through some of my shadow's fury. She knew she couldn't refuse the High Priestess out right, but she might be able to control the situation.

Except even if she controlled when, where, and how, it still didn't completely protect her. Not if Crane was still skulking around.

CHAPTER 32

Ash

THE SEVENTH BELL RANG, announcing dinner time, and with a collection of groans — the loudest from the inexperienced novices — all of the novices lowered their practice blades.

Rider called an end to training and jerked his chin toward the bags of rocks sitting at the base of the boulders marking the running trail.

"Extra lap time," he barked, and Sawyer marched across the practice yard with Tyon trailing a few paces behind him.

The pudgy human, a former chef's assistant, kept his distance from the boy, his round face carefully blank, but I knew if anyone was going to befriend Sawyer, it was Tyon.

They were closest not necessarily in age — especially since Sawyer was barely sixteen, if he was even sixteen — but in situation. With his limited physical abilities and his soft physique, Tyon was almost as much of an outcast as Sawyer.

If Sawyer hadn't completely fucked up by coming through the ring after dark, Mikel and his group would likely be picking on Tyon instead.

"You only have a bell to clean up and eat before class," Talon called out with a quick clap, earning another collection of groans from the tired novices. "Only two more to go then lieu time."

That perked the novices up enough to pick up their pace in handing back their practice sword and hurrying toward the Tower to clean up before dinner and class, all except Mikel, Durand, Hamelin, and Bramwell.

Sure, they handed back their weapons, but they held back, and from the tension in Durand's jaw and the hardness in Mikel's eyes as they watched Sawyer heft the bag of rocks on his shoulders, I knew they were pissed.

I handed my practice weapon to Quill, my friend's gaze sliding over me and confirming I hadn't fucked up and still maintained my cover. He shoved the sword in a canvas bag and hefted it over his shoulder before elbowing Talon who was staring at the mouth of the running trail.

Talon jerked and a hint of shadow flickered in his eyes, just a whisper of darkness through those pearlescent orbs that I doubted anyone who didn't know better would notice.

But I knew better, and the fact he'd been stuck staring after the boy would only make Sawyer's life more difficult.

With luck, Mikel and Durand hadn't noticed.

I turned back to the group. Mikel's eyes were narrowed and a muscle in Durand's jaw ticked.

Just great. Sawyer had the worst luck of anyone I'd ever met.

It was bad enough they still thought Sawyer was getting special treatment — even though he wasn't — but the fact that Talon was still obviously enthralled only made them angrier.

Best to keep on their good side.

With my expression flat, I strolled over. Ambrose didn't really care about Sawyer Herstind and what the Lord Commander and the Captains of the Black Guard did, but he was part of the special group of human novices who had military experience prior to becoming guardsmen, and he did agree that the boy needed to learn respect and become a better swordsman.

Which was the stupidest thing I'd ever heard. The boy didn't go around lording it over others and he was already a damn fine swordsman — better than Bramwell and soon to be better than Hamelin.

Behind me, Rider grunted. I glanced at him out of the corner of my eye. He glared at us, his expression hard, then he turned and stormed toward the Tower. Talon and Quill hurried after him leaving me with the four assholes who thought they knew best.

Well, really it was two assholes and two followers who weren't bothered by the assholes' plans.

Mikel huffed, his attention behind me, following Rider, Talon, and Quill. He rolled one shoulder, working out the stiffness from training, but his gaze stayed fixed on the retreating figures.

"I can't believe all we can do now is ignore him," he hissed, his voice low. "It's been days and he doesn't even look bothered."

"No shit," Durand growled. "Talon's probably fucking him every night. He's not being isolated at all."

My chest tightened. I didn't like the implication of that. To men like Durand, there was no other explanation for why Sawyer wasn't suffering. The isolation should have broken the boy, the silence crushing him.

But Sawyer was stronger than that. He'd proven that when he'd taken Mikel's ambushes and turned them into personal training, and when he'd finally had enough, he'd threatened us and broken my nose.

But in Durand's mind, someone had to be propping him up. And if Sawyer was getting fucked by the fae captain, that meant he was still getting special treatment, something he didn't deserve even if Durand thought it was disgusting.

Talon was going to lose his shit when he heard about this.

"Yeah," I drawled, "because Sawyer looks like someone who's taking it every night."

"It's not Talon," Hamelin said, his voice low and his gaze darting around the now-empty practice yard. "It's Kit's team."

The practice yard was quiet now, the other novices long gone. A breeze kicked up dust where dozens of boots had churned the ground during drills.

"But half of them are in the infirmary," Bramwell added.

"Which means the runt sits with them whenever he likes." Mikel's jaw tightened and he adjusted his sword belt, a restless motion. "Wouldn't surprise me if that's why he was given infirmary duty this rotation."

I resisted the urge to roll my eyes. Sawyer had been given infirmary duty because it wasn't nearly as strenuous as mucking the stables and he'd demonstrated that he was smart. Rider had hoped learning basic healing would make it easier for the other novices to warm up to him.

So much for that, since Reef had relegated him to cleaning duties and ignored him. Or at least ignored him until the moron had taken him and Garridan beyond the Tower walls and nearly killed everyone.

"And we can't do a damn thing about it," Durand spat, his shoulders bunched.

Every day Sawyer didn't break, Durand got worse. It was clear, the man needed to see suffering, and I didn't want to think about what he'd do if he didn't get it.

I shifted my weight, positioning myself so I could watch all four of them. The sweat from training had cooled on my skin, leaving a chill that had nothing to do with the evening air.

"And now Payne won't shut up about the hound attack," Durand added, his tone venomous. "Says he didn't even hesitate to fight back. Like that makes him one of us. Maybe he's letting Payne fuck him, too. We already know the big guy likes them smaller and skinnier than him."

Oh, Great Goddess! Was he that stupid? Did he really think that kind of attitude would work with the rest of the Guard? If he wasn't careful, one of the fae guardsmen was going to gut him and no one was going to care.

"Reef is saying it, too," Bramwell added. "He says Saw— *the runt* moved like he knew what he was doing and that he saved Garridan." Bramwell's voice stayed even, but he kept his gaze on Mikel, not even glancing at Durand. "The hounds would've torn him apart if Sawyer hadn't gotten him into the wagon."

"You mean Payne says *that,*" Durand sneered, his face turning red.

"No, Reef. I heard him in the line at breakfast telling the guardsman in front of him about what happened. And we know Reef didn't like Sawyer," Bramwell pressed. "We heard him complaining about him at lunch the other day."

"So what?" Durand replied, his hand falling to the hilt of his sword. "He didn't kill any of them. Real guardsmen kill shadows. They don't hide in covered wagons."

Which meant Durand had been paying attention to the rumors swirling around.

Mikel nodded as if Durand had made a significant point. "Surviving's not the same as doing your job."

Except someone had needed to protect the injured merchant and the frozen novice. Getting them into the defensible position of the covered wagon had been smart and ensured that Sawyer, with his inexperience, wasn't getting in Payne or Reef's way.

"And it doesn't change what he is." Mikel's voice was flat, but his gaze tracked the trail where Sawyer had disappeared. "Or how he got here."

"What's the point anymore?" Hamelin asked, his voice quiet, his attention on the ground in front of his feet. "He had Garridan's back when it mattered."

Durand whipped toward him, closing the distance between them in two sharp steps. "Are you fucking serious?"

Hamelin held up his hands, taking a step back. "I'm just saying—"

"You're saying we should back off?" Durand snarled. "Let the runt think he won?"

"Maybe…" Bramwell shifted his weight, his attention sliding to the Tower like he was calculating how fast he could get there.

"Maybe what?" Durand spun on him, and Bramwell flinched. "You going soft?"

Durand glared at Bramwell, daring him to answer, and Bramwell swallowed hard.

"Quill and Talon still treat him like a child," Mikel said. "But he's a guardsman now. He needs to be a man. We back off now and we're saying he earned it. That we were wrong."

"And we weren't wrong," Durand growled. "He's still the same arrogant shit who waltzed in after dark thinking he's better than us."

"So what do we do?" Hamelin asked. He crossed his arms, tucking his hands in his armpits, and hunching his shoulders. "Keep ignoring him forever? It's not working."

"We try something that works," Durand said.

His hands flexed, the violence in his posture barely contained. I could see what he wanted: Sawyer alone in the Tower, cornered in the barracks, or bleeding in the practice yard.

But then his gaze jumped to the Tower, and the knuckles of the hand gripping his sword hilt turned white.

Rider had made himself clear. Sawyer was untouchable. The best they could do was hit him harder than necessary during sparring and ignore him... at least I prayed that's what they were thinking.

Fuck, I didn't have time for this. I couldn't spend my nights keeping an eye on Sawyer's door to ensure one of these idiots didn't try something.

"I don't know about you," I said, "but I'd rather not piss off the Lord Commander. He can grow fucking claws from his fingers."

Bramwell shuddered at that and Hamelin paled.

Durand sneered but jerked his attention away from the Tower. He wasn't stupid. He knew how dangerous Rider was, but just because he was being more cautious, didn't mean he wasn't still a danger to the boy.

"Fine," Mikel said. "We wait."

"For what?" Hamelin asked.

Mikel's mouth pressed into a tight line, then he huffed and marched toward the pasture gate.

Bramwell's shoulders sagged, the tension bleeding

out of him. He glanced at Hamelin who also looked relieved, and together they followed Mikel.

With a snarl, Durand jerked away from glaring at the running trail and hurried to catch up.

That, I didn't like. Rider might have scared the others enough to stop taking direct action against Sawyer, but it was only a matter of time before Durand snapped.

I hung back, letting them pull ahead, trying not to look over my shoulder at the boulders. Sawyer was still somewhere on the trail, running with the bag of rocks, and I prayed he wouldn't crest the final hill until after Durand was well out of sight.

Durand was getting more dangerous, not less, and it would be best if he and Sawyer were never alone together.

My insides churned. I couldn't do anything until Durand did. All I could do was warn Rider, Talon, and Quill where the novice's mind was at, and that wasn't a conversation I wanted to have. Not with how fucked up his attitude was toward the fae-touched.

Hell, the man had almost assaulted Sawyer, and the best I'd managed to do was shove the boy away.

Goddess be damned. I was useless.

I was useless at protecting Sawyer and I was useless at protecting Sage.

All of my contacts, in the White Tower and in the fae realm itself, still had nothing. The knife was still missing, and the bracelet artifact was still a mystery, and the fact that Yarrow remembered a similar artifact found with other artifacts didn't mean anything if it couldn't be proven.

It didn't matter how good Yarrow's memory was. Someone had to prove the bracelet was connected to the other case for that to be a lead, but since the case details were missing it was a dead end. I couldn't even figure out what that other case was about.

Or at least it was a dead end for me. My contacts in the Order, because they weren't particularly high level, had already tried and failed to glean any new information about it. Yarrow, if it bothered him enough, could use all the resources of the Order to hunt down what had happened to the case files. But he had other problems to deal with, like where the hell Crane and the other men who escaped were.

And if I wasn't so useless, I'd be able to help with that.

But Crane, Thunder, Addax, and that last remaining man who'd attacked Sage in the sacred chamber had disappeared and no one knew where they were—

Well, that wasn't true. According to Rider, that last remaining man we hadn't been able to identify had stood outside the door to Sage's suite in the Divine Residence.

Nausea churned in my stomach at the thought as I crossed the bailey and pushed through the door to the right wing where the main barracks were.

My real room was a small, individual suite on the second floor of the left wing among the suites for the guardsmen with set positions like the blacksmith, the chamberlain, and the head cook as well as the suites for the elite hunting teams.

But since I was just a regular novice at the moment, I needed to climb to the third floor and head to the end of the hall of the right wing.

Fuck, I was tired and something deep in my chest that I didn't want to examine too closely ached.

Except I knew what it was that ached. It was that thing inside me that yearned to connect with a fae woman. I had a taste of it when I'd had sex with Sage and now I wanted more.

Except I couldn't have more.

I passed a group of guardsmen on the second landing, nodded at them, but didn't pause to talk. I needed to pull my shit together, and I couldn't do that while directing conversation to gather information regarding all the things I needed information about.

Picking up my pace, I hurried up to the third floor, through the door, and down the hall to my assigned room. It was small, like all guardsmen's rooms, with a narrow cot along one wall, a trunk at its foot, and a washbasin and pump on a stand, but it was private.

With a sigh, I shut the door behind me and let the mask slip.

Goddess, I wanted her again, wanted to be near her, to touch her, to hold her in my arms and never let go.

I shouldn't have let myself be with her, shouldn't have tormented myself with the knowledge that she was everything I craved, because she wasn't mine. She'd never be mine.

Except that small voice of hope, the one I was certain had died decades ago, whispered in my soul: maybe. Maybe she could be mine, maybe the Goddess would bind our souls together.

Sage hadn't been terrified of me, and she hadn't turned away in disgust when she'd seen me.

But how much of that had been because her mating marks were overwhelming her with desire and how much of that was the real Sage?

It was foolish to think it was anything other than her marks. They'd been unnaturally inflamed with power, turning her into a desperate sobbing mess. She would have craved a release from anyone, and me thinking otherwise was fucking idiotic.

Now that Her Brilliance had her eye on Sage, she'd never approve of me courting her. I didn't have a chance and I shouldn't want one.

I was smarter than this.

I was the Black Guard's spymaster, and I didn't let my feelings get in the way of doing what needed to be done.

And what needed to be done was to stand in the shadows, like I always did. My job was to protect her, my brothers-in-arms, and the fae realm. What I wanted and how I felt didn't matter. It couldn't.

CHAPTER 33

Sage

With a groan, I opened my eyes, rolled onto my back, and stared up at the ceiling in my suite in the Divine Residence.

Back again.

Because going to sleep and staying asleep would be too easy.

I could only pray Talon or whoever had arranged the one-on-one audiences with the High Priestess's prospective suitors and I wasn't going to be stuck, surrounded by all those men again.

A shiver of fear and disgust rolled through me at the memory of being touched and crowded and Crane staring at me from across the garden.

I squeezed my eyes shut and fought to control my breathing before the panic I'd managed to ignore all day overwhelmed me.

I could do this.

I had no choice but to do this. I certainly couldn't risk the High Priestess's ire.

Father, one day my thoughts would be different. One day I'd be in a situation I wanted to be in, and I wouldn't be afraid and forcing myself to get through just one more day, one more hour, one more minute.

But shadows, the suitor audiences were bad enough. I didn't want to attend Her Brilliance's ball, didn't want to be vulnerable like that. I could say something wrong, screw up etiquette... be taken by Crane again.

Someone cleared their throat and a shadow fell over me.

I opened my eyes and stared up into West's glowering face.

"The individual audiences you've requested have been arranged," Sir West rumbled. "Your first suitor is Cobalt. Whenever you're ready."

I bit back a huff. Whenever I was ready, hunh? *And if I'm never ready?*

The enormous knight's sapphire eyes narrowed as if he could read my mind. Was that his magic? Was mind reading even a magical ability a fae could have?

If it was, then he already knew everything: that I wasn't really fae, that I shouldn't be in the Garden, that I had no idea what I was doing.

Surely he'd have informed the High Priestess about me by now.

Lord Rider, Talon, and Lord Quill might have convinced him to keep my sleeping mating marks a secret, but I doubt he'd keep the fact that I was human to himself.

No, he couldn't possibly read my mind, but I couldn't discount the possibility that someone else could, not until I talked with Zinnia and confirmed whether it was a likelihood or not.

"My lady," Sir West said, reaching out as if I were waiting for his assistance to sit up and stand and not just lying on the floor trying to pull my shit together.

"Of course." I took his offered hand and rose, my gaze jumping to the couch to see who was on chaperone duty tonight. If the guys were sticking to their schedule, it should have been Talon, but he'd switched with Lord Rider last night so...

The couch was empty, and I swept my gaze around the room until it landed on Lord Rider standing at the open balcony doors looking out onto the gardens below.

The softly glowing light from the flowering vines framed his bulky form. He wasn't as big as Sir West, but he was bigger than Talon, Lord Quill, and Ash, and he looked exactly as he always did, whether he was in the Garden or the Gray.

He wore his black leather armor and his shoulder-length black hair half pulled back in a topknot. The only thing different between the Garden and the Gray was that here he wasn't wearing his sword and carried only half of his usual arsenal of daggers.

He turned to face me, the light and shadow from the vines playing over his ruggedly handsome features.

Father, why did fae men have to be so breathtakingly beautiful?

Heat rushed across my cheeks and down my neck. If he and Talon hadn't switched last night, I would have been forced to have sex with him.

And now I couldn't stop wondering what sex with Lord Rider would have been like. Would it have been strangely impersonal like it had been with Talon, like he was performing a necessary service? Or would he have released all that feral energy?

And why did my body ache in all the right places at that thought?

Jeez. What was wrong with me? I'd taken care of my desire last night, and I'd been fine all day. I hadn't even experienced a flicker of need when I met Talon's gaze across the practice yard that afternoon.

I. Was. Fine.

Really.

"West tells me he asked the High Priestess to give you the Lesser Rose Room for your audiences," Lord Rider said. "It's a good choice. Only a few windows and a single entrance."

Right. The audiences with the prospective suitors I didn't want and couldn't outright avoid.

I dragged my attention away from him and forced myself into the bedroom, struggling to find my determination and reminding myself that I could get through this.

With a sigh, I contemplated all the different colored dresses in the wardrobe but couldn't bring myself to choose something other than the first red dress I'd decided on.

I really needed to talk with Zinnia again and get another lesson on the fae court and their behavior.

My thoughts jumped to Cobalt and how polished and predatory he'd been. He'd found too many excuses to brush against me and touch me, and I prayed that however the room was set up, I'd be able to keep a table between us.

Maybe I should wear the black dress and match Lord Rider. Surely that would signal to Cobalt that I wasn't interested in him. Although given fae society, subtly indicating my interest in one man probably wouldn't be a deterrent since fae woman took multiple mates.

Once changed — into the red dress — I returned to the sitting room and we left the suite.

With Rider at my side and West behind us, we headed down the stairs and into the opulent halls of the Divine Residence. The wide, impressive majesty quickly gave way to narrower, less ornate passages, making me even more grateful for West's choice of room.

Here was hoping the suitors would think the High Priestess had seen my request for individual audiences with her chosen suitors as a slight and given me a simpler room in a less lavish part of the Divine Residence as a punishment. Maybe if they believed that, they'd lose interest in me.

We turned a corner and, halfway down, Cobalt stood from where he sat on a cushioned wooden bench. His expression flashed from annoyed impatience to surprise when he spotted Rider beside me — most likely not expecting me to arrive with another prospective suitor on my arm. But his surprise quickly turned to an overly pleasant smile that made my skin crawl.

West moved past us and opened the parlor door.

I opened my mouth to apologize for making Cobalt wait, but a low growl rumbled from Rider, barely audible, startling me.

Except he wasn't looking at Cobalt. He was looking inside the parlor.

I followed his gaze to the man sitting inside on a cushioned, highbacked chair placed against the far wall and facing the doorway. In front of him was a table and another cushioned chair with a lower back that wasn't nearly as fancy.

This was the setup I'd asked for, a secure seat where no one could sneak up behind me, positioned so I could see the only entrance with a table in front as a barrier discouraging potential suitors from sitting too close or reaching out and touching me.

Except this man wasn't a suitor. I didn't recognize him from the intimate garden audience last night, and even if I did, it wasn't supposed to be his turn, and he shouldn't have entered the room before me.

Like all fae, he was breathtakingly beautiful, almost as beautiful as Talon, with long light brown hair braided back at his temples and light green eyes that tracked my every movement. He wore the same green and gold doublet that Onyx, a Knight Captain in the Order of the

Sacred Grove, had worn, so I could only assume he was a knight as well.

I tried to surreptitiously glance at Sir West to see if he had a reaction to the man, but, as usual, West continued to glower, and I couldn't figure out if it was his usual glower or a more serious one.

I stopped at the threshold, not sure what to do, my gaze traveling around the parlor taking in its plush furniture arranged in a conversation area by the hearth, thick rugs softening the stone floor, and two wide windows open to the evening breeze carrying the scent of the flowering vines climbing the walls outside.

The man rose and gave me a deep bow that was more formal than any bow anyone had ever given me, instantly putting me on edge.

"I'm Sir Yarrow, Investigator Captain of the Order of the Sacred Grove, assigned to give you justice." His smile was warm, but it didn't reach his eyes, and he stared at my face a moment longer than what was comfortable before trailing down to my covered neck as if looking for my mating marks. "It's a privilege to finally meet you, Lady Sage."

"Sir Yarrow," I said, dipping my head.

I wasn't sure if I owed him the courtesy of a curtsey, but I refused to bend a knee for him. Everything about him put me on guard.

He was obviously ambushing me. Taking over the room I'd requested for my audiences and waiting for me as if I'd been summoned while sitting in the most powerful position in the parlor.

Clearly that was a move meant to intimidate me. I'd seen my stepfather, Edred, do similar things when meeting with other noble lords. Hell, he'd even sat on his throne in the great hall when Lord Quill had arrived to announce Sawyer's name had been drawn in the lottery.

It had also been days since Wells and Crane and those other men had attacked me in the sacred pool. Making me wait to interview me — if this was in fact an interview — was also another way to assert dominance.

I'd assumed telling Sir Onyx what had happened had been enough for the investigation or that, despite the High Priestess suggesting I was important to her, she didn't care enough to apprehend the men who'd gotten away. With those men still on the loose, she had an excuse to keep me close and under her control and spirit linked to Sir West.

"I hope you'll forgive me for borrowing your parlor," he said, gesturing to the chair across from him. "I had no idea when you'd manifest, so I figured this was the best place to wait."

I crossed the room and took the offered chair, demurely clasping my hands together in my lap. I could have been difficult and sat on one of the two couches by the hearth, but that left room for Sir Yarrow to sit beside me, and as much as I didn't want the prospective suitors touching me, I wanted Yarrow touching me even less.

Behind me, Rider closed the door, leaving Cobalt outside, and moved to stand behind my chair on the right while West took position on my left, as if they, too, didn't trust Yarrow's intentions.

Yarrow's gaze flickered to them, his gaze staying on Lord Rider just a moment too long. His smile remained firmly in place, but it hardened at the edges, making me wonder if he didn't like Rider, if there was some kind of competition between them, or if me having a second escort somehow ruined Yarrow's plans.

"I hope you're recovering well," he said as he sat back down.

"I'm fine." I tried to keep my skepticism from my voice, but I doubted he was actually interested in my well-being.

"I can only imagine how frightening your ordeal must have been." He frowned, but there was something off in his expression, like he was playing a part, not actually sympathizing with me. "A new arrival, marks only just awakened, and to have something so terrible happen..."

I fought to keep my expression neutral. He was trying to get a reaction, and I wasn't sure why, which only made me more determined not to give him one.

"I want you to know," he continued, "that I consider your safety my personal priority. I won't rest until all those responsible have been brought to justice."

The words came out smooth and practiced, making me wonder if he'd rehearsed them before ambushing me.

"Thank you," I murmured, not sure what else I was supposed to say.

Yarrow smiled, pleased, expectant, like he was waiting for me to say something more — to gush with gratitude, maybe, or to pour out the details of my attack without being asked.

When I didn't, his hand moved to adjust his cuff, tugging the fabric with a small, quick movement before settling back against the arm of his chair.

"In order to protect you properly," he said, "I need to understand your situation."

My pulse lurched. I had a bad feeling about this.

CHAPTER 34

Sage

Sir Yarrow asked when my marks first awakened, how many times I'd manifested before the attack, and I answered carefully, giving him as little as I could. Recently. Only a handful of times.

He nodded, his gaze softening. "So you're new, still learning your way around the Garden. That must have made it all the more disorienting."

His smile widened slightly, like I'd confirmed something he'd already suspected, and he looked overly pleased with himself.

"Where in the realm are you?" he asked, his tone gentle, almost casual, like it was just another routine question. "So I know where to send word if I need to reach you outside the Garden, during waking hours."

My chest tightened. "There's no need to trouble yourself with messages to anyone but Sir West." I glanced up at West, praying that both men would accept that I wanted Sir Yarrow to contact me through my unwanted knight guardian.

Yarrow's eyes narrowed ever so slightly and his lips pursed. Something flickered across his expression, but I couldn't tell what.

"Of course," he purred. "But just in case, I may need to contact your family?"

"Sir West is a more accessible contact. My family is... quite busy."

Yarrow's gaze dropped to my clasped hands, lingering on my lap for a too-long, uncomfortable moment before rising back up.

"I understand," he said. "Some women prefer their privacy. I... *respect* that."

But the slight emphasis on "respect" didn't make the word sound respectful. It sounded like he wanted to say something else, like he was storing the information away, adding it to a list that I was sure I wasn't going to like.

"I've spoken with the men who rescued you." Yarrow's gaze flickered back up to Rider. "Their accounts were helpful, though of course they arrived after much of the... unpleasantness... had already occurred."

And by unpleasantness he meant being hung under a waterfall, slapped and groped and cut in Wells' disgusting plan to force me to mate bond with him and the seven other men in the sacred chamber.

My stomach twisted tight, and I fought to keep my breathing steady. I didn't want to think about how close I'd gotten to being trapped — or how close I'd gotten to being murdered if the spell hadn't worked because I was actually human.

"Your rescuers described finding you in the sacred pool chamber and the fight that followed." His tone stayed light, like we were discussing the weather instead of a bunch of men attacking a single woman.

He leaned back in his chair, watching me with an intensity that made my insides squirm.

"A terrible thing to endure," he tutted.

My pulse pounded. He was watching me too closely, waiting for something. I just didn't know what.

"The witnesses reported you killed Wells," he said. "With his own dagger."

Somewhere beyond the parlor walls, voices, muffled and distant, passed in the corridor.

I nodded, not trusting my voice, my throat tight with the memory of my anger and desperation and fear that I'd be trapped with a man like Wells for the rest of my life.

"What a terrible thing to endure," Yarrow said again, shaking his head in false sympathy — it had to be false, nothing about him felt genuine. "I want to assure you that the Order is working diligently. Addax has already been apprehended."

His chin lifted slightly as he said it and Rider huffed.

"Addax was injured," Rider said. "I practically handed him to you on a platter."

I bit the inside of my cheek and a vein in Sir Yarrow's temple twitched.

"And what about Crane?" Rider asked. "He and Wells were the leaders."

Yarrow's gaze shifted to him, and his smile stayed in place, but his fingers went still against the arm of his chair. "The investigation is ongoing. Crane will be found."

"He was in the Garden last night." Rider didn't raise his voice, but something in his tone made a chill run down my spine. "Didn't West inform the Order?"

Sir West grunted and I could only assume it was a confirmation since I wasn't going to look away from Sir Yarrow to confirm.

The muscles in Yarrow's jaw flexed, and he brushed something— probably an imaginary something since I couldn't see any lint — from his knee. "The Order is aware."

"And?" Rider growled.

The fire crackled in the hearth, and a log shifted, sending sparks up the chimney.

I waited for more, for reassurance, for a plan, for some indication that Sir Yarrow and the Order of the Sacred Grove was actually doing something to find the men who'd attacked me.

"It would help," Yarrow said after an uncomfortable drawn-out moment, "if you could provide more details about your encounter with Wells and Crane before the attack. Had you spoken with them previously? Did they approach you in the Garden?"

So this was going to be his angle. He was going to suggest I encouraged them, that I invited the attack.

"They'd talked to me a couple of times," I said, fighting to keep my voice even. "But I told them I wasn't interested."

"And did you tell anyone about those encounters?" he asked. "Report them to anyone?"

I swallowed, my throat tightening. I should have said something. It was my responsibility, somehow, and lying and using Rider's name as a shield hadn't been the right way to go about it.

"No," I forced out.

Yarrow made a small sound. It wasn't quite agreement, but it wasn't quite skepticism, either. A sound that he made deliberately to keep me unbalanced.

He asked again about my family — not where they lived, since he'd already heard my deflection on that — but whether anyone in the Garden knew me. Whether I had kin who manifested here. Friends. Anyone who might vouch for me.

Except I had no one. No one to confirm my story or say who I was or where I came from.

"I'm new to the Garden..." I trailed off, not sure what else to say that wouldn't make things worse.

Yarrow's eyebrows lifted. "No one? You manifested with your marks fully awakened, drawing the attention of every unmated male in the Garden. Surely someone who knows you must have noticed."

"I've been disoriented. I preferred to keep to myself."

Outside, the wind stirred the flowering vines against the open windows, sending soft light and shadows dancing across the floor.

Yarrow smoothed his sleeve again. "Of course. I didn't mean to pry. I only want to understand your situation."

But something in his expression had sharpened. I'd given him exactly what he wanted, and I was sure that it was more proof that something about me wasn't right.

He glanced at his hands, perfectly manicured, not calloused and scarred like Lord Rider's, Talon's, or even Lord Quill's. Yarrow wasn't a swordsman. He didn't fight to survive. He played games just like the High Priestess.

"I find it admirable how composed you are," he said, almost casually, like he was making polite conversation. "Most women in your situation would be... I don't know. Distraught? Desperate for protection? Eager to share everything that might help?"

I opened my mouth, but nothing came out.

I wanted to yell at him that I'd tell him everything if I believed it would do any good, that I didn't trust him and I didn't trust that he wasn't working in the High Priestess's interests.

Back in Herstind March, I'd been nothing, free labor, chattel to buy influence — and not particularly precious chattel at that. No man would support me, find me justice, or care what happened to me unless it directly affected them. And everything within me said Sir Yarrow and the High Priestess were exactly like those human men.

Behind me, Rider shifted his weight, his hard-soled boots shushing against the thick rug.

"I suppose some women are simply more... self-contained," Yarrow continued, and his smile was back, but his eyes stayed cold. "Private. It's a quality I admire. Truly."

I'd seen that smile before — on men in Erellod when my mother needed a new husband. They thought they were being charming, but their intentions were obvious and disgusting.

"Enough of this," Rider snapped. "She's answered your questions. If you have concerns about the investigation, ask them plainly."

Yarrow's attention shifted to Rider, and the pleasant mask held, but barely. "I'm simply trying to understand Lady Sage's situation. Surely you appreciate the importance of thoroughness."

"What I appreciate is that she was attacked in a chamber that should have been guarded by the Order," Rider snarled.

"Why are you so defensive, Rider?" Yarrow asked, his eyes narrowed.

"Why is Crane still free?" Rider spat back.

Yarrow stiffened. "The Order is conducting a thorough investigation. Perhaps if Lady Sage were more forthcoming—"

Rider growled, the sound low and threatening. "She's told you everything she knows."

"She's told me very little," Yarrow hissed, all pretenses vanishing, his expression dark and suspicious. "Where do you come from? Why does no one in the Garden know you? Why won't you answer the most basic questions about yourself?"

Because I don't trust you.

I couldn't stop manifesting and I couldn't get trapped in the Garden. I just couldn't.

Yarrow jumped to his feet and glared down at me. "Why?"

"Enough," Rider barked. "This interview is over."

He stepped forward as West yanked back my chair. They moved as if they'd fought together for years, their actions quick and coordinated with Lord Rider stepping between me and Yarrow, and Sir West grabbing my arm and pulling me to my feet.

I was halfway across the room before I fully realized what was happening.

"This isn't finished," Yarrow snapped, the cold, sharp tone of his voice making my stomach churn.

Rider threw open the door and we rushed into the hall. Cobalt jumped to his feet, the action making my thoughts jerk. He'd sat on the bench and waited?

His expression flashed from expectation to confusion when I didn't pause. I barely gave him a glance. I couldn't deal with him right now. I could barely breathe.

Yarrow knew. He *had* to know that I wasn't who I was supposed to be, that I was human.

Except that was impossible. There was no way he'd be able to figure that out.

Lord Rider was right behind me, close enough that I could hear his breathing, rough and fast, and Sir West still gripped my elbow, his touch firm, almost painful.

They had sensed it, too. They had to have. They

knew Yarrow had figured out something about me and they'd defended me.

It didn't make any sense. They didn't know me, and as far as I understood fae culture, Yarrow was the law.

Why couldn't I just go to sleep and stay asleep? Why did I keep manifesting where I didn't belong?

CHAPTER 35

Sage

THREE DAYS LATER, I lay in my narrow, slightly lumpy bed in the Black Tower, listening to the men in the hall hurrying down to breakfast or the bathhouse in the Tower's basement to start their day.

Last night's suitor audience had been awful. He hadn't stopped talking about himself as if his life as Lord Treasurer for Her Brilliance was worthy of a minstrel's tale. And while his title sounded impressive, the details of his employment were all dry ledgers and financial audits, and I'd prayed even before we'd gotten to the halfway mark of the meeting that I'd stop manifesting and my spirit would return to my body.

That had only been marginally better than the night before with Cobalt. He'd been angry that Sir Yarrow had taken his original day — despite my meeting with Yarrow being anything but pleasant or planned or anything else.

Cobalt had insisted on sitting on the couch in front

of the hearth, not taking the hint when I'd sat in the highbacked chair against the far wall.

My insides had twisted tighter and tighter as the night went on, with everything inside me screaming that I needed to be polite, needed to appease him. Any human man would have been furious. Edred would have stormed over, hauled me from the chair, and dragged me back to the couch.

But it wasn't the human realm, and Zinnia had assured me I could stand my ground. So, I'd gritted my teeth and refused to move, making for a strange, awkward audience that I prayed frustrated Cobalt enough for him to give up on me.

I only had seven more suitors to meet with and then—

I had no idea what. I doubted the High Priestess would just give up on me. She was too interested in playing her games, and I was trapped because Crane and the three— well, I guessed now it was the other two men who'd escaped Lords Rider, Talon, Quill, and Ash since Sir Yarrow had said he'd captured Addax were still out there.

Father. It wouldn't surprise me if the High Priestess insisted I continue these audiences and meet with her prospective suitors multiple times.

And then there was the ball happening tonight. The thought sent a cold shiver down my spine. At least with these private audiences, I only had to face one man at a time with Rider, Talon, or Quill and Sir West watching over me. At the ball, I'd be surrounded by the entire court — every unmated male who thought they had a chance, every courtier curious about the newcomer, and Father forbid, Crane lurking in some shadow, watching, waiting. If he'd been bold enough to appear at my private suitor audience from a few days ago, what would stop him from attending a crowded ball where he could blend into the masses?

The ball would be the worst. Standing in some grand ballroom, exposed, with nowhere to run and every eye on me.

It didn't matter that I was sure Lords Rider, Quill, and Talon would all be there. I didn't want to keep playing her games.

But I didn't have a choice, not until I figured out how to stop manifesting in the Garden.

I rubbed my face and groaned. I was tired of just surviving, playing along with the High Priestess, keeping my head down and doing my work as a guardsman. It was just like my life before Sawyer and I fled Herstind March. It was endless, exhausting, and frustrating.

Except it wasn't.

As much as I'd been keeping my head down, grateful that the other guardsmen had decided I was more or less invisible, I kind of liked life in the Black Tower.

Sure, at times it was hard work, but I wasn't constantly afraid like I'd been after Edred had become my stepfather. And if I didn't think too hard about the kind of trouble Sawyer could get into by himself as he fled the Five Great Kingdoms and trusted the Great Father to keep him safe — or thought too hard about the fact that everything would eventually come tumbling down because someone would discover my secret — things were actually better than they were before. A lot better.

And with yesterday being the last day of my second rotation, today was officially my first of two lieu days.

I felt great... if I didn't think too hard about the fact that I was going to have to face the High Priestess's entire court by the evening.

Except, I had no idea what I was going to do. I couldn't catch up on sleep since I couldn't risk returning to the Garden, and I didn't want to join the other novices in Lehyrst. That was still too risky.

While the other novices might have decided my new punishment was to ignore me, I didn't want to push my luck and make them think I was doing something I didn't deserve. And leaving the Gray was definitely something I didn't deserve.

With a sigh, I got up, wiped myself down using the pump and basin in my room, and headed to the great hall for breakfast. After breakfast, I'd visit Kit and Payne in the infirmary. They'd at least be happy to see me.

My steps faltered. Kit wasn't in the infirmary anymore. The day before yesterday, he'd been moved back to his suite to finish recovering. The worst of his injuries had healed enough that Reef decided he no longer needed to take up a bed in the infirmary.

Kit's arm was still in a splint, and he wouldn't be back on duty anytime soon, but he no longer needed to be monitored. He'd mentioned just before he and Payne had left the infirmary, that there was a chance he'd get back into the field sooner than expected, but it all depended on what happened between then and the end of Reef's rotation — which was in four more days.

If Reef had an excess of magic when his shift ended, he could use it to heal his broken arm. But that was only if there wasn't anyone in more serious condition in the infirmary. The worst cases were healed first.

And all of that meant, I didn't know if I could or should visit Kit in his suite. I was sure he'd say it wasn't a problem, but I doubted the other guardsmen would appreciate me wandering around the left wing where all the elite suites were. Especially if my only goal was to go unnoticed for as long as possible.

With a sigh, I finished taking the stairs down to the great hall, stood in line for breakfast and was pointedly ignored by everyone while I made a sandwich, pocketed an orange, and returned to my room.

The hall outside my door was now quiet, and the weight of the silence pressed around me, making me acutely aware that I was surrounded by men but completely alone.

I shoved that thought aside, pocketed my orange rinds, and headed outside to dispose of them in the manure pile outside the Tower walls.

It was a bit of a walk, and it wasn't necessary to go all the way out there, but I didn't have anything else to do. I didn't have anyone to spar with, no one to chat with, no duty to do. I supposed I could run the trail, but my body was still a little sore from two rotations of physical training that I wasn't used to, and I figured I should probably give my muscles time to rest and recover for whatever the next rotation brought.

As I walked, my thoughts wandered from wondering what my chore for the next rotation would be, to if I could survive the upcoming ball, to what I'd do with my free evenings now that the basic classes on the Gray and the shadows were done — depending, of course, on the outcome tonight.

A part of me felt those lessons weren't enough. Ten days for the duration of a single bell for lessons didn't seem adequate. Sure, there were only a few categories of shadows and all we really needed was to know what to watch out for — like poisonous quills — or how to kill them.

More than half of us were only ever going to be regular guardsmen, which meant we did daytime patrols around the Tower and between the Tower and the gate, manned the walls, and ensured the Tower continued to function properly. We didn't need to know all the intricacies about shadow behaviors and habits.

And while I appreciated that the lessons were short and didn't extend beyond a single rotation, since I always found it difficult to sit still for extended periods of time, I felt like I was missing details.

Which, as I'd already learned with my catastrophic entrance into the Gray, could be a serious problem.

If I'd known that the sun set earlier in the Gray— Hell, if I'd known I shouldn't have entered the Gray at night, everything would have been different. I might not have been instantly despised by the other guardsmen.

I wasn't going to be caught unaware again if I could help it, and since I couldn't just ask all the questions I wanted to ask because there wasn't anyone around and because I didn't want to draw attention to myself, my best bet was to return to the library and see what I could find.

CHAPTER 36

Sage

HOURS LATER, I sat at the small study table across from the two chairs where Tyon and I did our first reading lesson, a book open in front of me and four others piled to the side, their leather spines cracked and faded. No one had been in the library when I'd entered and started randomly searching for anything of interest, and no one had entered while I'd sat here reading.

Dust motes drifted through the soft light emanating from the fae lights scattered through the room and the pale gray light coming from the skylight above, and the scent of old paper and worn leather filled my nose with every breath, making it twitch.

I didn't enjoy libraries, not like Sawyer did, but I did recognize the necessity for information, and I was more than willing to force myself to sit still long enough to learn what I needed to. Especially since this was information I couldn't just ask anyone about.

Sure, maybe Lord Quill might have information

about the things I needed to know, but I didn't want to bother him, and if I had, I doubt I'd have found the current book I was reading. Hell, from their location and the amount of dust covering them, I doubted anyone knew about the books I'd discovered.

I wasn't even sure why I'd wandered into that particular corner and then thought of looking at the bottom shelf. Well... actually I did. I just wasn't sure I wanted to acknowledge it.

I'd gotten a *feeling*.

It wasn't an actual vision or a sense of dread like I'd gotten before. It was just a sense that it was logical to search the library from the beginning and that bottom shelf in that far corner was somehow "the beginning."

And right there, tucked into a corner, were five books, all on fae-touched humans — the kind with magic, not the kind that were men attracted to men.

The first two books looked like philosophical theory on fae-touched humans: their possible connection to the fae, and why and how they had magic.

I skimmed the first couple pages of each of those books and they looked drier than dust. Something Sawyer would have loved and spent all day reading.

The next book, however, was more like a journal written over four hundred years ago by a scholar who, in his words, wrote "scholarly observations about particular cases." He'd interviewed fae-touched humans and gathered eye-witness testimony about the humans and their abilities.

The first three-quarters had been fascinating with

fae-touched humans who demonstrated magical abilities as strong as, sometimes stronger than, a fae's. He even interviewed and recorded information about a human sorcerer who could manipulate raw magical power to imitate almost any fae ability — as opposed to the other fae-touched humans who only possessed a single ability.

I finished reading about a man with the ability to summon fire, who singlehandedly held Zumar's pass in the Grimmar Mountains in the north of the Kingdom of Irialas for five days, holding off a monstrous horde until help could arrive.

The fourth bell rang, reminding me that I should probably get up and eat lunch, but I flipped the page instead, curious who the next fae-touched human would be.

Turi of the Stone Touch: freed slave from Helialonde.

I stared at the swirling, ornamented text — obviously a carefully made translation from the original fae language. Turi was a woman's name.

Up until now, all of the fae-touched humans mentioned in the book were men, and I didn't know if that meant mostly men had magical abilities or if no one had cared to pay any attention to the women who'd been gifted with magic.

I leaned closer, my elbows pressing against the worn wood of the table.

Turi, who yes, indeed, was a woman, had lived in the Kingdom of Helialonde a hundred and fifty years before the Shadow Gate opened... so about six hundred and fifty years ago.

She'd been a slave to the king of Helialonde, with a magical ability called Petrifying Touch that could turn any living thing to stone.

I shuddered at the thought. I couldn't imagine discovering I had that ability. My ability first manifested as a sense of unease and knowing. She had most likely accidentally turned something, hopefully a plant or bug or something and not a human, to stone.

Father, I couldn't imagine how terrifying that must have been.

And yet, from the scholar's account, Turi could control her ability. It wasn't random, not like my magic, and it didn't threaten her sanity.

Which of course then begged the question, why had she remained a slave? Her magic was powerful enough that she could escape her situation, flee to a different kingdom and hide what she could do.

The account told how Turi's magic manifested when she was a child, younger than even Sawyer was now, and how the king of Helialonde had used her to threaten his nobles into compliance and execute his dissenters. Turi was convinced she needed to comply to protect her family.

And six hundred and fifty years later in another lifetime that could have been me. If Edred had discovered my magic, what would I have agreed to in order to protect Sawyer?

I huffed a bitter laugh.

I'd have agreed to anything. My current situation was proof enough.

I turned the page, read the next paragraph, blinked, and read it again.

Turi was discovered by the scholar because she'd started manifesting in the Garden. There'd been rumors about the King of Helialonde's executioner's horrifying magic, but no one had known that executioner was a woman until she'd arrived in the Garden confused and afraid.

The scholar wrote that her ability to manifest her spirit form in the Garden had to be a second magical ability since prior to her appearance no fae-touched human, male or female, had ever manifested in the Garden. As well, no fae-touched human had ever been able to physically enter the Garden, just like any other human.

My pulse picked up. The book was over four hundred years old. Had other humans been able to enter the Garden since?

Perhaps my appearance there, while rare, wasn't an impossibility like I'd originally believed. Perhaps there wasn't something wrong with me.

The text theorized that the sheer strength of her magical ability gave her the strength to manifest her spirit. Her power was so potent that the magical spark in her soul was closer to that of a fae's than a human's.

Was that how I was doing it? My visions had been growing stronger and more frequent. Did that mean the spark in my soul was strong enough to defy the laws of nature?

Except I'd already read an account of a fae-touched human sorcerer who hadn't manifested in the Garden, and surely a sorcerer was more powerful than someone with a single ability.

Of course, that didn't necessarily mean the sorcerer hadn't been able to manifest in the Garden, only that he hadn't done so.

I turned back to the book. When Turi manifested, the scholar described that she had pale, partially formed mating marks that glowed with power even though she was clearly human with rounded ears and plain brown eyes.

Hunh. So even she'd had mating marks.

Except when I manifested, I looked like a fae woman, and my marks were fully formed. My ears were also pointed, my hair a deeper red, more like a fae hair color, and my eyes jewel toned.

Still. I had evidence that a human could manifest in the Garden, even if I manifested slightly differently than Turi.

The scholar went on to say that despite being human and despite the partial marks, fae men had been drawn to her, and she'd fallen in love with two of them. Those two men had eventually rescued her from slavery, saving both her and her family, and brought her to the fae realm where she was able to physically enter the Garden.

My throat tightened and I sat back in the hard wooden chair.

What would it be like to have someone care for you so much that they'd risk the ire of a king to save you?

Those men could have started a war between the fae and human realms, and they'd still saved her.

The thought caught in my chest, sharp and unwelcome. Would Ash save me if I told him the truth? Father, I wanted him to. But I doubted any of the other men would.

I wasn't sure why Rider, Talon, and Quill were protecting me, even though I was grateful they were, but I doubted they'd go to the trouble of saving both me and Sawyer. Especially when it became clear I'd been lying to them from the beginning about everything.

And really, it didn't matter.

I couldn't risk Sawyer's life by revealing myself. Not to anyone. Not until I knew he'd had enough time to escape the Five Great Kingdoms.

According to the scholar, Turi's marks had never fully formed. And although a few did eventually change color, she never created mating bonds with her men, even though she loved them and they loved her, and they never mated again after she'd lived out her short human lifespan. The scholar concluded that despite Turi demonstrating fae-like abilities in manifesting and even presenting with mating marks that glowed with an albeit weak power, a human never had the possibility of forming a Goddess-blessed mating bond.

At least that was good news.

I mean it wasn't good news for poor Turi and her mates who'd probably spent centuries mourning her. But it sounded like even if the power in my mating marks reawakened, I wouldn't be able to form a bond.

Or at least form a bond in a natural way. What Wells and Crane and those other men had tried to do had been unnatural, and the bond, even if it looked natural, couldn't have been.

So, as long as I didn't let some crazy man magically force a bond on me, I was safe. No matter what happened in the Garden, even if I had another desire spike or my marks reawakened, I couldn't accidentally end up bonded to anyone.

I closed my eyes and my heart ached to be in Ash's arms again. Talon and Quill had satisfied a need, and as much as I was attracted to them, desired them, maybe even craved them, I didn't feel the depth of comfort and safety I did with Ash.

Father, if I could resume what I had with Ash, I could get through anything. With Ash, at least my nights would be safe.

My body and soul ached for that, a soft place to be, a place where I could have desire and grief and all of my emotions without having to look over my shoulder or pretend to be someone I wasn't.

I needed to make that happen. No, it *would* happen. Once Crane was captured, I'd be free to move around the Garden like I wanted again. I had to. I'd only survived two rotations in the Gray and manifesting in the Garden, and I had at least three — better if it was four — more rotations to go to ensure Sawyer's safety.

A lot had already happened, and I feared a lot more

still would. For all I knew Mikel and his friends were planning a big attack, or Crane was plotting some other way to force a bond on me.

If I had Ash—

"Sawyer?"

I jerked backward, my heart pounding, furious that I'd been so lost in thought I hadn't heard anyone approaching in the silent library.

Tyon stood at the end of the aisle, his warm brown eyes wide, a thin book clutched to his chest.

"Did you find... *the books*?" he asked, his voice dropping low, a blush staining his round cheeks.

What books—?

Ohhh.

When we'd first met in the library on our last lieu days, he'd thought I was looking for the dirty books.

My own cheeks heated. "No. I wanted to do more research into— Ah... shadows."

His eyes narrowed, as if he didn't believe me, then he shrugged and sat in the chair he'd sat in before for our reading lesson. "Do you mind if I sit here?"

"Not at all."

I glanced back at my book. I wasn't sure I wanted to continue reading. I'd learned a lot and my thoughts were already swirling, trying to make sense of everything I'd read.

"How about you show me the progress you've been making," I suggested as I stood and stretched.

Hopefully, helping Tyon for a few hours would help

me forget everything else, even if it was only for a little while.

CHAPTER 37
Quill

I MANIFESTED near the side door of the Divine Residence, where the stone walls gave way to a half-wooden archway draped in flowering vines. The soft glow of pink and white blooms traced the edges of the alcove, but inside, shadows pooled thick and dark. The night air carried the sweet scent of the blossoms, and I breathed it in, letting it settle in my lungs.

The ball was tonight, there were still three attackers at large, and Sage was going to be surrounded by strangers who wanted her for themselves — and I doubted all of the men in the High Priestess's courts had honest intentions.

The alcove, our new meeting spot where we met with Ash for updates on the novices, lay only a few feet away, and I stepped inside its gloom intending to wait for him.

But a figure moved from deeper within the shadows at the back of the secluded space, and Ash stepped forward. He angled the scarred side of his face away from the faint glow of the flowers that ringed the mouth of the alcove, the habit ingrained so deeply he probably didn't notice he did it anymore.

The lines around his unscarred eye were deeper than usual, and his jaw was tight. He looked exhausted, worn down, and I didn't know if it was just because he was juggling too many duties or if there was more going on... like being separated from Sage.

Sure, her mating marks had been put to sleep, but some of them had already turned green. Her soul had picked a mate, and Ash was the only one in the Garden she'd gotten close to.

It made sense that she'd bond with Ash, even if neither of them had realized it yet, and would explain why he looked so worn down. Being separated from your mate when the bond first formed could cause exhaustion and pain.

Except that was just a theory. I had no proof and now wasn't the time to bring it up. Sage would manifest soon, I'd promised her that I'd be at the ball with her, and I needed Ash's report on the novices to ensure things hadn't taken a turn for the worse.

"How are the novices?" I asked, my thoughts jumping to Sawyer.

The need to protect him, to find his sister, to take care of them both flared.

Damn it. I'd managed to hold it back all day, despite not being able to see him and ensure he was safe because it was a lieu day.

I needed to pull myself together and focus. I couldn't afford to be distracted and endanger Sage.

"Sawyer and Tyon stayed in the Tower. Everyone else went to Lehyrst." His expression darkened. "Durand hasn't tried anything. Yet. But it's just a matter of time. He was still complaining about the boy scoring points on him in sparring three days ago."

The urge to send my spirit back to my body swelled through me and I gritted my teeth.

He. Was. Fine.

Nothing was going to happen tonight.

Goddess, what was wrong with me? I barely knew the boy. I'd spent even less time with his sister. Why couldn't I stop thinking about them?

Focus.

"The ball is in the main ballroom," I forced out.

"Of course it is," Ash said with a huff. "Sage is her new toy. She wants to make the biggest statement possible."

Which was exactly the kind of game my mother liked to play.

I shifted my weight. "We don't know when Sage will manifest. She usually arrives anytime between now and an hour from now, but there's no guarantee she'll keep the same schedule."

Ash shrugged, unsurprised. "There never is."

"And what about Crane? Anything new?"

"Nothing," Ash said, his voice clipped. "Whatever Yarrow's doing, it isn't obvious. I'll have to break into his office again soon."

Which wasn't good. Crane, Thunder, and a mystery attacker were still out there, and we had proof with Rider catching the scent of the mystery attacker outside the suite to Sage's door that they were still interested in her.

"Are you... staying?" I wasn't sure how to ask if he was going to stay in the Garden while we all attended a ball with Sage that he couldn't attend or not.

"I can get into Her Brilliance's private gardens without anyone noticing," he said.

"The rose garden runs along the length of the main ballroom. The edge of the night-blooming garden has a small entrance from the back of the room," I mused, wondering which of the gardens would be the best one.

Ash would have better coverage in the night-blooming garden, but it would be easier to see inside the ballroom from the rose garden.

"The rose garden has better visibility." He gave a tight nod as if coming to a decision. "I'll watch from there."

He'd be close enough to watch her dancing with other men, maybe even close enough to hear her laughing if the patio doors were left open. But not close enough to touch her, to talk to her, to just be in her presence.

The injustice of it sat heavy in my chest. Ash had done nothing wrong except exist with scars he couldn't do anything about. And for that, he was banned from the Divine Residence, unwelcome in polite society, too ugly to exist among the beautiful.

My throat tightened. I understood his pain. We were

both looked on with disgust, both whispered about and stared at. He, because he'd gained his scars, and me because I lacked magic.

And, whether he acknowledged it or not, we were both yearning for someone and something we could never have. A mate, a connection, a soul-deep bond bestowed by the Goddess herself.

But at least Ash had a chance.

Once the danger with Crane was over, once the investigation was closed, he could find a way back to her. She wouldn't be trapped in the Divine Residence.

Even if my mother never gave up toying with her, Sage wasn't a prisoner. She and him could connect, develop love, and deepen the bond I suspected he'd already formed with her.

But for me—

The ache in my chest deepened, and I struggled to force all of my feelings, for myself, for Sage, and for Sawyer and his sister, as deep down as possible.

Feelings wouldn't get the job done.

I gave Ash a tight nod, gave his shoulder a reassuring squeeze, then forced myself out of the alcove.

I entered the Divine Residence through the narrow side door, the structure's opulence, even in this lesser-used hall, stretching before me.

With a thought, I changed my clothes from my usual doublet to a fancier, more detailed one and black pants made from a finer fabric. My clothing changed as I moved without impeding my movement or slowing me down like it would have if I hadn't been in my spirit form.

I climbed stairs, moved through wider corridors, and made my way up to the guest suites.

A few minutes later I stood outside the door to her suite and knocked.

West opened the door, his expression as grim and unreadable as always. He studied me for a moment, then stepped aside and let me enter.

Inside, Rider stood by the hearth, his shoulders squared and his jaw tight. Fur rippled over the back of his hands, a sure sign that his wolf was close to the surface, perhaps even fighting for control, something he was going to need to get a hold of before stepping into my mother's ballroom.

Talon lounged on the couch, appearing relaxed, almost disinterested, but I knew him intimately and could see the tension in his eyes and feel the whisper of allure bleeding past his control. Both of them wore fancier clothes than I knew they were comfortable with.

West closed the door behind me then moved to the center of the room where he always stood when waiting for Sage to manifest.

I'd arrived before her. Good.

I dropped onto the couch beside Talon and leaned into him, offering him comfort with my closeness. "Shall we review the plan?"

Talon's arms wrapped around me and he pulled me into his lap. Rider grunted, and West continued to glare.

"My mother will be furious if it looks like I'm

publicly courting her, so I'll head down early and keep close but won't interact with her."

Fur rippled higher up Rider's forearms. "I'll go down with you. I don't want anyone thinking I'm courting her, either."

I was pretty sure it was too late for that. The servants talked and without a doubt he'd been seen stomping up to her suite every third night since the High Priestess had taken an interest in her.

"You don't want anyone thinking you're courting her?" Talon rolled his eyes at him. "So you weren't glaring at all of her suitors during her private audiences?" His tone clear that even though he hadn't been there, he was certain he knew how Rider had behaved.

Rider's rumbling growl in reply didn't help his case.

Talon barked a bitter laugh. "Thank the fuck being the Lord Commander and a Captain of the Black Guard ensures us an invite to this ball. If we were anyone else, we'd be left in the cold right along with Ash."

His grip tightened around me, and he nuzzled his nose against the top of my head, breathing in my scent. He was trying to calm himself and also offer me comfort. But why?

Talon's fingers traced idle circles on my shoulder. "I *will* dance with her. One of us needs to look like we're courting her."

Ah, so that was why.

He'd already figured out there was no way we were going to convince Rider to look like he was courting Sage — even though Rider would have been the best choice out of the three of us given his shifter nature — but didn't want to upset me.

I wasn't quite sure why he thought I'd be upset. He knew I cared for him, but not to what extent, and I knew he needed to have sex with multiple lovers to keep his shadow controlled.

Except he hadn't taken a female lover since the shadow infection.

"I wish you'd be the only one to dance with her," Rider said. "It'd make our job that much easier."

"If you wanted to piss off Her Brilliance," Talon replied. "But this ball is to introduce her to all the eligible bachelors. She'll probably be pissed if Sage doesn't dance with half the room by the end of the night."

Rider huffed and turned to West. "The guard uses all the same hand signs as the Order. Are you familiar?"

West grunted.

Rider took that as a need to review them all just to ensure that The Order hadn't changed theirs.

Most of our guardsmen didn't know the discrete hand signs the Order used when protecting the High Priestess or significant dignitaries, but the Black Guard elite who protected the nobles in the Gold Tower did, and as the Lord Commander and Captains of the Black Guard we were all familiar with them.

West glowered at Rider the whole time, but I couldn't tell if it was West's usual glower or an *"I'm pissed at you for wasting my time but you outrank me"* glower.

Regardless, it made me feel better. If the worst

happened, West, with his soul link to Sage, was the only one who could find her.

Now here was hoping he'd actually use the hand signals if the worst occurred.

No. Here was hoping absolutely nothing happened tonight.

CHAPTER 38

Sage

I OPENED my eyes to find myself lying on the floor beside Sir West like I always did. Every damn night. Except this night my stomach was tight with nerves, and I'd seriously prayed while lying in my bed in the Black Tower that tonight could be the night Quill's meditation technique would keep me from manifesting in the Garden.

For a moment I just lay there, hating that I was back. I hadn't really expected it to help in only a few days — that and it wasn't supposed to help me with manifesting, it was supposed to help keep me sane from my magic. I'd just really hoped it would.

Especially tonight.

Because tonight was the High Priestess's ball.

The ball I'd been dreading since Her Brilliance had first announced it. The ball where I'd have to stand in a crowded room full of strangers — possibly dangerous strangers — with everyone staring at me, unable to hide.

But I couldn't refuse the most powerful woman in the fae realm.

Really, I didn't have the power to refuse anyone. I never had.

With a sigh, I pushed myself to a seated position and West, who'd been glaring down at me the entire time, offered me his hand.

His grip was firm and brief, letting me go the moment I was steady.

Which was fine. I didn't really want to hold hands with the man in the first place, even if he seemed ever-so-slightly softer in the last few days while I'd been suffering through my personal audiences with the High Priestess's handpicked suitors.

And I was probably just imagining that because the soul link ensured I couldn't escape him and it was impossible to escape.

I wrenched my gaze away from him and swept it over the room.

Lord Rider stood by the hearth, firelight catching on the silver streak in his black hair. His jaw was locked so tight I could see the muscle jumping beneath his skin, and fur rippled along the backs of his hands. He looked like he was bracing for a fight, not a party.

Talon was sprawled on the couch, looking too relaxed. But there was a subtle tension about him, a stillness, hinting that he wasn't as carefree as his posture suggested.

Beside him, pressed shoulder to shoulder as if he'd been leaning against Talon a moment ago, sat Lord Quill.

His gaze found mine and his expression softened, making my chest ache with a longing I didn't want to examine.

I couldn't afford feelings tonight. I needed to be ready to face all of the fae court, and I couldn't let myself be distracted by my confused, unwanted emotions about anything.

All three of them were dressed in finer clothes than they usually wore in the Garden. Rider in a fine black and silver doublet with only a single long dagger at his hip instead of his usual array of weapons, and Quill was in a finer green and gold doublet.

Talon was the most changed. He wore a two-toned silver doublet, instead of his usual gold. The doublet had a detailed silver embroidered vine swirling down the front and intricate silver clasps. He also had more braids in his long silver hair than usual, and his gold earring — the one that was adorned with tiny pearls, capped the tip of his delicately pointed ear, and looped through three holes pierced down the side — had been replaced with a silver version adorned with larger pearls.

They all looked like they were attending a fancy event, even if their expressions implied they weren't going to enjoy it.

Across from Quill and Talon, sitting in one of the highbacked chairs, was Zinnia. She wasn't dressed to attend a ball, wearing her usual blue healer's robes, and I frowned in confusion as she stood and offered me a warm smile.

"I'm here to help you prepare," she said. "Quill thought it might be a nice treat."

"Oh. Thank you."

I didn't know what else to say to that. I didn't want to prepare, but I was grateful Lord Quill had thought to get me help. I had no idea what I was supposed to wear or how I was supposed to style my hair.

Even if we'd been in the human realm, I wouldn't have known. My mother had passed before I was old enough to talk to her about such things.

After that, Edred had treated me like a servant so fancy clothes and fancy hairstyles were just a fantasy... not that I'd actually fantasized much about that. No, I'd been more interested in forbidden swordplay and becoming a Sayorian Swordmaiden.

"Come." She gestured toward the large fancy bedroom that I'd claimed as mine. "We've got work to do."

"Right."

I followed her, glancing back at the men as I crossed the room. Rider's silver gaze tracked my movement, Quill's expression was still soft, and Talon watched me without any expression at all, his stillness too deliberate to be natural. None of them looked away, and I couldn't tell if that made me feel safer or more exposed.

Safer.

It had to be safer. They didn't know me, didn't care for me, just wanted to protect me for some reason.

And really, I had nothing to worry about. I was just putting on a gown and going to a party. People did this all the time. Normal people. People who weren't terrified of crowded rooms and powerful High Priestesses and attackers who were still out there somewhere.

I could be that. I could pretend I was a normal girl in a normal situation.

If my parents hadn't died and if Edred hadn't become my stepfather, I would have gone to balls. I'd been a noblewoman before I'd given everything up to save Sawyer. What I was doing right now, should have been my life.

Zinnia moved to the wardrobe and opened its intricately carved doors. The gowns Lord Quill had arranged for me still hung inside, silks and gauze and lace in every color imaginable, more beautiful than anything I'd ever owned or even touched before my life had become this strange, impossible thing.

My thoughts jumped immediately to the question that had been nagging me since I'd first seen these dresses. What color should I wear?

In the human realm, wearing a specific color could signal allegiance or romantic interest. I'd been sticking to red, my manifestation color, since they'd arrived because it seemed like the safest choice and everyone had already seen me wearing it.

But there was only one red dress and compared to some of the other dresses, it wasn't particularly fancy. Would it be good enough for the ball? Or would the High Priestess be insulted that I was wearing the same thing I always wore?

"So," I said slowly, "in the human realm wearing colors to match your escorts or to match someone of a higher rank than you symbolizes an association, be it political or... romantic."

"Ah," Zinnia replied with a soft smile. "And you've been afraid to wear anything other than red for fear of someone getting the wrong idea?"

"How—?" I pressed my lips closed. Without a doubt everyone in the Garden was talking about me and everyone knew what I'd been wearing.

"Color doesn't carry any meaning in the fae realm. You can wear that emerald dress tonight and no one would assume you've chosen Quill." She chuckled softly. "If you spend all night dancing with him then that's a different story."

She gestured for me to follow her into the bathing room and then sit at a large vanity almost taking up one whole wall near the window.

I sat, and she began working on my hair, her fingers gentle as she gathered the strands.

"Is there anything else you've been worrying about?"

How I'd had sex with Talon, how I felt an attraction to Lord Quill and even Lord Rider, and how I ached for Ash.

But that wasn't what she was talking about, and I couldn't act on my feelings so there was no point in bringing them up.

"I know you're concerned about tonight," Zinnia said, her fingers twisting my hair into something elegant, "but you don't have to dance with anyone you don't want to. You can say no. To anyone." She twisted a braid into an artful curl and secured it with a pin. "You can walk away from any conversation that makes you uncomfortable. That's your right." She caught my gaze in the mirror. "I know things are different in the human realm, especially for you, but these men should be nervous about approaching you. Not the other way around. You're the one with the power tonight. You're the one who gets to choose."

"Of course," I murmured.

I wanted to believe her. Father, I wanted to, but the voice inside me, the one Edred had trained so well — and the one that understood that the High Priestess was very much like Edred in her need to get exactly what she wanted — said I couldn't refuse.

Engaging with Her Brilliance's court while she watched wasn't as simple as what I wanted, and I needed to be careful.

If I refused too many men tonight, the High Priestess would notice. If I didn't play the role she'd carved out for me, she would find a way to remind me of my place. I'd seen the way Edred operated. I recognized the tactics. The only difference was that Her Brilliance wielded them with more elegance.

My stomach tightened, and I swallowed against the pressure forming in my throat.

The High Priestess wanted me mated. She'd made that clear when she'd paraded me in front of her court the very first time, when she'd drawn attention to my magic despite not knowing what it was, and when she'd spirit-linked me to West without asking if I wanted it. I was useful to her for some reason, and useful people didn't get to say no.

My hands curled in my lap, nails pressing into my palms. My breath came too shallow, and I forced myself to take a deeper one, but it didn't help much.

I didn't want to do this.

"Sage?" Zinnia's hands stilled in my hair. "You've gone pale."

"I'm fine." I uncurled my fingers, but they trembled when I tried to smooth them over my skirt. "I'm fine."

Without a doubt, Her Brilliance's ballroom would be crowded with countless strangers, all of them watching me.

And any one of them could be working with Crane. He was still out there. Four of my attackers had escaped, and Yarrow had only found Addax, the injured one.

What if Crane had allies among the courtiers? He and Wells had managed to find six other men willing to force a mating bond on me. I didn't doubt that Crane would be able to easily find more.

The memory of his magic draining my strength slithered down my spine. My limbs had gone heavy, my vision spiraling into a dark tunnel. I'd been overwhelmed with the helplessness of knowing I couldn't fight back.

"Let's choose a dress," Zinnia said, and I was grateful she didn't push.

I stood and went back to the wardrobe in the bedroom, scanning the options with new eyes. Now that I knew color didn't matter, I could choose based on what actually mattered: hiding my marks and satisfying the High Priestess.

My gaze caught on a gold gown near the back. It was the fanciest one in the wardrobe, with delicate beading that caught every flicker of faelight and fabric that shimmered when it moved.

The back dipped dangerously low, the fabric along each side of the gap and at my waist resting in loose, voluminous folds, and deep slits ran up both sides, revealing more thigh than I was comfortable with, but it was flashy. Eye-catching.

Like all the other dresses Quill had brought me, it would cover all my mating marks, but it was also, certainly, the kind of dress the High Priestess would expect at her ball.

If I was going to be forced to play this game, I might as well look like I was playing it well.

I pulled it from the wardrobe. "This one."

Zinnia helped me into the gown, and the weight of the silky fabric settled over me, cool and heavy against my skin. I smoothed my hands down the front, feeling the intricate beading beneath my fingers.

Despite its coverage, I still felt naked.

Of course I'd probably feel naked in any of the dresses, so there was no point in changing my mind.

I turned to catch my reflection in the mirror, and for a moment I didn't recognize the woman staring back at me.

She looked like she belonged, with her jeweled eyes, and her delicately pointed ears. She looked like a fae courtier who'd spent her whole life preparing for nights like this, who knew all the rules and all the games and how to navigate them without getting destroyed.

She didn't look like the woman who'd cut off all her hair with her boring brown eyes and her too-severe features.

She looked beautiful. Polished.

And utterly foreign.

Zinnia placed a hand on my shoulder and met my gaze in the mirror.

"You look beautiful," she said. "Those men out there should be thanking the Goddess you're even willing to speak with them."

"Thank you, Zinnia. For everything."

"You'll be fine." She squeezed my shoulder gently. "You're stronger than you know."

I turned away from my reflection, and for a moment I just stood there, trying to steady myself.

It was just a ball. I had Lord Rider, Talon, and Lord Quill to protect me. If I believed I could trust Sir West, I had him as well.

I drew in a slow breath, let it out, then walked through the door back into the sitting room.

Every eye in the room turned to me, and I froze, uncertain about their reaction and uncomfortable with the attention.

"You look—" Rider growled. His gaze darkened with an almost feral heat, sending a shiver of unwanted need racing down my spine.

I yanked my attention away from him, sending it to Quill. Surely, he was safe to look at.

But he rose from the couch with an expression so tender and caring it made my breath catch and my chest ache with longing for the one thing I could never have: unconditional love.

A heartbeat later, a flicker of heated desire caressed my skin, drawing my gaze to Talon.

He looked unaffected and maybe he was. Maybe his shadow was just hungry and saw a potential easy target in me, and that's why a hint of his allure had caressed my skin.

Except if that was the case, why hadn't his shadow fed off me when we'd been forced to have sex? I'd seen its appearance but hadn't felt the chilling cold I'd expected.

I shoved that thought aside. I didn't want their reactions. I couldn't *afford* their reactions because I wasn't fae.

I wasn't who they thought I was, and no matter what I tried or wanted, I could never be what they wanted.

But even as I thought that, warmth spread through me that these men, these beautiful, stunning, powerful men looked at me with desire.

It reminded me of another man who'd looked at me with longing and heartache and a little bit of fear because he thought I'd reject him.

The warmth chilled, the moment turning sour, because the one man I wanted to see me as beautiful and feminine couldn't be here because of the High Priestess's cruelty.

An ache cut deep around my heart. I wanted him with me, wanted his warmth and safety and comfort, and like with everything else in my life, I had to make do without.

But soon. Soon Yarrow or Rider and the others would find Crane and bring him to justice. Soon I wouldn't be trapped in the Divine Residence and I'd be able to be with Ash.

I squared my shoulders and raised my chin. "I'm ready."

It was a complete lie. I wasn't ready, I didn't think I'd ever be ready, but I really didn't have a choice.

CHAPTER 39
Sage

The High Priestess's ballroom stole my breath the moment I stepped up to the wide, open double doorway.

Crystal chandeliers hung from a high ceiling covered in intricately stamped gold panels, their faelight fracturing into a thousand glittering shards across the marble floor. Gilded columns rose like sentinels along the walls, wrapped in flowering vines that pulsed with soft luminescence. The entire right side of the room was a bank of impossibly tall windows filled with fae glass so clear it might as well not have existed. Beyond them, a rose garden glowed with fae lanterns, the blooms swaying in a gentle breeze.

It was beautiful and terrifying.

Because everywhere I looked there were fae men.

Hundreds filled the space, their faces flawless, their clothes dripping with jewels and silks and lace.

"Lady Sage and Captain Talon of the Black Guard,"

the servant at the door called out, his voice carrying over the roar of voices and music.

In an instant, every head turned toward me, every eye fixed on me with that hungry, assessing look I'd seen too many times in the Garden.

My pulse jumped, and I locked the muscles in my legs before I could take a step back.

Stepping back would show fear. That, and stepping back would bump me into Sir West who stood directly behind me.

The urge to run squeezed my insides, and I scanned the room for doors or windows I might be able to slip through and escape.

There, three glass doors in the wall that I thought were just windows, one by the back of the room, and another discreet one beside the royal dais sitting against the lefthand wall where the High Priestess reigned over the event.

Except large, masculine bodies filled the space between me and any escape, and even if I could reach the doors, where would I go?

This was supposed to be a ball in my honor. I couldn't just run away.

"Sage," Talon murmured, while my thoughts and emotions spun out of control. "Dance with me."

"I—" Heat rushed across my cheeks. "I don't know how."

I'd barely begun dance lessons when my mother had passed, and I had no idea if human dances were the same as fae dances.

Shadow shit, why hadn't I thought about dancing? That's what happened at a ball, and it hadn't even occurred to me to ask for lessons, to prepare myself with what little time I had.

"If you're dancing, you won't get swarmed," he said, his voice low.

And with the High Priestess watching, she'd want me to perform. If I wasn't dancing, I'd have to be talking.

"Right. Let's dance."

I placed my fingers in his and let him lead me onto the floor. The musicians shifted into something slow and formal, and Talon pulled me into position, one hand still gripping mine, the other settling against the small of my back.

My pulse skipped, and the colors in his eyes swirled in that mesmerizing way that made it hard to look away.

I knew I shouldn't react to him, knew I couldn't afford the complications, but my body tried to lean closer anyway, drawn to him whether I wanted it or not.

Father, why was he so beautiful?

The chandelier light caught the sharp lines of his jaw, and the perfect slope of his cheekbones. I couldn't stop thinking about the alcove and him pushing inside me, his breath hot against my ear.

I wanted that again. Wanted him to look at me the way he had in that one unguarded second when his forehead had rested against mine and he'd seemed to forget himself and the distance he'd kept between us.

But despite me staring at him, *he* wasn't looking at me. He was looking past me, scanning the crowd over my shoulder, even as we started to move, and I realized his movements were too precise and practiced. His hand sat exactly where it was supposed to and he hadn't pulled me close.

This was a job for him and I needed to remember that.

I let my gaze wander as we twirled across the dance floor, his skill at leading me was so effortless my feet seemed to know where to go before I did.

Most of the dancers were men partnered with other men, their movements graceful and mesmerizing. There were a few women with skirts swirling around them like me, but not many.

Which was probably why the stunningly beautiful blond woman with the red eyes standing at the edge of the dance floor caught my attention.

Ember. I recognized her from the courtyard in the Garden when she'd stalked up to Talon and pointedly ignored Lord Quill who'd been sitting at the same table.

Ash had said Ember had been trying to mate with Talon since her marks appeared, and from the way her gaze burned with resentment as she glared at me and Talon dancing, it was clear I'd just made an enemy.

Which was ridiculous. Surely it was obvious that Talon wasn't interested in me. His posture, lack of eye contact, and lack of conversation while we danced said it all.

The music ended and Talon released me with a small bow, but before I could catch my breath, the Lord Treasurer stepped forward.

"Lady Sage." He extended his hand with a bright, hopeful smile. "Might I have the honor of the next dance?"

Every gaze in the room shifted toward us. Waiting. Watching to see what I would do.

Refusing would make a scene and likely draw the High Priestess's ire.

The musicians played the initial few chords for the next dance, and I dipped my gaze demurely to my feet.

I didn't want to dance with him, but I didn't want to get swarmed with men, either, and I had no idea what the safest response would be.

If I said yes, he'd know the moment we started dancing that I didn't have a clue. If I said no—

"I'm unfamiliar with these dances," I replied.

Please let it be logical that I might not know all these dances.

"Worry not," he said with a soft warm smile — with no hint that I'd said anything wrong or concerning. "I'm as skilled a dancer as Talon."

If he hadn't been so boring during our private audience — and if I'd indeed been looking for a mate — I might have considered him. He seemed kind.

"I'd be honored." I took his offered hand and he led me deeper onto the dance floor.

Kindness, however, was not enough to guide me through the unfamiliar steps without me stepping on his toes half a dozen times.

But it was enough for him to not let it interrupt his

steady, boring conversation about expected wheat yields in the coming fall.

I made what I hoped were appropriate sounds of interest at what I hoped were the right moments and, as boring as it was, wished it wouldn't end.

At least with—

What was his name? It started with a D? or was that an A?

At least with the Lord Treasurer, I knew he wouldn't get upset when I stepped on him or tripped over my own feet.

But the musicians played the final chords of the piece, and the Lord Treasurer bowed and thanked me for the dance.

Pine, one of the other handpicked suitors, pushed his way in front of me. He flashed a brilliant smile and swept me into the next dance without even asking permission.

The beat of the music picked up, and Pine deftly whirled me around the dance floor, chattering all the way.

"—and then she said the flowers were the wrong shade of pink, can you imagine? As if there's more than one shade of pink—"

"—so I said, if you're going to bring a gift, at least make sure it's not the same lute you gave her sister last spring, but did he listen—?"

"—and then he tried to claim he'd written the poem himself, but everyone knows it's from the Third Age, and honestly, did he think no one had read it before—"

Thankfully, his ability to lead me was almost as skilled as Talon's and I didn't step on his toes.

After Pine, I was passed to another suitor and then another and another, all who ended up with very sore toes and sour expressions despite being warned.

The musicians kept the tempo lively and my legs started to burn. Every spin left me more breathless than the last, the air in the ballroom felt thick, and sweat gathered at my temples and between my breasts.

But the men just kept coming, one dance ending and another suitor appearing in an endless line I couldn't escape.

I searched for West in the crowd but couldn't find him. Too many bodies, too many faces, and I was about to use my ability to refuse a request and to hell with what the High Priestess thought when turquoise eyes met mine.

Raven. Another of Her Brilliance's handpicked suitors.

CHAPTER 40
Sage

"LADY SAGE." Raven held out his hand, and I stared at his long fingers, fighting the urge to shiver in disgust and outright refuse him.

Would the High Priestess be furious if I turned him down?

Zinnia had assured me I could, but I couldn't stop the niggling doubt that refusing someone, especially someone who the High Priestess had picked herself, would be seen as a tremendous slight.

He raised an eyebrow in silent question, his hand inching closer to me.

Something about him put me on edge. He seemed familiar but I couldn't remember from where.

I glanced toward the dais. The High Priestess's pale gaze bore down on me.

Refusal would definitely be seen as a slight.

And I really didn't want to piss off the High Priestess.

"Of course." I took his hand, fighting the shiver of trepidation that raced down my spine.

I braced for wandering hands, for him to press too close like the others. But Raven guided me through the steps with a grace almost as easy as Talon's and his hands stayed where they belonged. He even kept a respectful distance between us, and some of the tension in my shoulders eased.

"Overwhelming, isn't it?" he said, his voice low. "All these people staring, all this attention. I imagine it's the last thing you wanted."

I frowned at him. "How did you—?"

"You moved to individual audiences immediately after that first group audience." His lips curled into a soft smile. "And I did a little research."

I didn't know if I liked the sound of that.

"After you fled, I was... concerned." He twirled me through a complicated series of steps, and I managed to avoid stepping on his toes. "I realized I didn't know anything about you and asked around."

His soft smile deepened and a warm understanding filled his gaze. "You're very shy, aren't you?"

Heat bled across my cheeks, but I wasn't sure if it was from a blush or just the exertion of dancing. "Groups of strangers make me uncomfortable."

"And you are currently surrounded by strangers," he said, his tone sympathetic.

Maybe I was wrong about him and he wasn't someone I should be wary of. He'd come across too aggressively during our initial meeting, but we hadn't had a chance for our private audience yet, and it looked like he'd taken the time to try to understand me.

The music carried us across the floor, the fast tempo stealing my breath, and when the final chords played my gold gown clung to my sweaty skin and I gasped for air.

A cool breeze swept over me from an open door, and I realized we were at the back of the ballroom, the windows here overlooking a magical garden with softly glowing flowers.

"You look overheated," Raven said, still beside me. His hand rested lightly on my arm from the dance.

"I am." I pressed a hand to my chest, willing my heart to slow. "I just need a moment."

"We could step outside," he offered, indicating the open door. "Just for a moment. The other suitors won't notice if we slip through here."

I hesitated. The garden was right there, just through the door. I could see people in it. If something went wrong, I could yell for help. And West could find me anywhere through our unwanted spirit link, no matter where I went in the Divine Residence. I was never truly out of his reach.

The cool air called to me, my body desperate for relief from the heat, and Raven had been kind.

"Just for a moment," I said.

We stepped out onto a narrow patio and down a few stone steps into the garden. The music faded behind us, and the air was even cooler here, carrying the sweet scent of flowers.

Raven huffed and released my arm.

The people milling about the garden vanished.

I blinked. The wandering trails with softly glowing flowers and bushes were empty.

What the—?

I whirled to face Raven, who now sneered at me, sending every instinct I had screaming that Raven was exactly who I'd first thought him to be.

I brushed my arm where he'd touched me and his sneer deepened.

"Just a little trick." He raised his hand in a flourish. "But I've got to be touching you."

Horror swept cold through my chest. He'd used his magic to make me think I was safe and surrounded by witnesses.

Now I was completely alone with him and he stood between me and the ballroom doors. I could try to run, but he was bigger and faster.

Would it be better to run deeper into the garden and try to lose him?

Except I had no idea what lay in the garden's shadows.

I could scream for help, but would anyone hear me over the music. Fighting him was out. I had no weapon, and I doubted I could hold my own in a fight without one. I was just too small and weak compared to a man.

No, I had to—

Something massive surged toward me from the side, and a hand clamped over my mouth and wrenched me backward. My heels scraped across stone, then grass, and a tall shrub swallowed my view of the ballroom.

No. No no no no.

I would. Not. Be. Taken. Again.

I clawed at the arm locked around my chest, bit down on the palm covering my mouth, and kicked backward.

I caught a shin and heard a harsh masculine grunt, but whoever it was, his grip didn't loosen.

Then two more figures stepped out from the deeper shadows. One I only sort of recognized from the sacred pool but knew from his turquoise eyes and similar face shape that he had to be Raven's brother — that was why Raven looked so familiar.

The other man sent fear racing through me. His white hair gleamed in the dim flower-light and his yellow eyes were fixed on me with that same hunger I remembered from the sacred pool and the alcove where he and Wells had grabbed me.

Crane.

My pulse stuttered into a rapid, desperate beat. If he touched me, it was all over. His magic had knocked me out before I'd had a chance to fight back last time.

"Lynx, watch the path. Make sure the others stop the knight," Crane said to the man I didn't recognize before turning to me and drawing a horribly familiar dagger from a sheath at his hip.

It was the same dagger Wells had used during the ritual to force a mating bond on me, the one with the swirling fae words carved over the blade.

Everything within me froze. Zinnia and Lord Aster had said there was a strange magic still inside me.

If it was the magic from Wells' ritual, I couldn't risk discovering that a single cut would awaken my marks and I'd start bonding with Crane.

And with Crane's magic, he could just incapacitate me and I wouldn't be able to fight back like I had with Wells.

Oh, Father! Please. Don't let this happen.

CHAPTER 41
Talon

I SHIFTED AWAY FROM EMBER, angling my body to see past her, pissed that she wouldn't leave me alone. I'd been trying to extricate myself for too long already, and she stood directly in front of me, blocking my view of the dance floor.

I stepped left. She mirrored the movement, her yellow mating marks glowing faintly as she leaned closer. Her fingers trailed up my arm, and her too-sweet perfume swirled around me in a suffocating cloud, choking me.

My shadow heaved with irritation, also pissed that Ember was getting in the way.

If this woman didn't move soon, I was going to cause a scene.

I scanned past her, trying to find that flash of gold silk that told me where Sage was. After our dance, I'd watched her get passed from one suitor to the next, the

Lord Treasurer first, then Pine, then a string of others whose names I hadn't bothered to learn.

I'd lost track of her somewhere in the endless parade of partners, my attention pulled away by Ember's relentless pursuit. Now the press of bodies and the roar of music conspired to hide Sage from view.

Ember touched my arm again. "You're not even listening to me."

I shifted slightly to the left. She shifted with me.

"I heard you."

Goddess, this woman!

I'd rejected her years ago, firmly and without ambiguity. The fact that she continued to pursue me despite that rejection, despite the utter lack of reciprocation, moved past flattering into insulting territory.

"Perhaps we could take a walk in the garden." Her voice dropped to something she probably thought was sultry. "The night-blooming flowers are lovely. And private."

My shadow heaved, sending cold fury spiking through my chest.

"Find a partner who actually wants your company." The words came out sharp, exactly as I intended — not that I expected her to take them to heart because it seemed she never did — but I didn't have time for this shit. I needed to confirm where Sage was, and nothing else mattered.

Ember's face flushed and her spine went rigid. She opened her mouth, and for a moment I thought she was going to argue with me, then she turned on her heel and stomped away.

Here was hoping it stuck this time.

But I doubted it. Ember was nothing if not persistent, and she was determined that I'd be her mate.

I swept my gaze over the dance floor, determined to find Sage.

Nothing. Nowhere. Every glimpse of gold or red belonged to someone else.

The shadow within me lurched and my pulse picked up.

There were too many bodies, too much movement. The swirl of silk and jewels blurred together as I looked from face to face, searching for red hair, for gold fabric, for anything. The music that had been pleasant was now discordant and jarring.

Where were the exits? Who had been near Sage last?

Around me, the crowd remained oblivious. Laughter rang out near the refreshment table, courtiers chatted and flirted, and dancers kept spinning and stepping across the floor as if nothing was wrong.

My gaze found Rider across the room. Fur covered the back of his hands and forearms, and his fingers were curled as if his claws were about to extend. A few feet away Quill slowly edged around the dance floor, his head turning this way and that as if looking for Sage as well, confirming what I already suspected.

Something was wrong.

Someone yelped, jerking my attention back to the dance floor. A couple had crashed into another couple, knocked aside by West's bulk as he cut a straight line through the dancers toward the garden doors.

He drove through the dancers like a battering ram, scattering couples in his wake, not caring about who he interrupted or bumped into. A woman shrieked as she stumbled out of his path, but he didn't acknowledge her or anyone. His attention stayed locked on the back of the ballroom.

Except I couldn't see Sage there, only—

Fuck.

My attention zeroed in on the garden door to the smaller, more intimate night-blooming garden.

Sage had to be outside.

And from West's determined stride and his darker than normal glower focused straight ahead, she had to be in trouble.

I hurried to follow after him, but I was coming from a different angle and had to twist and turn my way around the groups of people who'd stopped to stare at the massive knight since I wasn't nearly as bulky as him and couldn't just shoulder everyone aside.

Rider was already in motion, cutting across the dance floor with predatory determination along West's path while Quill cut around the edge of the dance floor from the other direction.

From the corner of my eye, I saw the High Priestess, in all her brilliant shining glory sit forward. Was she smiling? I didn't have time to figure that out, but Goddess help us all if she was.

West barreled through the garden door onto the

patio. Rider was close behind him with Quill on his heels and me a few steps farther back — because these damned courtiers didn't know when to get the fuck out of the way.

They were halfway down the stairs into the garden when half a dozen armed men stepped out from the garden's shadows.

Shit.

I leaped forward, clearing the doorway and manifesting a sword in my hand.

West didn't stop. He barreled through the men in front of him, blocking a sword strike to his head by drawing one of his two swords in a fast, fluid motion and letting another slam against his armored ribs.

He grunted from the impact but didn't slow down, storming down the path, leaving us behind, while the men still standing closed ranks, blocking Rider and Quill's way.

Behind me, more men stepped out of the ballroom, closing the door behind them — as if that would hide their actions from those in the ballroom despite the glass door and massive windows.

They, too, manifested weapons, and I turned to face them, inching closer to Quill and Rider so our backs were protected.

My shadow heaved under my skin, desperate to break free and attack.

"Ten of them," Rider growled.

"They must have forgotten what wc fight on a daily basis." I slid my gaze over them, sizing them up. Some looked dangerous, some nervous, none of them I recognized. "Ten men is nothing compared to a pack of hounds."

"You're just the Captain of the Gold Tower. When was the last time you even swung your sword?" a muscular, dangerous looking one said with a sneer.

"Come here and find out." I flashed a wicked smile and let my shadow lash out from my skin.

Right now, everyone looking at me would just think I was manipulating the shadows around me, fully in control of my magic.

And thank the Goddess for that, because I had no idea how I was going to hold my shadow back and fight these assholes at the same time.

One of the attackers, a man with a shaved head — an unusual style for a fae — raised his hand and shot a bolt of fire at Rider.

Rider dodged, rolling to the side, and the fire bolt slammed into a flowering trellis, with a flurry of sparks and the scent of burning wood.

Beside him, Quill blocked a swing from another attacker's sword, their blades crashing against each other. A second man thrust his hands forward, and a wall of air slammed into Quill's back, making him stumbled into a stone planter.

Crap, in a matter of seconds they'd broken our formation apart.

Through the windows and the closed glass door, I could see chaos in the ballroom, courtiers shoving past each other going in all directions, others moving to press against the glass to watch, while a few more stood stunned, staring at the sudden violence.

Two of the attackers came at me at once, both wielding swords. I blocked the first man's attack, dodged the second man's, and countered with a jab at the first man's gut.

He twisted out of the way, avoiding the strike, but stumbled in front of his friend, ruining his next attack.

My shadow clawed at my insides, its rage and fear for Sage burning cold and feeding my own fury. Its black whips swept over my arm and curled down my blade, and I yanked at the shadows around me from the plants, the planters, and our assailants to hide the fact that the shadow on my sword didn't come from anywhere.

Snarling, I swept my shadows around my first assailant, yanking him back, while parrying a strike from the second assailant with a different shadow before sliding my blade through the man's throat.

With a spray of blood and a gasping gurgle, the second assailant dropped dead then vanished, his dead spirit returning to his very soon-to-be dead body.

I spun to face my first assailant, everything in me screaming to hurry up, kill him, and get to Sage.

West might have gone on ahead, and he might be an extraordinary swordsman, but there was no way of knowing how many more men Crane had hired to stop us or what their magic might be.

Someone screamed on the other side of the garden, and one of the assailants collapsed to the ground with a real dagger, not a manifested one, protruding from his eye. The man beside him, a skinny man with wide orange eyes, jerked away as Ash leaped from the bushes, the dagger in his left hand lengthening into a sword as he moved.

He swung at Orange Eyes, who flung his hands up in front of him with a yelp. Vines exploded from the ground between him and Ash, wrapping around Ash before he could finish swinging his sword.

Fucking hell. That looked like a vine weaving ability, a powerful magic that was useless in everyday life, but devastating in a fight. That man could immobilize all of us — if he wasn't in the middle of panicking — and it'd be a struggle to break free... at least that would be the case if we weren't spirits manifested in the Garden.

Still, he could seriously slow us down and trip us up.

I raced toward Orange Eyes, but another man jumped toward me, swinging his longsword, while yet another shot ice bolts at me.

Crap. I didn't have time for this.

I blocked the sword strike and swept up a shadow to block the ice. The shadow trapped inside me heaved, and my vision darkened, just like it had when it had taken over and attacked Sawyer.

Fuck fuck fuck.

I tried to will it to understand that it wasn't helping, but it didn't understand. It needed to protect Sage, the desire so overwhelming it nearly brought me to my knees.

I know, I mentally hissed at it. *Let me save her.*

Ash disappeared from the vines in a swirl of black smoke and a clatter of real, non-manifested weapons that he'd been forced to leave behind, but — because of the telling black smoke — he wouldn't be able to manifest right beside anyone without the risk of being stabbed.

A few feet away, Rider lunged at Shaved Head, dodging another blast of fire, while Quill blocked and countered sword strikes with two other men.

Ash manifested on the opposite side of the battle from where he'd been and started to race toward Orange Eyes.

"We've got this," Rider yelled at Ash. "Get Sage."

Ash didn't even hesitate. Black smoke swirled around him, and he vanished mid step, reappearing on the path where West had gone. One of the men closest to him turned to chase after him, but I whipped a rope of shadow around his ankle, tripping him.

He fell with a thud, and I yanked him toward Rider, away from Ash so he could get away, while whoever it was who possessed the wind magic shoved me into the oncoming jab from the swordsman in front of me.

I twisted away from the blade, but it still caught my shoulder, pain flaring hot and sharp.

This was taking too fucking long. West had disappeared down the path, Rider and Quill were still caught up with at least two men each, and I had no idea how many more men Crane had hired or what they were doing to Sage right now.

My shadow heaved inside me, clawing at my control. She could be hurt. Bleeding. Dying. And I was stuck out here fighting these assholes when every second mattered.

CHAPTER 42

Sage

"We only need to stall your guard dog for a moment," Crane said with a sneer that sent cold fear flooding my body.

I squeezed my eyes shut and strained to send my spirit back to my body. I didn't want to be here. I couldn't be here. I wasn't real when I was here, just a spirit and I belonged in the Gray.

Now. Right now. Please now.

They'd dragged me deeper into the garden, and now we stood in a small clearing, illuminated by a patch of red glowing flowers, and backed by a tall stone wall that I wouldn't be able to climb.

I strained to hear the sounds of fighting, yelling, anything to indicate the spirit link had alerted Sir West to the danger and he was coming after me. Even if there were other men and they were stalling him, surely I'd hear something.

Unless, of course, the spirit link didn't actually work and Sir West had no idea I'd been taken.

Crane twirled the ceremonial dagger in his hand, the engraved blade catching the red light, looking like it was dipped in blood.

I didn't know if he needed to perform the spell in the sacred pool or not, and I sure as hell didn't want to find out. I could only pray an accidental nick wasn't going to be enough to start the spell.

I thrashed and clawed against the man who held me. I had to get free.

But whoever had grabbed me was so much bigger and stronger than me. I didn't stand a chance.

Crane stepped forward and I kicked out at him.

With a snarl he jerked back. "Hold her still."

Raven rushed forward, bending to grab my legs. I pulled them up to my chest and kicked out, slamming both into his chest and knocking him back.

"You fucking bitch," he yelled.

The man holding me laughed and his hands started to move as if he were trying to get a better hold of me. The hand on my mouth lifted while the one on my waist loosened.

With a scream, I twisted and stomped down on his instep. Hard.

Something crunched, he howled in pain and let go.

I dove out of the way — away from the direction of the ballroom but it was the only direction I could go — before any of them could think to grab me.

Crane lunged for me, his fingers brushing my arm. A

wave of exhaustion swept over me and I scrambled out of reach before he could incapacitate me.

Great Father that was too close.

And now I was even farther from the ballroom with all three men between me and escape or even help.

Lynx raced around the edge of a bush and stumbled to a stop, his eyes wide with surprise as if he hadn't expected me to break free.

And really, looking at the only other man in the group I hadn't already seen, I was surprised I had gotten free.

I recognized the man from the sacred pool. Crane had called him Thunder, and he was enormous, not as big as Sir West but almost as big as Lord Rider.

"Come on now," Crane cooed, "stop making this hard on yourself. We already know you can't send your spirit back to your body."

"What makes you think I'm not just biding my time?" I spat back, my voice sounding way more confident than I felt.

"Because you would've been gone by now," Crane said. "The moment Thunder grabbed you." He laughed, the sound dangerous and deadly and chilling. "You would have vanished the moment you saw me in Her Brilliance's private garden. But you didn't. You needed West to drag you out of there."

My pulse lurched with horrified realization. Letting me see him had been a test. He'd wanted to know if I could control my spirit form, and I'd proven to him that I couldn't.

"For fuck's sake," Crane snapped, pointing the dagger at the others. "Would you get the bitch? This doesn't work if we can't cut her marks."

Lynx and Raven leaped forward just as a massive shadow crashed through the bushes behind them.

Thunder turned just in time to dodge the swing of a massive sword, and Sir West stepped fully into the eerie red light.

West's expression hadn't changed from its usual grim, but there was a hardness in his gaze that made me almost as nervous as Crane holding that dagger.

"He tore through half a dozen men already?" Lynx squawked as he spun around, raised his hands, and shot bolts of ice at him.

West blocked the bolts with his swords, moving with a grace and speed I didn't think possible for someone so large.

Both Raven and Thunder rushed at Sir West—

And Crane lunged at me, wrenching my attention to my own fight.

I heaved back, his fingers mere inches from my face. My chest tightened and my breathing picked up, panic turning it shallow.

One solid touch. That was all it would take. Hell, not even a solid touch. I still felt slow and tired from when he'd grazed me moments before.

Behind Crane, Lynx threw his arms forward and ice exploded around Sir West's feet. Thick and heavy, it raced up his shins, climbing his thighs, and encircling his waist.

Lynx's head tipped back with a wild laugh, and West's swing at Thunder went wide.

Shit. Shit shit shit.

If Lynx could immobilize someone with ice, I was going to be next.

I darted my gaze around the clearing but couldn't see beyond the shadowy bushes on either side of me, and the wall at the back was too tall.

With a grunt, light flared from West's eyes, and he brought down the pommels of both his swords onto the ice in front of him.

The ice shattered with a sharp crack, the pieces spilling around him, and he surged toward Lynx, who yelped and scurried out of the way, while Raven turned and dove at me.

My pulse lurched, I'd been distracted by Crane and desperate for an escape, I hadn't realized how close he was.

I twisted out of the way, but he caught the folds on the side of my open-backed dress, his grip high by my shoulder, and ripped open the neck of my dress.

Cool night air hit my now bare skin and he gasped, his gaze locking on my neck where my sleeping mating marks were.

"What the fuck?" Raven snapped as I tore my dress from his grip.

"No," Crane screamed as he barreled toward me. "You think that will stop me?"

I dodged out of the way, my heel hitting a root, threatening my balance. He twisted back around and dove at me. I wasn't going to be fast enough. He was going to tackle me.

Desperate, I dove to the side. I tucked and rolled but he landed first and seized a handful of my skirt.

The fabric pulled taut, and I toppled forward. I hit the ground hard, the impact knocking the breath from my lungs and sending pain shooting through my palms and knees.

Oh shit oh shit oh shit.

I scrambled forward, desperate to get away, but Crane yanked on my dress dragging me back.

My pulse raced, rushing in my ears, and I fought to catch my breath.

I kicked back, my heel hitting his shoulder and drawing a snarl of pain. His grip loosened and I lurched forward, my hands slipping in the damp grass.

"You won't get away, bitch," he screamed as I fought to get to my knees.

Another yank, jerking my hands out from under me. My face hit the ground, sending lights flashing across my vision.

No.

"Got you!" His cold hand seized my ankle and exhaustion swept through me. "You're mine now."

No. Please no.

I kicked back as I swept my hands through the grass, scrambling to find a weapon. I needed a branch, a stone, something to stop him.

There. On the ground. A few feet away. A dagger.

I didn't know who'd dropped it and I didn't care.

I grabbed for it, my fingertips skimming the pommel.

Shit.

I heaved forward. I had to get closer. Just a little closer.

But my arms and legs already were heavy with sudden exhaustion, my whole body weighed down despite everything inside me screaming to keep fighting.

My fingers brushed the pommel again. I wasn't going to make it.

Come on. Come on!

I just needed a weapon. Any weapon.

Please!

Warmth filled my palm, and my hand spasmed. My fingers closed around a familiar leather grip, and I stared at Sawyer's dagger, the dagger I'd taken with me into the Gray and had worn every day since.

My vision blurred, Crane's magical fatigue threatening to drag me under, and the desperate need to close my eyes was overwhelming.

No. Fuck no. I wouldn't let him have me.

With a scream half of determination and half desperation to find the strength to move, I threw myself back at him.

His yellow eyes flashed wide, as if he hadn't expected me to fight back even though he'd already seen me stab Wells to death.

"No," I yelled, plunging the dagger into his eye — the closest vulnerable area I could get to — drawing a shriek of agony. "I'm not yours. I'm not anyone's."

I wrenched the dagger back and plunged it into his neck.

With a snarl, I twisted and pulled the dagger free with a wild spray of blood.

His grip on my ankle loosened, and the magical drain of strength and vitality stopped, leaving me so tired it was a miracle I was still conscious.

I stared at his body, my chest heaving with each strained breath.

I'd killed another man.

And I didn't feel a damn thing about it.

Maybe once I wasn't so tired I'd care, but I wasn't sure that would be the case.

Something thudded a few feet away and I dragged my attention to West, who stood surrounded by Thunder, Raven, and Lynx's bodies.

No one was left alive. No one able to answer questions. Had he meant to kill them or was that just the way it had turned out?

His expression hadn't changed and he didn't even look winded, so I had no idea if it had been necessary for him to kill all three of them or not.

Movement from the garden path made me flinch, my hand tightening on the dagger that I'd somehow manifested into existence.

Ash burst into the clearing and skidded to a stop, his eyes wild, his beautiful, heartbreaking face tight with fear.

He held a bloodied sword in his hand and there looked like there were a few wet patches on his black doublet that could have been blood and not water but it was impossible to tell.

All I knew was I was relieved and happy and overwhelmed to see him again.

His gaze swept over the bodies, over West, over me on the ground with blood on my hands and my dress and my face, and he opened his mouth to say something but Lord Rider, Talon, and Lord Quill burst into the clearing and rushed right past him toward me.

"Are you hurt?" Rider dropped to one knee beside me.

"Just bruised," I said, exhaustion slurring my words and thoughts.

Quill checked me for injuries, his hands steady and gentle as they moved while Talon stood guard, his gaze scanning the garden.

I set my dagger on the ground beside me and it vanished just like Lord Quill said it would, proving that I had finally managed to manifest something in the Garden.

It felt so strange that something so impossible could have saved me.

But I guess it didn't matter. Crane was dead, and I was—

My pulse stuttered.

I was free. I didn't have to hide from Crane. I wasn't trapped in the Divine Residence, a prisoner in the guise of protection.

"It's over," I said, searching the clearing for Ash.

He stood back from the others, his head tipped so

that his hair fell forward and veiled the scarred side of his face.

"We can be together again." I reached for him, but he didn't move. "Ash?"

"Every time I turn around, you're in another mess," he said, his tone cold, void of the warmth and comfort I'd become familiar with.

"What?"

"You're constantly in trouble. Even the High Priestess could see that. That's why she gave you West." He jerked his thumb at the enormous knight.

"What the hell, Ash?" Talon asked, taking a step toward him.

Ash held up his hand, stopping him. "No. I'm done. Crane is dead, and she's got more than enough nursemaids to take care of her."

No. This wasn't right. This wasn't Ash. He wouldn't behave like this. He was kind and caring and safe.

"But I thought—?"

"You thought what?" Ash asked.

That there was something between us, a safety, a comfort that I desperately needed. He'd helped me when the pressure from my mating marks had overwhelmed me. He'd teased and flirted with me. He'd been my friend when no one else cared about me.

"I thought it meant something," I said, my voice small, my confession ripped from a throat tight with tears I didn't want to cry.

He shrugged. "Maybe to you."

Then he vanished in a swirl of black smoke.

Don't miss the next book in the series!

Strike Among the Shadowed Gray

Desperate Disguise: Book Five

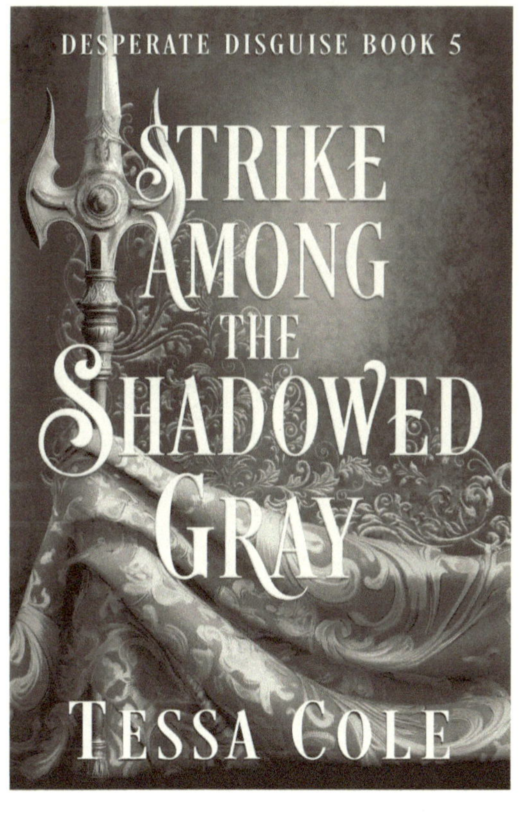

Other Books by Tessa Cole

DESPERATE DISGUISE

Lies Within the Darkest Tower, book 1

Stand Against the Rising Storm, book 2

Whispers Within the Midnight Garden, book 3

Hidden Within the Secret Heart, book 4

Strike Within the Shadowed Gray, book 5

NEPHILIM'S DESTINY

Destined Shadows, prequel story

Destined Darkness, book 1

Destined Blood, book 2

Destined Fire, book 3

Destined Storm, book 4

Destined Radiance, book 5

ANGEL'S FATE

Fated Bonds, book 1

Fated Winter, book 2

Fated Fear, book 3

Fated Despair, book 4

Fated Resolve, book 5

Fated Heart, book 6

ENSNARED BY THE PACK

Wolf Deceived, book 1

Wolf Denied, book 2

Wolf Desired, book 3

Wolf Distressed, book 4

Wolf Decided, book 5

Wolf Devoted, book 6

THE GRECIAN GODDESS TRILOGY

Written with Clara Wils

Kiss of the Goddess, book 1

Power of the Goddess, book 2

Bonds of the Goddess, book 3

SECRETS GODS KEEP

Written with Clara Wils

Craving Demons, book 1

Chaos Demons, book 2

Claiming Demons, book 3

HER BAD BOY WOLVES

Written with Clara Wils

Pack Against the Wall, book 1

Want you Pack, book 2

Pack in Business, book 3

www.ingramcontent.com/pod-product-compliance
Lightning Source LLC
LaVergne TN
LVHW050924080826
845145LV00001B/198

* 9 7 8 1 9 9 0 5 8 7 6 7 2 *